Seduced By Flames

Hidden Realms of Silver Lake
Book 2

Vella Day

Can this dragon shifter fight against all odds to win her human mate?

If it weren't for bad luck, safety expert, Nessa Caspian, wouldn't have any luck at all. Just when she thinks things can't get worse, an explosion traps her in the mine. Really? If she hadn't been a dragon shifter, capable of clawing her way out, she'd be dead!

When she learns the mining inspector, Kyle Harper, has to shut down her family's legacy because of all the safety issues, she's livid—that is until she realizes the super hot man is her future mate. Well crap. Now what is she supposed to do? Bite him?

Kyle hates dragon shifters. After all, one nearly killed his sister. When he meets the highly tantalizing and intelligent Nessa though, all his preconceived notions fly out the window. Part of him wants to keep her at arm's length and the rest of him wants to ravish her...

Chapter One

THIS DAMN MINE would be the death of her yet.

"Come on, come on. Where are you?" Dragon shifter Nessa Caspian tapped her nails across the rock face, determined to find the gold vein. Her ability to locate metals by touch had yet to fail her, so why couldn't she sense any now? She was sure the gold was there.

Nessa closed her eyes, throwing out more energy to sense the vibrations. Her father's words of worry came back to her, cutting short her concentration. "You have a gift Nessa, but opening a new vein is dangerous, especially at two hundred feet below the surface."

Dangerous? Hah. Even if the electricity failed—shutting down the elevator between here and the surface—she could still fly up the shaft to escape.

You better be right, her dragon said. *If you aren't careful, and there's another accident, the Mining Consortium will close us down.*

Her hands shook at that terrible thought.

Sure, the wealth that this gold could bring her family and their miners would be great, but more than anything, she wanted to prove to her dad that she had the ability to find the perfect mother lode. She'd inherited this talent to read vibrations from rock from her father's great-great grandfather. No one else in the family could find gems and metals the way her ancient relative had—until now.

Once more, Nessa ran her nails across the cold rough rock, sensing small tremors. Before she could identify the source, the wall suddenly shook, and her pulse soared. This was it! Nessa could almost taste success.

Her dad hadn't wanted to dig this deep, but she'd promised him that she'd take every precaution. It was why she'd refused to allow any other workers down here with her.

An even larger vibration tingled in her fingers, returning her attention to the elusive vein. When a high tinny sound accompanied the trembling, her heart slammed against her rib cage. The frequency coupled with a distinct pitch signaled a metal was present. She wouldn't celebrate yet though. There was a fine line between gold and copper and between silver and platinum, and Nessa needed to be right this time.

After absorbing the sensations for a full minute, she was convinced the frequency and intensity of the trembling matched gold's signature. But the only way to be sure was to dig into the rock face and see the metal in its pure form.

Leaning back, she extended her arms and pointed to the area she believed contained the thick gold vein—not merely gold flecks embedded in the rock—and partially shifted her hands into her dragon talons.

She smiled at what she was about to do. If anyone on Earth had a mother lode like this, they'd celebrate for years. Hell, it might even make the history books in her realm of Tarradon.

Unlike other dragons, the fire coming out of her talons had laser precision and was coupled with an extremely hot flame, better than any store bought blowtorch. Mouth breathing fire just went everywhere, which made it useless in this situation. Plus, she'd have to be in her dragon form to do that.

With total concentration, Nessa bored through the rock, sending bits and pieces of sediment in every direction. A shard of rock flew at her, cutting through her shirt and slicing open her skin.

Oh crap. In her excitement at the discovery, she'd been careless and had forgotten to initiate more of her shift. Stopping for a moment, she concentrated on turning her human skin into protective dragon scales.

Phew. That was close. She then continued drilling. Even though the heat blew back in her face, forcing her to squint, it didn't stop her from making progress. After a minute though, her hands shook from the intense power needed to keep the flame going.

Don't fail me now, she demanded of her body. Two minutes turned into four. Then, on the next push, the shine of pure gold bounced back at her. "Yes!!"

Heart pounding, she cut off the fire and extended her claws on one hand to dig out a sample. The gold had somewhat melted, making it easy to scoop out. Extracting a small container from her pocket, she lifted the exquisite metal to her nose and sniffed, hoping it had the scent of a rose or some exotic flower. It didn't, but a girl could dream. As much as she wanted to paint her body with the stuff in celebration, she placed the scraped metal inside the box. Impossible to remove all of it from her hands, her talons glowed yellow.

She wiggled them before letting her hands return to normal. With the exploration complete for now, Nessa fully returned to her human form.

Excited about her find, she collected her light and headed back to the elevator. *See, Dad? This is the mother lode. Told you I could do it.*

Ten steps from the metal cage that would take her swiftly to the top and let her bask in her glory, the entire wall exploded, jettisoning her backward. Her mind failed to comprehend what was happening other than to tell her she was in deep shit.

Without any conscious thought on her part, her dragon took over and did the shift for her, taking the brunt of the blast. The force slammed Nessa's animal into the stone wall so hard that she crumpled to the ground. She tried to bring in her wings to avoid more harm, but something stopped her. As much as she wanted to check out the damage, between all the dust and the flying rocks, she had to keep her eyes closed until the dust settled. A sharp object pierced her skull, and she moaned at the intense ache. Where had the detonation come from? She was the only one down there.

Rocks continued to fall on top of her, and dirt lodged under her scales. Seeking as much safety as possible, she lowered her head and waited for the onslaught of rubble to stop, hoping against hope she wouldn't be buried alive.

Seconds passed and then minutes, as more aftershocks shook the area. When silence finally surrounded her, she took a deep breath to assess the situation and was immediately sent into a coughing fit. Her dragon had never coughed before, and she didn't like it one bit.

When Nessa opened her eyes to check for injuries, she had to shut them immediately. Rocks were pressed against her snout and silt fell into her eyes. While she didn't usually jump to conclusions, it was pretty obvious she was trapped hundreds of feet below the surface—all alone and with no means of communicating with anyone. Damn.

While both of those facts made her situation dire, she was a dragon after all—one with some magic at her fingertips—no pun intended. Nessa should be able to get out of there. The big question was how long would it take her, and would she live long enough to reach the surface?

The one glimmer of hope was that everyone on the surface would have heard the explosion. Sadly, there was little they could do about it. She was too far down for them to drill a new tunnel. Hell, it had taken them a month to build the shaft in the first place.

When she blew out a breath, her chest screamed in pain. Really? She chanced opening her eyes a smidge and found a mammoth rock sitting on her chest. Not only that, one wing sat under a ton of rubble. Well, double damn. It was worse than she'd feared.

Sure, she was scared, but she was more pissed than anything. This was the third accident in as many months at her family's mine. It might be better to die down here than have to go through the humiliation of having the Mining Consortium shut them down. Her father had already received two warning letters. After this, it would be lights out for them for a long while. Since she was in charge of the safety of the mines, she'd be the fall guy.

It would be one thing if Caspian Mining had been guilty of neglect, but they hadn't been. Nessa had been meticulous at keeping everyone out of harm's way.

She grunted. She wouldn't reach the surface by feeling sorry for herself. No one was going to save her, which meant it was up to her to figure something out.

The first thing Nessa had to do was move that huge boulder off her body. To do that though, she needed her claws—claws that were trapped under a mountain of debris. Ugh. This wasn't going to be easy or painless. Using much of her energy, she worked her claws upward inch by inch. Because one of her wings was not accessible, it wouldn't be of much use until she could free it.

Slowly but surely, Nessa edged her talons to the surface, tossing small rocks aside along the way. When one talon broke into view, she took a big breath.

"Ouch. Damn it." Why couldn't she remember that inhaling deeply was painful?

Move the damn rock, her dragon complained.

"I was planning on it." Sheesh. The only reason she vocalized her comment was to help feel less alone. "I'm sure help is on the way."

In a month maybe, her dragon shot back.

She refused to listen to such negativity. Grabbing one side of the boulder, Nessa pushed while she lifted her right wing a few inches. While not totally free, it was enough to help her move the rock to the side. In the process of shoving it out of the way though, several ribs cracked.

Don't move, her dragon said. *Let me heal you.*

"I have no place to go. Have at me."

As much as she wanted to pick the debris off her half-buried wing, she waited. And waited some more. *Hurry,* she pleaded.

I'm working as fast as I can.

To save energy, Nessa tried to slow her breathing and relax, but that was no easy task.

Okay, I've done what I can to repair the ribs, her dragon said, *but you will be sore for a while.*

I'm okay with sore. Thank you.

She didn't need her animal wasting any more energy healing her—energy she needed to help her get the hell out of there.

Moving more rocks, she finally managed to free her right wing completely and part of her left wing.

Exhausted from the exercise, Nessa leaned back and tried to figure out what had happened. Where had the explosives come from? She hadn't brought any into the shaft, so what had gone off? This mine was far from all of the others, so there was no reason for anyone to be excavating near there. She didn't want to consider that someone wanted her dead. She'd always believed the employees were grateful to her and her family for keeping them safe, but clearly she'd been wrong.

Nessa pounded a stone in frustration and instantly regretted her burst of anger. More pain sliced across her chest. After waiting a minute to catch her breath, she opened her mouth and shot a hot stream of fire straight at the rock in front of her. The scorching force blew right through the middle. Having a bit more room to maneuver, she began to claw away the rest of the rocks and dirt from the bottom half of her body. Because she was fifteen feet tall, it would be a huge chore to create enough room for her to stand and then spread her wings—but she had to try.

After several hours of labor, she finally had that space and stood up—or as close to standing as she could manage. Her left wing hung at an odd angle, and both of her legs were severely cut, but that wasn't going to stop her from carving her way out of there, no matter how long it took.

Knowing what she had to do, Nessa began shoving the larger rocks to the side. By heating them to a high degree, they fused, providing stability to the walls. She just hoped like hell she didn't have to repeat this process for two hundred feet straight up. She'd never make it.

KYLE HARPER'S CELL phone rang. When he saw it was his sister, Lily, calling, he smiled and pushed back his office chair to get more comfortable. "Hey, there."

"Kyle, there's been another accident at the Caspian mine," Lily spit out.

He bolted upright. She worked for Avonbelle Insurance Agency—the agency that insured miners. "When? Was anyone hurt?"

As the head of the Mining Consortium, he would be in charge of investigating the disaster—the third one in three months at this particular mine. He straightened his shoulders and inhaled. As much as he didn't like shutting anyone down, he'd do it if the miners' safety was at stake.

Closing this particular one wouldn't upset him too much either. After all, it was run by dragon shifters, and he knew quite well that most of the fiery creatures were evil.

"I don't know any details," she said.

"I appreciate the heads up. I'll head on over there now to find out as much as I can."

Lily huffed. "I bet it was the owner's fault."

He understood why she was a bit prejudice against dragon shifters. Her last boyfriend, a dragon shifter, had burned her back so badly she'd been hospitalized for two months. Her hatred of the species seemed well deserved.

"It's my job to keep an open mind, or at least pretend to."

She grunted. "I'll have to stop by at some point too. Whoever is injured will want to be compensated."

After he hung up, Kyle grabbed the folders from the last two incidents and headed out, ready to get to the bottom of what happened.

Chapter Two

ON THE DRIVE over to the Caspian mine, Kyle called his second in command, Dennis Taylor, who confirmed that he and the team were already at the site. Pride filled Kyle at his proactivity.

When Kyle arrived at the mine, he was met by total chaos. Laird Caspian, the mine's owner, was shouting instructions to his men. Many others, including dragon shifters, were circled around a large pit.

Kyle stepped up behind the owner and tapped him on the shoulder. Mr. Caspian spun around so fast Kyle feared he might hurt himself. "Oh, fuck. You heard."

That wasn't a pleasant greeting, but he'd heard worse. "Can you tell me what happened, sir?"

"My daughter, Nessa, is down there, and she's trapped. We have no way of getting to her before she runs out of air." His blood shot eyes changed from brown to a teal-colored hue, a sign that he was in a high state of agitation. Kyle couldn't blame the man for his panic. No one deserved to go through losing a child—dragon shifter or not.

"Are you in communication with your daughter?" Kyle asked.

The father looked off to the side for a moment. "No. I don't think she took any communication device with her. Even if she did, the rock walls would block any signal." The man stabbed a hand through his disheveled hair.

"You don't know her condition?" Kyle didn't want to say she was most likely dead.

"No, but Nessa is a fighter. She'll find a way out."

From where Kyle stood, it appeared as if the entire shaft had collapsed. "Do you know the cause of the cave-in?"

"We have no idea since it just happened. No explosives were scheduled, and this isn't an active mine."

Kyle nodded his sympathy. "My men would like to take a look around—away from the site, of course. One of my other assistants, Tom Delaney, worked in some of the other mines before he came to work for me. He knows a lot of these men and will be a good liaison."

"That's great. I want to get to the bottom of this as much as you do—maybe more so. Something evil is going on at my mine, and I want it stopped."

The man seemed almost too cooperative, but Kyle chalked it up to the owner being in shock. "From what you've said, I take it you suspect sabotage?"

"Hell yeah, I do."

"Any suspects?"

"Several, but I'd rather not point any fingers until I have more proof."

Kyle could respect that. "If you don't mind, I'd like to speak with some of your men to see if they know anything."

"Of course. Just make sure you don't get in the way of the dragons. They're trying to dig down to find Nessa. I'm using them since they can move the debris faster and more carefully than any bulldozer."

Kyle had no intention of getting anywhere near those beasts. "My men and I will respect their space." As much as Kyle wanted to mention that he'd be closing the mine, the man's grief had reached him. There would be time later to tell him all operations would have to be stopped in order for Kyle's team to investigate.

As Kyle headed over to check with Dennis, he studied those standing around, wondering if any of them had a hand in the destruction. Those who were in human form seemed terribly distraught at what had happened—hands waving, voices raised, and frequent glances at the collapsed tunnel. Two men stood off to the side, and Kyle headed toward them.

"Excuse me," Kyle said, "Did either of you see what happened?"

They both shook their heads. "This mine isn't operational yet. Both of us were at another site when we heard the explosion. We hopped in our vehicles and came right over," the taller of the two said. Because they weren't in the trenches digging, Kyle assumed they weren't dragon shifters.

"Did you see anyone skulking around this mine in the last couple of days?"

The shorter, beefier of the two stood up straighter. "No. I can tell you this. It wouldn't be anyone who works here. The Caspians take care of us. No one would hurt Nessa."

"Who else is down there with her?"

"Nobody. She went alone."

Humans would never be so foolish. "That doesn't seem very smart."

"Nessa said it was too dangerous for workers to go down there since the walls hadn't been certified as safe."

Something wasn't adding up. "Yet she went."

"Yes. She didn't want her father to invest any more money into the venture until she was positive gold was down there."

Either the girl was fiercely loyal to her father or not very bright. "How long was she below before the explosion occurred?"

They both shrugged. The taller one nodded toward his friend. "As Ernie said, we weren't here."

"Could Ms. Caspian have accidentally set off a charge?"

"No, way," Ernie said. "She's an expert. Hell, she gives classes on how to use explosives safely and effectively. Besides, this was her baby. She fought to have the mine excavated in the first place."

Kyle mentally crossed her name off the list. "Do any employees have any grudges against the family?"

They both looked at each other. "Like we said, the Caspians treat us well."

"Darnax Gorman didn't think so," Ernie said, looking over at his partner. "He was pretty vocal about wanting more pay and fewer hours." He returned his gaze to Kyle. "He was the foreman here before he was fired."

"I remember now. He was let go right before the first incident," Kyle added.

"Yes."

Kyle had personally checked him out, but he had an alibi at the time the cart carrying some minerals derailed and pinned Ed Hollix, causing him to lose his leg.

"Do you know where I can find Darnax now? Last time I checked, he'd moved from his downtown apartment."

"Gorman cut off all communications with us. He could be in another province by now for all I know."

"Thanks for your time."

"I hope you find out who did this," Ernie said.

"So do I." In too many of the smaller mines, the workers were closed mouthed. It was refreshing to meet with men who believed he was trying to find the source of the problem.

Kyle approached his second in command. "Did you find out anything useful?"

Dennis shook his head. "I spoke with their new foreman. He said once they dug the shaft and rigged up the car to take Nessa to the bottom, they removed all explosives—for safety purposes."

"Can he explain what happened?"

"He refuses to speculate. I think he knows something, but he isn't talking."

Interesting. "It's not looking like we'll be able to get down there. That means we'll have to look around the surface."

Dennis nodded. "I have my men searching the area for any signs of explosives now."

"Good."

The dragons were making incredibly fast progress digging, but it might take days if not weeks to reach the end of the mine. Losing a daughter would devastate anyone. Kyle totally understood why Laird

Caspian had almost come unhinged.

EXHAUSTION WAS TAKING a toll on Nessa. She needed water in order for her dragon to heal her. The cuts on her legs were closing up, and her wing was slowly repairing, but her energy was draining too fast. Fixing her crushed chest had taken a major toll on her animal.

Nessa was forced to stop and catch her breath once more. She had dug up a good fifty feet, and it seemed as if she'd spent several hours doing that—or had a full day passed? While she was pleased with her progress, she'd had to support herself with her legs while she pressed her damaged wings against the walls. Her muscles constantly quivered and threatened to give out. The width of the tunnel was now about eight feet wide, barely large enough to wedge her dragon body into the space. Even though it was a tight fit, it took strength not to slip.

She opened her mouth and aimed her fire once more at the wall of rocks and soil directly overhead. Clay and dirt rained down on her and caused her to lose purchase again. Nessa slipped a few feet, forcing her to press harder against the wall to keep from tumbling back to the bottom. Tears fell, but she refused to admit they were tears of desperation. She wanted to believe it was her dragon's way of cleaning her eyes.

Nessa refused to give up though. Never in her life had she quit, and she wasn't about to start now. "Blast away the dirt, scrape, scrape, scrape, melt the walls, and then climb upward. Repeat, repeat, repeat," she huffed. Her mantra was the only thing keeping her going.

Nessa's legs were like rubber, and her talons had dulled to nubs. Worse, her breath was giving out, meaning her fire was growing colder.

Since her fingers didn't have much strength left, she closed her eyes for a second, but awoke with a start when wind flew past her. Oh, shit. She was tumbling. On instinct, she stretched out her wings and flapped, forgetting she wasn't outside. The result of that momentary mental lapse caused one wing to fold in half, preventing her from stopping her descent.

It was the adrenaline from the intense ache that reminded her to extend her claws in search of an outcropping to hang onto. After several misses, she finally latched onto a thick rock protruding out of the side. Her muscles shook as she tried to keep a hold. When Nessa finally succeeded in stabilizing herself, she looked up. Well crap. She estimated she'd dropped over twenty feet. Defeat blanketed her, but she pushed it aside.

Once her breath settled down, she gathered the courage to push upward once more. This time, however, the pain from the broken wing made traveling more difficult.

Her dragon wanted to heal Nessa's wing, but she told her inner animal not to waste her strength. Nessa needed energy for her fire.

Because she couldn't sleep, it was wreaking havoc with her ability to stay focused. Each foot of progress took more and more out of her. It seemed like she'd been trapped for days, but it probably wasn't more than ten or twelve hours.

On her next fire blast, she stilled then shook her head. She must be hallucinating because she swore she heard voices. That was impossible though—wasn't it?

Fueled by the fact that help might be on the way, she inhaled then shot out a big flame. Even though her talons were next to nothing, she clawed and dug while clinging to the sides of the shaft. One thing she promised herself was that she would not fall again.

Inch by inch, she traveled upward. She estimated she'd already cut through about one hundred feet of the collapsed shaft. Only one hundred more to go. She could do it. Her progress might be slow, but she would get there.

Nessa wasn't sure what happened next, but suddenly large talons broke through the dirt above her and grasped her wings, tugging her upward. Her wing ached, and her chest hurt, but the fresh air was totally glorious. When those same claws placed her on her back, she let out a sigh of relief and passed out.

THE SHOUTS CAUGHT not only Kyle's attention but that of the worker he was speaking with.

The man turned to him. "It sounds like they found her!" He took off at a sprint toward the large pit.

Kyle and many others followed. The big question was whether Nessa Caspian was alive or dead. The dragons who had been excavating crawled up the shaft and then shifted into their human form. Their bodies were covered in dirt, and while exhaustion was clearly written on their faces, a sense of excitement bounced off them.

"We have her," someone shouted from deep down in the pit. "She's alive. Someone call for the ambulance."

Nessa Caspian had been trapped for only twenty-four hours. How had they reached her so quickly? The man he'd been speaking with said it took weeks to dig the tunnel the first time.

Her father pushed his way through the crowd. "Where is she?"

The pain in his voice tore at Kyle. What he wouldn't have given for such a caring dad. Hell, he would have been satisfied to have had a dad at all.

What am I thinking?

Sympathy played no role in his job. He also couldn't lose sight of the fact that these were dragon shifters. While he hadn't known many, the one he did know had hurt his sister badly.

A siren off in the distance moved toward the collapsed mine, jarring him out of his less than pleasant mental ramblings. A short while later, a vehicle arrived with the name *Caspian Ambulance* blazoned on the side. Having their own medical team on site was a necessity since they were far from town. Two men dressed in blue uniforms, carrying a stretcher, rushed to the pit.

Not able to see her because of the crowd, Kyle edged his way back to the ambulance to wait.

A few minutes later, about twenty men emerged from the crowd carrying a huge dragon—one that wasn't moving. She was covered in reddish brown dirt, but a hint of purple scales were interspersed throughout the black ones. Kyle had never seen a dragon up close and personal, and despite his intense dislike for the creatures, this one was rather beautiful.

"Is she alive?" he found himself asking one of the men huddled around her.

"Yes, barely. Please move out of the way, sir." They set Nessa down carefully.

Kyle did as the man asked, though he wasn't sure how they were going to take her anywhere. The ambulance certainly wasn't large enough to hold her.

Kyle studied this woman who had somehow managed to survive despite the odds. She cracked open one eye, and he could have sworn she looked straight at him. Pain, along with something else, filled her ever-changing eyes that went from forest green to purple. As much as he wanted to ask her questions, the woman deserved time to heal.

Her wing fluttered, and then when she opened her claw, it was as if she were trying to tell him something. She grunted, and his pulse soared. Kyle looked around to see who else she might be looking at, but no one else was in her line of sight.

As much as he wanted to ask how she was doing, she couldn't have answered him. A loud rumble sounded off in the distance and disrupted his thoughts. A flatbed truck, large enough to hold Nessa, rolled toward them.

Mr. Caspian charged up to Kyle and got in his face. "I want you to find out who did this to my daughter. I don't care what it costs or how many men you need. I'll pay whatever it takes to find the guilty party."

Kyle was stunned by his offer. Lack of funds had always been an issue at his firm until recently. After the first incident at the Caspian mine, the government had suddenly upped their funding. "I will do my best, sir."

The air in his chest seemed to deflate. "I appreciate that."

Nessa was loaded onto the back of the flatbed, and Mr. Caspian hopped into the passenger side. A second later, the truck took off.

Conflicting emotions soared through him. Kyle wanted to find the Caspians guilty, but from what he'd just seen, they might not be. Without a doubt, this would be the hardest case Kyle had ever worked.

Chapter Three

NESSA AWOKE TO a darkened room and had to blink several times to rid the grit lining her eyes. Only when she reached up to swipe her face, did she realize she was still in her dragon form. Why hadn't she shifted? Her mind spun. Oh, yeah. She'd been trapped in a mine, and her dragon had protected her. From the way her chest and wings throbbed, her dragon was working to heal her.

The horrible memory of the dirt pummeling her body over and over again raced back, sending chills from her head to the tip of her tail. An image of her shooting fire at the large stone tunnel walls surfaced. Somehow, she didn't remember making it to the top. Yet here she was—safe on the floor in the large gathering center of her family's mine building.

Not quite sure if she was healed enough to shift, Nessa did it anyway. The moment she changed though, she realized that had been a mistake. Blood covered her pant legs, while her shoulder, chest, and wrist screamed in pain. Clearly her dragon hadn't finished healing her. Nessa should probably shift back into the dragon form again, but she needed answers first.

Nessa slowly sat up and then rose to her knees. When her head stopped spinning, she chanced standing. No sooner had she taken three steps toward the exit when Greer, her younger sister, rushed in. "What are you doing up? Sit down."

Nessa looked around at the empty room. "Where, on the floor?"

"It doesn't look comfortable, does it? Let's move you to a more private place. I want to check you out."

Not only was Greer her younger sister, she was a healer—and a very good one at that. Greer wrapped an arm around Nessa's waist and led her out of the large room. Birk, her older brother, was standing watch in the hallway.

His eyes lit up when he saw her, and he placed a hand on her shoulder. "Are you okay, Nessa? You gave us such a scare."

She felt broken and weak, but if she told him every muscle ached, he'd insist she return to her dragon form. "I'll be fine. Greer will heal me." Her sister must not have believed her injuries were life threatening or she would have called in their cousin Declan, who was an even more powerful healer.

Nessa turned to Birk. "Why are you standing watch outside the room?"

His eyes widened. "Seriously? Someone tried to kill you. Once word gets out that you survived, it's possible he'll try again."

She waved a hand. "I don't think the explosion was aimed at me but rather at the mine in general. Once we excavate the gold that's down there, it might put other miners out of business."

"For your sake, I hope they were only targeting the mine." He nodded at Greer. "Where are you taking her?"

"Just to the office at the end of the hallway. It'll be easier to work in there."

"Sounds good. Can I get you anything, Nessa? Coffee? Water? Food?"

She smiled, but even her cheeks hurt. "You are sweet. Ask me again once Greer does her magic."

"Sure thing." Worry creased his eyes, indicating he wasn't convinced Greer's magic hands were strong enough "I'll stay here and pretend you're still inside in case someone tries to harm you again."

Birk was being his usual overprotective self, but she loved him for it. Nessa stood on her tip toes to kiss his cheek when her ribs protested. She winced. "Thank you."

"Nessa?" Birk asked.

"I'm good, or rather, I will be soon."

Once they entered the small office down the hallway, Greer

made her sit. "Everyone has been so worried about you."

"How long have I been unconscious?"

"About fifteen hours," Greer said.

"Holy crap." Her dragon never took that long to heal her. The injuries must have been more serious than she realized. "Who saved me?" Her memory had blocked it out.

"At least twenty men worked together to reach you. I think almost every dragon shifter volunteered to help dig out the collapsed shaft. It was incredible to watch. Other than to drink something to keep hydrated, they never stopped. One of the men finally saw your talon poke up through the dirt, and he reached in and grabbed onto you. Then all of them together lifted you out." Greer sniffled and swiped a finger under one eye. "I swear I thought you were dead. How did you get so far up the shaft? I would have thought the explosion would have collapsed the whole thing."

"It did." Nessa explained her method. "I was so tired. My wing was damaged in the blast and my chest was crushed, but I figured if I didn't do something, I'd die down there."

Greer very gently hugged her. "I'm glad you didn't. You're not out of the woods yet though. I want you to close your eyes and relax so I can do my thing."

Nessa held up her hands, indicating she'd obey. "Does Dad have any idea who set the charges?"

"Are you sure it was explosives?" Greer asked.

Nessa tilted her head. "From the sound and force, it had to be."

"Well, you don't need to be worrying about that yet. Think healing thoughts."

Her sister could be pushy when it involved using her magic, which was a good thing since Nessa was very determined to find out who had been responsible for the mine's collapse. Its safety was her responsibility.

While she'd seen Greer do her magic numerous times, Nessa hadn't been the recipient of her talents in a long while. With her eyes closed, Nessa could only imagine that her sister's hands were hovered over her ribs and sore shoulder.

"I'm going to touch you, so this might be a bit uncomfortable," Greer said. "The injuries are worse than I first thought."

Great. "Go ahead."

Greer started with Nessa's shoulder. Heat poured into the sore area and nearly burned her. Soon, however, the ache dissipated and Nessa finally relaxed. Just as her sister ran her palms over her ribcage, Nessa opened her eyes.

"What's wrong?" Greer asked. "Did I hurt you?"

The odd sensations pouring through her body were anything but painful. In fact, they were highly pleasant. Truth: they were downright erotic. "No."

Shouts sounded down the hallway, and Greer glanced at the doorway. "Sounds like Birk has his hands full."

"Do you know who it is?" Nessa asked, her blood zinging through her body too fast.

"Probably someone who shouldn't be here. Don't worry; Birk will take care of whoever it is. You need to rest," her sister said, wagging a finger at her.

While it was true Nessa wasn't fully healed, a different kind of energy charged through her. "I need to see who it is."

"Why?"

"I don't know; I just do."

Greer held up a hand. "You stay seated. Let me check it out." Just as Greer opened the door, her father rushed down the hallway. His footsteps halted, and a second later, he stepped into the room.

"Nessa? You're up! How are you feeling?" He cupped her face and leaned over, his gaze checking her out from head to toe.

"Better. Greer did her magic on me."

More shouts came from down the hallway—mostly angry ones.

"Give me a second," her father said. "I see our resident mining inspector is at it again."

Her heart thumped. So that was what the ruckus was about. "Is he going to close us down?" Nessa could barely say those words.

Odd as it was, she'd never met the man who held such power. The head of the Mining Consortium was new in town, having taken over for old man Dougherty a year and half ago. After the first incident at the mine, in which her foreman had been killed, she'd only spoken with Kyle Harper's second in command, Dennis Taylor. Nessa had been so devastated and angry at the time that she'd nearly torn the poor man in two. Her father decided the Consortium should deal with him.

"I imagine he will ask us to close the mine, but I'm going to agree with him, at least short term," her father said. "We need to find out who is responsible. I couldn't live with myself if you had died, or if you are injured again."

She appreciated his sentiment, but Nessa didn't agree. "Closing the mine, no matter for how short a time, will have dire consequences on our production. We have clients to serve. Promise him we'll beef up security or something."

Her father rubbed her arm. "You heal and leave the running of the mine to me."

Before she could argue, her father took off. While she couldn't hear the conversation at the end of the hall, it wasn't long before her father returned—with the mining inspector in tow.

Once the inspector stepped into the tiny room, blind lust shook Nessa so hard she couldn't fathom what was happening to her body. Heat swamped her lower half, and even her nipples hardened. Okay, that was wrong on so many levels. This had to be an aftereffect from Greer's treatment. The alternative was unacceptable.

Mate, mate, her dragon chanted.

No way! Sure, this man had as many muscles as a dragon shifter and was nearly as tall as one, but he was human. Not that her family over the ages hadn't mated with his kind, but he was the mine's archenemy, and therefore her enemy.

She had to look away or chance embarrassing herself, but even then she failed to gain much composure. Her heart refused to calm.

"Nessa, I'm glad to see you're okay," this man said as he held out his hand. "I'm Kyle Harper, the head of the Mining Consortium."

"I know who you are." She pretended as if she was too weak to shake his hand.

"I don't know how it is we haven't met before, but I'd really like to ask you some questions if you're up for it."

Nessa finally dragged her gaze back to him. Whoa. His eyes mesmerized her. They were a deep blue, the color of the ocean on a clear day. But it was the flecks of green and brown that drew her in.

"Nessa?" her father asked. "Are you okay?"

Heat raced up her face. "Yes."

No, she wasn't okay. Kyle's presence jumbled her thoughts. Needing him to leave, she rubbed her head and moaned slightly. "I mean not really. Even after I'm healed, I don't know how I can be of any help. I don't remember much. One minute I was headed to the elevator and the next, I was under a ton of rocks and dirt."

He shot his gaze between her and her dad. "Just so you understand, by law I have to shut down the mine until this is resolved, so whether you talk or not won't affect my decision."

Nessa's anger spiked at what he was implying, and her energy tripled. She jumped up from her seat and was in this man's face in a second. "That's not fair." She poked his chest. "We need the mine to stay up and running. You have no right—"

"Nessa," her father said in that stern voice she recognized very well.

She spun to face him. "What? You know we weren't negligent. This was sabotage."

"I know," her dad said in the softest voice she'd ever heard him utter.

Harper didn't seem upset by her outburst. Calm bastard. "Nessa, can you at least tell me who you suspect sabotaged the mine?" Kyle asked. "I'll make sure he is included in the investigation."

"That's easy. It had to be the Royals."

His eyes widened. "You think our government is responsible for this? What evidence do you have?"

She had none, and that was the problem. "They kidnapped my cousin a while ago. After she escaped, they came after her again, and in the process Prince Rathan was killed in battle. Now they want to take it out on us."

Kyle seemed to think about this. "I was aware he had died, but not the circumstances. If they are out for revenge, why not sabotage the Sinclair's mine instead of yours?"

Those lips. They moved in such a sensual way that she had the urge to kiss him right then. Nothing like this had ever happened to her, and she didn't like it one bit. His soft confident words soothed her soul and scrambled her mind at the same time.

Before she could answer, her father stepped between them and faced her. "He's right, you know."

Her senses returned. "No, he's not. Why are you taking his side? We have to think about the men who work here. They have families to feed." Even to her own ears, she sounded a bit irrational.

"You know as well as I do that insurance will pay their wages," her father said. "I'm sure once Mr. Harper learns who is guilty, he'll reopen our mine." Her dad rubbed her arm. "Honey, we can weather the loss of revenue for a few weeks. Don't worry. Please."

Kyle nodded. "Thank you, Mr. Caspian, for being so open minded. Like I mentioned before, the more you cooperate, the faster we can resolve this."

Despite her dad's warning, Nessa spun to face Kyle again. "Fast you say? Neither you nor the police have learned who killed my second-in-command, and that accident happened a month ago. And don't try to tell me Wendan was careless. He wasn't. He knew as much about explosives as I do."

The outburst weakened her, but Nessa was not going to be deterred. No one, no matter how sexy he might be, was going to claim her family had been at fault. Not that he'd come out and accused them or anything, but he must be thinking it.

Kyle held up his hands. "Hey, I'm on your side. My men have been investigating non-stop since that particular incident occurred.

We too think he was targeted."

His words softened her, but she wouldn't relent. Nessa crossed her arms. "What have you found?"

"Not much, but that doesn't mean we won't keep looking."

"Someone tampered with those explosives between the time I looked at them and when Wendan got them."

Kyle pulled out a small tablet from his jacket pocket. "Do you suspect the Royals of that crime too?"

She skewed her lips to the side, mostly in disgust of her own attitude. "I don't know. That incident happened before my cousin was kidnapped."

"Nessa, you need to rest," her father said. He turned to Kyle. "Maybe this isn't the best time. I'm sure my daughter will be more cooperative after a good night's sleep."

From the way his chest rose and fell, he was debating how to handle her. Kyle faced her father. "I'll return tomorrow then. A representative from the insurance company will probably want to speak with her too." He faced Nessa. "Or should I tell her that you won't be filing a claim?"

Was he kidding? "Of course I will. Even if I weren't a Caspian, I know what happened was out of our control."

"Let's hope you're right." Kyle spun on his heels and left.

As soon as his footsteps disappeared down the hall, she faced her dad. "Can he really shut us down without cause?"

Her father clasped her shoulders. "Yes, he can. We need to find the culprit. Mr. Harper reminded us that we might not be safe against more attacks."

"You also told me he said we might have been negligent on the first two cases."

Her father nodded. "*Might* have been. He's leaning more toward sabotage now. Who *is* responsible though, I don't know."

"I told you the Royals are. They don't care if they hurt us or the Sinclairs. To them, we're the same."

"I wish we could prove that."

"Me too, Dad."

Chapter Four

Between Greer's magic hands and Nessa's dragon's healing powers, the ache in her chest was gone by morning, and her legs had totally healed. As much as Nessa had wanted to return to her apartment last night, her father had been against it. Greer suggested Nessa stay with her for the next few days, and she had reluctantly agreed. As fun as it was to catch up with her sister, Nessa was too independent to have someone watch her all the time.

Once Greer went into work, Nessa headed to the mine. Needing to discuss a few things with her father, she knocked on his office door and stepped inside.

He looked up from his large wood desk and smiled. "Hey, sweetheart." He came around his desk and gave her a hug. "How are you feeling?"

"I feel great, which is what I want to talk to you about." She sat in the chair facing him while her dad leaned a hip on the edge of his desk.

"What's up?"

"As nice as it was to stay with Greer last night, I'd feel more comfortable in my own apartment." Nessa didn't need his permission, but ever since Kyle Harper appeared in her life, she doubted her ability to think clearly.

"I'm surprised you'd want to stay alone. You're the one who said the explosion was sabotage. Since they failed to kill you, they might try again."

"If someone is targeting me, I want whoever it is to try again. It might be the only way we can capture him."

Her father slipped off the desk and looked down at her with the most soulful eyes. He leaned over and rubbed his hands down her arms. "My brave Nessa. When will you realize you don't have to carry the weight of the realm on your shoulders?"

"I'm not." Not much anyway. "I need to find out if anyone knows anything about the explosion. Someone must have seen or heard something, even if they don't realize it."

Her father straightened. "Nessa, do not get involved. Not only is it dangerous, the investigation is a job for the police and the Mining Consortium."

She had no intention of sitting on the sideline while others tried to do what she was perfectly capable of figuring out for herself. "Sure." *Not.*

"Good."

Oh, shit. "With everything that happened, I forgot to tell you that I found a vein of gold so big it will rock all of Tarradon—no pun intended."

He scowled. "That's wonderful, but I've decided we're not going down there again. It's too dangerous."

That was the last reaction she expected. "Are you kidding me? The find could be worth millions. We could buy more land with that money. I also know you've wanted to reforest the ten thousand acres to the west of us."

"That mine is bad luck, and you know perfectly well we can afford to reforest the land without any gold mine. I just need some time to get to it."

He'd never believed in back luck before—or good luck for that matter. Once this mess was cleared up, he'd change his mind. "After we find the culprit, we'll talk."

"There is no *we* about it. Someone else will investigate. I need you to stay safe. I want to be able to sleep at night." He squatted in front of her and clasped her hands in his big ones. "You gave us a huge scare, sweetheart." His words were thick with emotion. "Your mother and I don't want to go through that again. Ever."

She blew out a breath. "I admit I was scared a few times, but it wasn't like I was helpless."

"I know." Her dad stood and returned to his corner of the desk. It was as if he needed a moment to think. "Look, if you feel compelled to do something with your time, how about checking out the rest of the mines in the next few days? No one will be working them, and it will give you an opportunity to run safety checks. You've been asking for time to do that for a while."

Her mind wasn't on that work now, but if she told him she had no intention of letting the incompetent Mining Consortium handle things, he'd probably ask Birk to stay by her side. "Great idea, Dad. I'll do that."

As much as she trusted a few of the men in the Avondale Provincial Police—specifically her detective cousin, Anderson Caspian—an insider like herself would have a better chance of learning the truth.

She'd almost made it out of his office when her father called to her. "Don't forget that Kyle Harper is not the enemy. He didn't set the charge that nearly killed you. He wants to find the answers as much as we do."

She highly doubted that. The Mining Consortium was created and basically run by the Royals. The man would be biased. After all, if he found his employers guilty, he'd lose his job. "I know."

Nessa headed out, but she didn't go to the other mines like her dad had suggested. Instead, she wanted to check out the collapsed mine herself, if for no other reason than for closure. She was the demolition expert. If anyone could locate where the charges had been set, it would be her.

Wanting to test whether her wings had healed enough, she shifted and was pleased that she was able to soar upward. The first few wing flaps were painful, but the joy from the rush of the wind across her snout was worth the small ache. She was alive, and that was all that mattered—that and finding the bastard who'd done this to her family.

When the gold mine—as she liked to call it—came into sight,

she landed. The moment she shifted back into her human form, waves of lust hit her a second before she spotted Kyle Harper.

Damn it. Why would Fate pair the two of them? Kyle Harper didn't even like her kind. He might say sabotage was involved, but she could see it in his eyes that he wanted her family to be guilty.

Seduce him and then we'll find out if he wants us, her dragon chimed in.

That wasn't going to happen. Nessa wasn't up for the rejection. It didn't matter that she found him hot. Hell, it was hard enough to keep her libido in check just being around him let alone if she flirted with him.

Kyle must have sensed her presence because just then he turned around and strode toward her. Was that a hint of a smile? Probably not. Most likely he'd tell her to leave—that this was his investigation. He dragged what she would call an appreciative glance up and down her entire body, and heat swamped her.

"Nessa, you're looking better."

"I'm feeling better too." If she had any idea that Kyle would be at the site, she wouldn't have come. On the other hand, if they were destined for each other, she didn't want to start off on the wrong foot, so she painted on a smile. "How can I help you?"

He cocked a brow and then relaxed. "How about telling me what happened down in the mine?"

That was a reasonable request. Once she explained the series of events, he'd see that she'd done nothing wrong. "Several days ago, after the tunnel was complete, the men installed the mine elevator. It was tested and proven to be safe so I figured it was time to go down and have a look."

"If it was so safe, why not ask others to go with you?"

She appreciated that his tone wasn't accusatory. "All of the walls hadn't been tested for stability. Besides, I didn't need help to look for veins of metal."

He nodded. "Go on."

"Once I checked out the area to my satisfaction, I headed back to the elevator to return to the surface. I was maybe fifteen feet from the cage door when the world caved in on me. My dragon shifted to protect me from the blast, but even so, I was thrown against the wall." One of her biggest regrets was that the sample she'd been carrying had been lost.

His brows pinched, and his lips thinned. Hell, he acted as if he cared. "I can't believe you survived. I'm guessing the explosives must have been planted fairly close to the surface or you would have been buried alive."

She had basically been buried. It surprised and slightly delighted her that they were on the same page. "I was thinking that too."

Kyle stepped closer, and her brain short-circuited for a moment. His beautiful eyes turned a darker shade of blue, and his nostrils flared. If she didn't know better, she'd say he was checking her out and finding her acceptable.

Mate, mate, her dragon chimed in.

Not now.

"Did you notice any kind of tripwire that would have caused the charge to go off?" he asked. She shook her head. "Did you have any cameras installed to monitor the mine's building process? Maybe they caught someone on tape."

A trickle of embarrassment seeped in. "I wish. The cameras were scheduled to be installed after I made my initial assessment of the mine's viability. Once we begin any operation, we keep the area well lit and the cameras running all the time. Since this was not a functioning mine yet, those safeguards were not in place."

"I see."

Even she had to admit that Kyle appeared to be keeping an open-mind. As much as she should dislike him, she was finding it more and more difficult. It wasn't helping that when he drew in his bottom lip, she found it so freaking sexy.

What was wrong with her? This was more than being in lust. It was downright messing with her mind and her body.

"How long had you planned to stay down there to check things out?" Kyle asked.

Nessa looked over at the large hole that had once been the shaft. "Two hours max."

"Hmm. Then how would this person know when to set the charge? The window of opportunity was small."

She shook her head. "He wouldn't. I only decided at the last minute to go down that afternoon."

"Someone must have followed you."

No one followed her. Kyle must think she was totally incompetent to ask that. "I would have noticed." His brows rose. "Oh, shit."

"What is it?" He leaned forward.

"A dragon shifter could have cloaked himself and hovered above the mine. Normally, I can sense his presence, but I was so focused on exploring that I wasn't really paying attention to what was above me."

He scribbled something on his tablet. "That helps. I think. On a different note, could you tell from the sound or the strength of the blast what type of detonation was used?"

As much as she didn't want to tell him, he'd know if she lied. Everyone in her family knew the moment she made something up. "It's probably what we use here. The XY21 brand we use is strong yet accurate. Because it's so expensive, we and the Sinclairs are the only two mines in this province that use it."

"You're that sure it was the same brand?" he asked.

"Fairly certain. As a dragon shifter, I can tell the difference between sounds quite well."

"Even though you were taken off guard?"

Nessa lifted her chin. "Yes. I'm particularly sensitive to vibrations too."

"Got it." He made another note. "Could this person have raided your storage locker then? Or would he have been able to buy this brand someplace else?"

"He could buy it elsewhere, but it makes the most sense that he'd take the sticks from here. He wouldn't know when to detonate them unless, as I said, he was watching me from above."

"Who has access to this storage unit?"

The sun bounced off his eyes, distracting her once more. He inhaled and straightened his shoulders. Okay, he was trying to distract her. "Uh, only three people. Other than me, only my dad and Acton Draco, my new second-in-command knew the combination to get into the shed. I know for a fact Acton was in another province at the time of the detonation. He was purchasing more explosives."

"Then it had to be someone else."

Kyle was actually listening to her! Her inner dragon cheered. "Yes."

"I know demolition experts, like yourself, have a signature, if you will," he said. "If you could find the location of the detonation and see how it was rigged, would that narrow down the suspect pool?"

"I can't be sure. The only thing I'm certain about is that this person isn't human."

His eyes softened, and she swore he licked his lips to entice her. "How do you know that?"

"The electricity to the elevator wasn't turned on until the morning of my descent. To set the charge meant someone would have needed to fly down the shaft, implant the charges, and return the same way. Only a dragon shifter could have done that."

"Why have an elevator in the first place then?" he asked.

"Because humans and other shifters needed access to the mine once production began."

"I see. It makes sense then that a dragon shifter is most likely responsible."

From the way his lips firmed, he wasn't fond of them. Great.

"Yes, but even if we find where the charges were set, considering the level of destruction, I doubt I can identify the person who did this," she said.

"Don't be so sure. If we can find the box that held the charges, there might be fingerprints on it. Maybe we can trace it back that way."

Nessa's partially shifted her hands, and Kyle jumped back. His eyes widened and changed to a richer change of blue. "Holy shit. How did you do that?"

Damn. She shouldn't have demonstrated without explaining first. He already disliked her kind. Now he'd think she was trying to antagonize him or something. Her lack of judgment had to be a result of being too close to Kyle. Her hormones were interfering with everything. Nessa quickly returned her hands to their human form.

When he shoved his fingers through his dark brown silky hair—hair that she wanted to touch—her nails sharpened. Jeez.

"I didn't mean to scare you. I only wanted to show you that we can open boxes without leaving fingerprints."

"You didn't scare me. I was a bit startled, that's all. So basically, any dragon shifter could have set the charges?"

His defeatist attitude didn't help. "Yes. We have cameras pointing at the building where we keep the explosives, so that might help." His eyes brightened, and she'd never seen anything more beautiful or alluring.

"Can I check that out?"

The normally skeptic Nessa would have said no, but it was as if her dragon had put some kind of spell on her. "Sure. I'd love to catch the bastard in the act."

"Fantastic." Then he had to go and smile and light up every one of her cells—including her purple dragon scales under her skin. Damn him.

"We'll need to go back to the office."

He glanced around. "Great. Can I give you a lift?"

Maybe he hadn't seen her fly in. She could say yes, but being in a confined space with him might cause more issues. "I'll just fly back, thanks." She smiled to show him she wasn't a horrible person. "I can give you a ride if you'd like though. We can pick up your car later."

No, no, no! She didn't just offer that! Her mind must have been seriously affected by the blast.

It didn't matter. He'd never agree. Her cousin Kaleena had told her about her mate's first ride with her dad. Her mate, Finn, had screamed. And that man was a shifter—albeit a wolf shifter.

"For real?"

Oh, shit. He sounded interested. "Yes, but I fly rather high."

She had to admit that when they weren't talking about the mine, Kyle Harper was fun to be with.

He waved a hand. "Um, I think it's better if I take my car. I'd just have to come back and pick it up."

Aha. She figured he'd chicken out. That was okay. Holding him in her talons would have tested her resolve to the max. "See you back at the office then."

WHEN NESSA SHIFTED into her dragon form, Kyle couldn't help but stare at her grace and beauty. Then an image of his sister's burnt back came into his mind's eye, and he quickly sobered. Dragon shifters might seem normal on the outside, but they were not to be trusted.

Or could they be? Nessa Caspian had been open and honest with him. She'd told him things that implied she'd been careless in not installing cameras or making sure the storage locker was better secured. So maybe, she was one of the good ones. Nessa sure as hell was the prettiest dragon he'd ever seen. He bet those khaki pants and that baggy shirt hid a killer body too.

His cock hardened at that thought. Shit.

As for going for a ride with her, he had been tempted, but if he liked it, he'd be one step closer to earning his way into hell. Kyle Harper with a dragon shifter? No way. If he weakened and fell for Nessa, his sister would never forgive him. While it was his life to live, he didn't like heaping more pain on Lily.

As he turned to go back to his car, the sight of the collapsed mine caught his attention once more, and his admiration for Nessa grew. When she had told him how she'd managed to claw her way toward the surface with injured legs and a damaged wing, he had to admit the girl had guts. Most humans would have given up.

The more he was around Nessa, the more he was changing his mind about dragons in general. Some were bad, like the one Lily had dated, but he wasn't so blind that he couldn't see that some humans were just as evil—like serial killers. Just as there were other humans who gave their lives to help others, there might be good dragon shifters who did the same.

Or was he now rationalizing because Nessa was hot? Fuck, he was so confused.

Not wanting to keep her waiting, he jogged to his car then headed to the office. He didn't need to piss her off, especially since she was giving him the chance to find whoever might be responsible for these incidents.

Once he arrived at the main office, he spotted the mounted camera above the door. Good. Having surveillance would hopefully solve this case sooner rather than later. But why hadn't Dennis been given access when he'd investigated the first incident? Maybe he had, but he hadn't found anything. Kyle would have to ask him.

He knocked on the office door, and Nessa opened it up right away. For a split second, he allowed himself the luxury of drinking her in. She was tall for a woman—about three inches shorter than his six foot two height—but then again, most dragons came large. And strong. But what he hadn't heard was how beautiful they could be. Her long black hair was windblown and contrasted nicely with her warm, tanned skin. Her most striking characteristic by far was the color of her devastatingly beautiful green eyes that he'd seen morph into purple. Even her full lips and straight nose were just about perfect.

His cock pressed hard against his zipper once more. He worked to halt the testosterone coursing through his system, but he failed miserably. Damn, working side by side with Nessa was going to be rough.

"Come on in. The camera monitoring room is in the basement."

She sounded professional. Good. He could deal with that. Kyle followed her down several wide corridors, trying not to watch how her black hair swayed and caressed her body.

From the outside, the building didn't appear large, but looks were clearly deceiving. They came to an elevator about one hundred feet from the entrance.

"It's down a few floors," she said.

"How big is this complex?" Talking about facts would help keep his mind focused where it belonged.

"Big." She laughed and something inside him heated. Damn it.

Cute. Once they entered the small elevator, her scent permeated his senses. Nessa didn't seem the type to wear perfume, but she smelled like a gardenia—fragrant yet delicate.

She smoothed her hair. "Ah, you're staring," she said. "Is something wrong?"

Damn. "No. I'm just thinking about something. Sorry." That was lame, but thankfully she didn't question him further.

Several seconds later, they arrived deep underground. "It's to the right," she said, moving her gaze away, almost as if she were uncomfortable being here with him.

Even though there were no windows, the space was so well-lit that it didn't seem depressing or confining. Halfway down the hallway, Nessa knocked and then pushed open a door. She led him inside a small room that contained a bank of monitors. Seated in front of one screen was a man who looked to be about twenty-five.

He turned around. "Hey, Nessa, how are you doing? I haven't seen you since…well, you know."

"I'm fine. Thanks for asking. Vic, this is Kyle Harper, the head of the Mining Consortium."

Vic shoved back his chair, stood, and held out his hand. "Nice to meet you. I've worked with Dennis Taylor."

"Great."

"I want to check out the tapes of the storage room holding the explosives," Nessa said. "Can you pull them up for us?"

"How far back should I go?"

Nessa turned to Kyle. "What do you think?"

He loved that she was willing to have his input. It was almost as if they weren't on opposite sides anymore. "Two months maybe?"

She twisted her lips into a sexy pose. "Why that far back?" she asked.

"If what you claim is true, it's possible whoever was responsible for the first explosion came into the storage room, tampered with the explosives, and then stole extra ones."

"I hadn't thought of that."

He appreciated that she would admit that. "Do you keep records of how much is removed on a daily basis?"

Nessa glanced to the side. "Yes and no. I mean, we're supposed to document everything, and I'm usually the one to take them—or Wendan was. But after his death, I kind of lost control of things for a while." She sucked in a big breath through gritted teeth. "Shit. I'm sorry."

Poor Nessa. The man's death had shaken her. "Let's take a look at the tapes and see what comes up."

"Do you want me to stay?" Vic asked.

"Go ahead and take a break. I imagine we'll be here for a few hours. I'll keep my eye on the rest of the stations."

He smiled. "Thanks."

Be with Nessa for a few hours? Kyle wasn't sure he could keep from daydreaming about her. As much as he wanted to think of her as the enemy, by not hiding anything, she was making it damned hard for him. To make matters worse, her delicious scent and sensuous movements made him want to know what was underneath that boring beige uniform of hers.

Nessa looked over at him. "This will be tedious. If you want, I can look through them first."

He smiled. "Nice try, but I want to see what you do."

As if she'd hope he'd say that, she returned his smile, and his damn cock turned stiff again. He shifted in his seat. "Let's do it."

Chapter Five

WHY, OH, WHY had Nessa suggested she and Kyle watch hours of boring tapes together? It was hard enough to talk to him, let alone sit next to him, especially when her dragon was panting and clawing at her insides to put the moves on him. Those inappropriate comments about what they should do with Kyle once Nessa stripped him naked wasn't helping with her concentration.

She sighed. "This is pointless. No one other than me or my foreman ever entered this room."

Kyle placed a hand on her arm, almost as if he'd just thought of something, and the touch caused her inner scales to glow. Thank goodness for her long sleeve shirt. Since Kyle had freaked when her hands had turned dragon, he'd totally run if she started to glow. She sensed he wasn't used to being around her kind.

"Could your foreman have removed the explosives and given them to someone?" He almost sounded excited to find someone to blame.

"No way. He never would have done that. As for Acton, who replaced Wendan, he doesn't have a bone of deceit in his body." Even after Kyle removed his hand, the heat remained. "Yet the perpetrator had to have gotten them from somewhere."

"You mentioned that, but even if we could get the company to divulge their customer list, there would be no way of knowing who used the explosives at your mine."

She blew out a breath. "I think our only hope is to remain more vigilant and hope we catch him the next time he tries something."

He glanced over at her. "The mine won't reopen until this is solved, you know."

She tried to convince herself that Kyle was just doing his job and not being spiteful or following orders from the Royals.

"What if you never figure this out?" she asked, trying not to let her frustration show. "If the mine remains closed, the perpetrator will have won. We'll never catch him."

"There is that risk. My men have spoken to most of the workers here, but they claim to know nothing."

"I'll talk to them," Nessa said. "With a little encouragement, they'll be open with me. I'll ask them to think outside the box."

Kyle shook his head. "It's too dangerous. If they think we are getting close, that person might harm you again. I won't let that happen."

His words stunned her. Before she could respond, Birk charged into the room, the lines around his eyes deeper than usual, and Nessa's heart shot to her throat. She shoved back her chair and jumped up. "What is it? What's wrong?"

"A dam burst over in Grindale Province close to where Gregor Kearn lives. People are losing their homes from all the mudslides, and our men want to help." He turned to Kyle. "I see no reason not to let them go, unless you've figured out who is responsible and plan to let us reopen our mine."

Didn't she wish?

"I'm afraid not," Kyle said. "We don't have many leads. Yet. How did a dam burst?"

Had it been sabotage? Or was she so focused on evil that she couldn't think of anything else?

Birk shrugged. "Right now, it doesn't matter what caused it. We'll figure it out eventually. These people need our help. I'll let our dragons know they can fly over there to help with the rescue."

She pushed back her chair. "I'll come with you."

Birk held up a palm. "Nessa, someone needs to stay here. I don't like the mine being exposed."

He had a point, though she suspected that wasn't the whole

truth. "How many men are going?"

"Almost all of them. With the mine shut down, they are eager to be useful. Even the humans want to help."

She glanced over at Kyle. "Do you think it's some kind of ploy to draw our people there so that the mine will be vulnerable?"

"Possibly."

She turned back to her brother. "Is anyone speculating if the dam breach was due to sabotage? If I recall, it's not very old."

"I don't know."

She tapped a finger on her lips. "If our men all go, it would give the person the chance to swoop in and do more damage."

Birk blew out a breath. "When did you become so distrustful?"

When I was trapped in a mine. "My job is to make sure this place is safe."

He dragged a hand down his jaw. "Tell you what. I'll make sure enough men remain here. They'll stay on high alert until the rest of us return."

Nessa had the best brother and the best workers. She hugged Birk. "Thank you and stay safe."

"You too."

Kyle stood. As soon as Birk rushed out, he faced her. "What are you planning to do now?"

"How about you stay here and finish looking at the tapes, while I speak with the men who are staying. I want to make sure we have all of our bases covered."

"Good thinking. What could someone do now to harm the mine? It's already shut down."

"That's easy. They could plant remote detonation devices to go off whenever they choose. Once we are back up and running—which we will be at some point—they could orchestrate another cave in. Only this time it could kill a lot of people. If I had been down there with any humans, they all would have died. If that happened, we'd be the first to close our doors."

"Or I would have."

"We wouldn't need to be told. We care about each other. All of the workers would be compensated." She shook her head. "I don't know what happened to you growing up to make you so distrustful of others, but you need to be more open-minded." Nessa hadn't meant her voice to rise to a near shout, but she hated people who were prejudiced. "Dragons shifters are everywhere on Tarradon. Some good. Some bad."

Kyle held up his palms. "I'm sorry. You're right. It's just that a dragon shifter abused my sister, Lily, horribly. It's where my distrust stems from."

"Well, I've been treated poorly by humans and dark lighters, but that doesn't mean I hate all of them. Okay, maybe I do hate the dark lighters since they are born to be evil, but not all humans are bad."

He leaned closer, and her pulse soared, forcing Nessa to step back to put some distance between them.

"My sister wasn't just treated poorly, she was badly scarred," he said, his voice elevating.

Nessa stilled. "Emotionally or physically?"

"Both. She dated a man who she thought was the love of her life. He was good looking, strong, smart, and had a great job. Then one day, he lost his patience and accused her of things that were completely untrue. Back then, Lily wasn't one to fight back."

"What did she do?"

"She walked away from him."

"Good for her."

"That's when the motherfucker shot fire at her back and scorched her from shoulder to waist."

Nessa sucked in a breath and almost grabbed his hand to console him. "She could have been killed from a burn that size."

Nessa had been harmed once by a dragon's fire when her back was turned, but with the help of Declan, the injury had been quickly reversed. She'd never forget the excruciating pain before he arrived to help her though. Even her dragon had struggled to cure her.

"It almost did kill her. I don't think I slept for weeks. Between my job and tending to my sister, life became a blur."

He loves her. Okay, she hadn't seen that coming. Maybe Fate did know what he or she was doing when she'd paired the two of them together. "How is she now?" Nessa asked, keeping her tone soft.

His lip curled. "How do you expect? It's been three years, but she rarely dates. For the most part, except for when she needs to be out and about for her job, she doesn't leave her apartment."

This time Nessa placed a hand on his arm to give him some comfort, and that one touch caused her scales to glow. She immediately lowered her hand. "I'm sorry."

Kyle glanced away. "So am I. You can see why dragons aren't my family's favorite creatures." He chuckled.

He considered her a creature? Or was that merely a figure of speech? "Do you think all dragons are bad?" Nessa was pleased that she didn't sound too accusatory.

He returned his gaze to her and held her trapped in its intensity for several seconds. "I don't know."

Not the response she was hoping for. "Do you think the men who flew out of here to help those in need in Grindale province are bad?"

He shook his head. "You're twisting my words."

Was she? She didn't need to get into an argument with him. "Keep watching the tapes. I need to talk to the men who've elected to stay."

Without waiting for him to respond, she rushed out.

KYLE'S HEAD SWAM with confusion. He'd spent his life battling his prejudices. When his dad walked out on him, his mom, and Lily, Kyle had decided at the ripe age of seven that marriage wasn't for him. Then, when he was nine, several large men, who he later learned were dragon shifters, evicted the three of them from their trailer for not paying their rent for two months. At the time, he thought that was terrible and that the government should help instead of forcing them to live in a tent. He later learned his mom had been too strung out to apply for any kind of aid. It shouldn't have come as a surprise that when Lily started dating Nelor, Kyle was not happy with her choice. Unfortunately, his innocent younger sister was a romantic, and Nelor knew just what to say and do to convince her that he was the perfect man.

Kyle's fists clenched at how he'd held his tongue and stood by while Lily blissfully fell for the asshole. She'd told him that Nelor had shoved her once, but that she'd deserved it. Kyle had tried to explain that no one deserved to be treated with disrespect. Unfortunately, his brotherly advice fell on her deaf ears, and no matter what he said or did, Lily defended the man until the day he used his deadly dragon fire and burned her. Now, his sister was damaged both inside and out.

Kyle probably shouldn't have told Nessa dragons were terrible. After all, the entire crew had spent tireless hours digging in an unstable pit until they found her. Humans would have assumed the person was dead and abandoned the effort. Then there was the call to action regarding the flood victims. He'd never seen anything like it— or rather never heard about that kind of fast response.

Wanting to learn more about the disaster, Kyle yanked out his cell to check on the story of the broken dam. It didn't take long to find coverage. He stared at what appeared to be a swarm of black birds scooping up people and then carrying them to safety. While the rescue would be unnerving for the victim, the terror would be short-lived once that person was deposited in a safe and dry location.

Okay, maybe a few dragons were good, but that didn't mean he wouldn't be cautious.

"This just in," said the commentator. "We have footage of someone sneaking into the turbine room carrying what is believed to be explosives in his backpack. The former dam worker, Jax Delinia, had been laid off two weeks before and allegedly wanted retribution. The dragon shifter is now in custody."

Great. Another bad dragon shifter. At least the culprit had been identified.

Enough playing around. Needing to tackle this job, Kyle returned to watching the tape feed from the room that contained the explosives. He was just about to press the play button to cycle through a few more days, when he noticed a man with his back pressed to the side of a building on one of the live feed screens. Kyle leaned forward to study the slightly blurred image. The man, whose face was averted from the camera, appeared to have something in his hand, but Kyle couldn't tell what it was. Perhaps it was the story of the dam that made him think something bad was about to go down.

The man tugged on a locked door, kicked it, and when it didn't budge, he moved down the building and tested each entrance. Okay, this wasn't good. Needing to report this, Kyle slipped out of the monitoring room to find Vic. Unfortunately, neither Vic nor anyone else was around.

That left Nessa. Once outside, he looked for her, but the whole place seemed to be abandoned. Great. He wasn't about to stand by and let this guy do damage to Caspian property. Kyle hopped in his car and headed in the direction of the building where he'd spotted the man on camera. Thankfully, someone had labeled each of the monitors to indicate where the camera was pointed. The map of the complex on the wall across from the monitors told him all he needed to know.

Kyle suspected the man was long gone, but just in case he wasn't, Kyle parked a couple hundred feet away and headed in on foot. While he wasn't trained to take down intruders, he had grown up on the streets and learned to fight the hard way. He already had a broken nose, a broken jaw, and a few stab wounds to prove it.

Learning the art of stealth during his troubled youth, Kyle darted toward the building and pressed his back against the side. He could only hope that Vic wasn't back in the room to see him.

A slight shuffling sound caught his attention, but a quick scan of the area showed no one was near. Darn. As Kyle made his way down the length of the sixty-foot long building that housed equipment, he listened for more movement but found none. Perhaps Nessa or one of the crew had sent this man to retrieve something, and he'd come and gone.

Even though Kyle relaxed a bit, he stopped right before he rounded the corner, and then glanced around it but spotted no one. Oh, well. As soon as he completed a full sweep, he'd return to the office, find Nessa, and tell her what he'd seen. Kyle walked down the last side of the building, and right before he'd reached the end, he felt a pain the size of Tarradon crash down on his head. When his face hit the dirt, darkness surrounded him as he passed out.

Chapter Six

ONCE NESSA SPOKE with the men who would be standing watch, she fluttered down the shaft of the collapsed mine, her wings scraping against the walls. Yes, she'd told Kyle that she was just going to speak with those who'd remained behind, but that only took a few minutes. Not wanting to go back into that confining room for another few hours where she'd have to tamp down her desires, Nessa decided to follow up on something Kyle had asked her: if she found the spot where the explosives were placed, could she identify the person?

She didn't know the answer, which was why she was at the semi-collapsed tunnel now. When the passageway turned too narrow, she dug her talons into the side and hung on. The problem with this method of descent was the instability of the dirt. A few times, a quick movement resulted in her sliding down twenty feet or more. Eventually, she figured out the technique of keeping hold while meticulously looking for evidence of the blast.

Nessa was about sixty feet down when she spotted a piece of explosive sticking out from the wall. This wire, along with an attached piece of paper, would hopefully point her in the direction of the culprit.

When Kyle saw this evidence, it would only add fuel to his already dim view of her species, but it couldn't be helped. Facts were facts. Nessa dug into the wall and extracted more bits and pieces of the device. She lifted the paper and metal scrap to her nose and sniffed. Yup. It was the same kind Caspian mines used. Damn. She didn't dare speculate who might have set this charge. It would be too painful to learn there was a traitor in her midst.

Once she was satisfied she'd found the majority of the device, Nessa crawled upward until the passage widened, and then she flew to the surface.

With her found prize in her claw, she returned to the office and shifted. Lunchtime had come and gone, so maybe she could convince Kyle to join her for a meal.

She also just wanted to spend some time with him—away from that small room—despite the fact he jacked up her libido something fierce. She not only lusted after him, she also liked the guy. His concern for his sister spoke volumes about him. Sure, he was a little one-sided in his thinking about dragon shifters, but if he learned more about her and realized she had the same hopes, dreams, and work ethic that everyone else did, he might decide she wasn't that bad after all.

At the office, she headed down to the monitoring room. When she pushed open the door, she stilled. No one was there. Okay, that was odd. Either Kyle needed a break or he'd found something and had driven out to find her. He hadn't come to the mineshaft though. Then again, Nessa hadn't told anyone where she'd be.

She slipped her phone from her pocket. Because she didn't have Kyle's number, she called Vic, hoping he'd know where Kyle was.

"Hey, you guys finished?" he asked.

That wasn't good. "I'm not with Kyle. I went out to do something, and when I returned he—oh, shit." She suddenly caught sight of a man face down at the equipment building.

"What is it?"

"Something's happened. Can you get back here and rerun the tape of building eight? I need to check it out in person."

"I'll be there as fast as I can."

Fearing the prone man was Kyle, she raced down the hallway and jumped back into the elevator. Once she made it outside, Nessa shifted, took off, and bore down on the building. When she spotted his parked car, her heart sped up.

Please don't let it be Kyle.

Nessa landed, shifted, and ran to where she'd seen the injured man. Her anxiety level shot through the roof when she realized it was him. Blood covered the back of his head, and her legs weakened at the implication.

She dropped to her knees next to him and placed two fingers on his neck. *You can't be dead. You just can't be.*

When a thin beat registered, she let out a breath. The dark pool of blood beside his head was quite large. If she thought Declan or Greer could get there quickly enough, she'd wait for them, but from the severity of the injury, it would be best if she took him to a human hospital right away.

By now, Vic should be watching what was happening, so she looked up and waved. A second later, she returned to her dragon form. Gently, she picked up an unconscious Kyle. *I'm sorry you won't be awake to enjoy your first ride.*

Once he was securely in her grasp, she soared upward and headed into town. His limp body tore at her. Who the hell had done this to him? And why? Her intense worry morphed into anger, and by the time she arrived at the Emergency Room entrance, she had to work to control herself from tearing something apart.

Nessa landed off to the side of the entrance, set a still unconscious Kyle on the grass, and shifted into her human form once more. While she could have carried him to the front door, it would be more efficient if she found assistance and asked for help. She'd heard enough stories from Kaleena about the Emergency Rooms in the US to know they prioritized their patients depending on the seriousness of the case. She suspected it was the same on Tarradon.

In order for the medics to take her seriously, she smeared some of his blood on her hands as well as down the front of her shirt. Leaving Kyle safely in the grass, she ran into the Emergency entrance and acted rather hysterical. Truth be told, it wasn't far from the way she felt.

Once she told them what she believed had happened, the attendants rushed outside with a gurney and placed Kyle on top. As much as she wanted to go with him, she had to fill out paperwork first.

As they wheeled Kyle into a curtained room, she approached the front desk. The insurance forms were rather problematic since she didn't know where he lived, what his cell phone number was, or how to reach Lily. She did the best she could, filling in her own information in places. After she gave her SinCas insurance card to the hospital to pay for Kyle's stay, Nessa settled back to wait.

Her stomach grumbled, but she wasn't sure she could eat even if she found a vending machine. Poor Kyle. What had possessed him to leave the monitoring room?

Needing answers, she called Vic again. He answered on the first ring. "Nessa, how's Kyle?"

"The doctors are treating him now, but I don't know if he has regained consciousness. Did the tapes indicate what happened?"

He explained about seeing a man at the equipment building who was trying to gain entrance.

"I take it you didn't recognize him?" she asked.

"No. He kept his face away from all of the cameras. It was almost as if he'd cased the place beforehand and knew where not to look."

Right now, she had to worry about Kyle getting better. Once he recovered, she'd get even. "Then what happened?"

"Kyle was checking out the building when he collapsed."

"He didn't just collapse. He has a huge gash in the back of his head, which was not the result of the fall. He landed on his face."

"I don't know what to tell you."

"Maybe the assailant cloaked himself." She kept her voice to a whisper. Sure, everyone knew about dragons being able to shield themselves, but the extent of their magic was often kept on the down low so as not to frighten people.

"That's what it seems like."

That would mean he was either in his dragon form when he hit Kyle, or he was a powerful dark lighter imbued with the ability to become invisible. "That could explain why Kyle might not have heard him approach. Did you see the guy go into the building?"

"No, but I'll keep looking."

"Thanks, Vic."

Once she disconnected, she slumped in her chair. This was worse than she thought. How in the hell could they catch this person if he possessed so much magic? In her mind, she recreated each of the accidents. Stealing the explosives while invisible would be easy to accomplish, as would speeding up the metal cart that jumped the track, crushing Ed Hollix's leg. As for the incident that involved collapsing the mine where she'd been trapped, the security had been lax in that area since the mine hadn't been fully operational yet.

So who was the guilty party? As far as she knew, none of the Royals possessed that ability. Even though they received some of their power from the dark lighters, she believed she would have heard if any of them had the ability to become invisible.

"Ms. Caspian," said a deep voice.

She jumped up. "Yes?"

"We've finished treating Mr. Harper. His wound was deep and required stitches. He's regained consciousness, but he has a major headache from the concussion."

"When can he be released?"

"Not until tomorrow. We'll need to monitor him overnight."

"May I see him?"

"For a short time."

Nessa wasn't sure what to expect, but she doubted it would be good. When she entered Kyle's room, his eyes were closed. A patch was taped to the back part of his head, and an IV was hooked up to his arm. Even in his injured state, her body exploded with not only concern but overwhelming need. If she ever doubted Kyle Harper was her mate, this erased it.

Nessa waited at the end of the bed, not sure if she should disturb him. Then the unthinkable happened. Her nails began to grow, and her scales glowed. Damn. She didn't know how to stop her body from reacting in such an erotic way.

He must have sensed her because he opened his eyes, but then closed them right away.

Great. He didn't want to see her, and she couldn't blame him. Nessa turned to leave.

"Stay," he said in a wobbly voice.

She hadn't expected that request, but maybe he wanted to tell her about the attack. She dragged over a chair and sat next to the bed. Too bad moving so close to him made her body react even more violently. Seeing him wounded must have ratcheted her need to protect him. That or her horny dragon just wanted her to slip into bed next to him and hold him tight.

"How do you feel?" She rubbed a hand down his arm, wanting to show her support, but that only pooled heat between her legs.

"Like I got run over by a truck." He gave her a brief smile, and her pulse rose.

"Do you remember what happened?" she asked. Needing to put some distance between them, she stood, walked over to the window and looked out at the garden behind the building.

He told her about seeing someone acting suspiciously, and how after watching the news on the burst dam, he got it into his head that this person might be up to something.

She twisted to face him. "No offense, but you're only human." When his jaw clenched, her heart dropped to her stomach. "I mean, most of the people working for us are shifters, and most of them are dragons."

"I'm a mining inspector. It's my job to investigate."

She was blowing this. Wanting to change the subject, she returned to the chair, determined to keep her focus. "You're right. I'm sorry. I trust you didn't see the person who hit you?"

"Only on the monitor. When I got there, he was gone, or so I thought."

Wanting to give him some hope that the culprit would be caught, she told him about her find. "I located evidence of the explosive caps, and as I suggested before, only a dragon shifter could have put them there."

"What?" He winced. "You went to the site again? That's dangerous. It's cordoned off for a reason."

"Sorry, but I was careful." Or so she believed. "I couldn't get the question you asked me out of my mind."

He raised a brow. "What question?"

"About whether I would recognize the signature of the shifter who placed the explosive. I had to check it out."

"Did you figure it out?" he asked.

"No."

He shook his head and then winced. "Nessa. When will you learn this is my investigation?"

Fuck. "I won't go again. I promise."

"Good." Kyle tried to sit up but then grimaced and dropped back down. "Did you take the evidence to my office so we could document what you found?"

"As for getting the evidence documented, if I had been in my human form, I would have taken pictures. Dragons do have some limitations." She smiled, but he didn't return the cheer. "But I will do that once I get back to the mining office."

"Thank you."

Nessa stood, in part because she was way too tempted to lift that one strand of hair that had flopped over his forehead. Thankfully, she refrained from touching him again. "I should let you rest. The nurse said to stay only a few minutes. I can come back later if you'd like."

"Yes, please do." His eyes closed, and a second later, he was snoring.

Nessa chuckled. Kyle Harper was all male. Even a few feet outside the room, her body continued to vibrate.

All during her short flight back to the office, she tried to sort out why someone had attacked Kyle. This person could have let him walk around the building, and when Kyle saw no one, he would have left. His attacker must have believed Kyle was close to finding out his identity. It was the only thing that made sense.

Back at the office, Nessa headed straight to the monitoring room to watch the incident on tape, hoping she'd spot something Vic missed. Then she planned to check out the warehouse to see if anything had been taken. She told herself she wasn't investigating a crime, but merely keeping the mine safe.

Vic was inside the room when she entered. "Did you find anything else?" she asked.

He shook his head. "I played the video over and over again. The man was there just like Kyle said, but then he disappeared into thin air. It took me several rewinds to notice some dust kicked up behind Kyle."

"What does that mean?"

He stopped the tape. "Take a look at this big rock."

"What about it?"

He fast-forwarded for two seconds. "It's here one second, and then it's gone. The man or dragon must have picked up the rock. When it disappeared, he hit Kyle with it," Vic said with a fair amount of sureness.

"It has to be a dragon shifter who's also a dark lighter." That scared the crap out of her.

"Know anyone like that?" Vic asked.

"No. I'll ask a few men to keep a close watch on the area. If the perpetrator didn't get what he wanted the first time, he might return."

"I'll note any suspicious behavior too. Did you call the cops yet?"

Shit. "Not yet, but I will."

Nessa stepped outside and called her cousin Detective Anderson Caspian. She told him what happened.

"How is Mr. Harper?"

She explained about the stitches and that the hospital was keeping him over night.

"I'm glad he's going to be okay. As soon as someone is free, I'll send him over to investigate."

"Thanks." She'd also give him the evidence she'd found. She trusted the police more than Kyle's office.

While she waited for the police to show, Nessa wanted to keep busy, mostly to keep her focus off her desire for Kyle. It was always possible this attack was aimed at her and the mine and not at him. After all, the explosion that collapsed the gold mine occurred first.

Once she left the office, she shifted and flew to the area where Kyle had been attacked. Before she landed, Nessa hovered slightly above the building to see if anything was out of place. No telling if the person Anderson sent to investigate would be a dragon shifter or not. It took her three sweeps before she noticed recent marks of a dragon landing. The tracks changed to human footsteps halfway across the top of the building. Because the roof hadn't been cleaned in forever, it aided in seeing the tracks.

Considering the person's extensive talents, she had to scratch off the Royals as possible suspects, unless they'd hired some powerful dragon shifter to do their bidding.

Nessa landed alongside the building and looked for clues. It didn't take long before she located the bloody rock ten feet from where she'd found Kyle. Her stomach churned at the thought of his head being cracked open. While she doubted the attacker left any of his own evidence, she'd let the police make that call. Hopefully, the shifter's ability to become invisible caused him to be overconfident.

After entering the warehouse that contained the mining equipment she had planned to use for the gold mine, Nessa mentally ran through a list of what was there. After a thorough search, nothing seemed to have been taken. If they ever did excavate again, she'd be sure to check that nothing had been tampered with though.

The only leads so far were the rock and the small piece of explosive. As much as she wanted to go back and check on Kyle, she didn't want to overstay her welcome. Right now, he needed to rest.

After an hour of waiting for the cop, she called Anderson again. "It's Nessa. I was looking over where Kyle was injured and found a rock that has some blood on it. Is your man going to show up or would you like me to take it to the station?"

"Did you touch the rock?"

Damn. "I did. I'm sorry. I wasn't thinking."

"Then you might as well bring it here. Sorry about my man not showing up. There was an incident outside of town, and I needed the whole crew to check it out. I'm heading out there now, but I should return in an hour."

"Not a problem. I'll see you soon."

With the rock safely in her grasp and the piece of explosive in her pocket, she hopped in Kyle's car, knowing he would need it when he was released from the hospital. Because of her bloodied shirt, she had to stop at the SinCas building first to change. No way could she waltz into the police station like that. It would cause too many questions.

Once on the bottom floor of SinCas, Nessa headed to the changing room where she placed the evidence in a bag in her locker. She then slipped off her bloodied top and put on a nice white button-down shirt she kept there in case she needed to attend a meeting. She'd change her pants later.

Anderson wouldn't be back at the station for a while, so Nessa decided to spend a few minutes confiding in Greer about what had gone on with Kyle's attack. Nessa found her sister hunched over the jewelry counter at the front of the store.

"Hey!" Nessa called.

Greer jerked upright and smiled. She was dressed in a black pencil skirt and a rather conservative white silk blouse that hugged her body. Her reddish blonde hair was pulled back into a bun, making her look elegant yet approachable at the same time.

Her sister's eyes widened. "This is a nice surprise. What are you doing here?"

"The mine is closed, and most of the men, including Dad, are over in Grindale, helping out with the emergency from the break in the dam."

"I heard about that. It's terrible. I donated to the cause, but I wish I could do more."

Greer was such a caring person. "If you want, you could tell people that since the mine is basically empty right now, they could drop stuff off there and we could fly it to Grindale. Or the humans could drive the donations to the next province. I know everyone wants to help."

"That's a great idea."

Greer came from behind the counter and placed a hand on her arm. "I don't think you came here to tell me that. What's really troubling you?"

Her sister wasn't psychic, but her ability to heal made her highly intuitive. There was no use lying. "It's Kyle."

"The mining inspector?" Nessa nodded. "What about him?"

So much had happened today, Nessa had forgotten to tell any-one, other than Anderson and Vic, about the incident. "He was injured today." *And I'm really upset because he's my mate.*

"Oh, no. How?"

Nessa went through how they were watching tapes to determine if anyone around the gold mine looked suspicious. "I needed to speak to the men who were there to protect the mine, so I went outside. I also wanted to take a break from being around Kyle. He jumbles my brain." *And my body.*

Greer shook her head. "Since when do you take breaks—especially when you're on a mission?"

Nessa hadn't come here to spill the beans, but she needed to explain herself.

Oh, damn. There was no use keeping it a secret from her sister. Greer would find out soon enough. "As hard as it was to accept, it turns out Kyle is my mate."

Chapter Seven

NESSA DIDN'T EXPECT the squeal and subsequent hug from her sister. "That's wonderful. I know Kyle's human, but does he possess some white lighter abilities?"

The words spewed out of her sister's mouth so fast Nessa found it hard to keep up. "He could have some abilities. I never asked him. Remember, we are adversaries—or rather we were. It's not like we met at a bar and struck up a conversation, so finding a way to get to know him is hard—and vice versa."

Greer waved a hand. "It doesn't matter. What does matter is whether you are happy."

"I am, though it's hard to have too much enthusiasm when he basically distrusts all dragons."

Greer whistled. "That is tough."

"Tell me about it."

"Does he know you are mates?"

Nessa laughed. "Hardly. Right now I'm betting he wants to keep his distance, especially after he was attacked on our property."

"You can't let him get away. If you mess this up, you'll lose your one chance at happiness."

Nessa shrugged. "Things always have a way of working out."

"Only if you're willing to wait a long time. I think you need to go after him now."

"If I come on to him, he'll think I'm trying to sway him into opening the mine or something."

"Not if your passion is real." Greer clasped her hands together. "This is so exciting." She then sobered. "Why aren't you by his side?

You need to show him that he matters to you; that you want him in your life."

Nessa sighed. "I saw him briefly a little while ago. I'm letting him rest."

"Then you need to go back there this evening to show him your support. I bet even for a guy, it's scary being alone in a hospital."

Nessa wanted to see him, but every time she was around him, signs of her lust became more evident. "I imagine it is, but what if I say something inappropriately suggestive, and it turns him off? Besides, I'm more used to being gruff than soft and feminine."

"Now that you've found your mate, I bet that will change." Greer's eyes sparkled. "I get off work in a little while. How about stopping over at my place, and I'll find something for you to wear when you visit him?"

Nessa chuckled. "Wear?"

Greer sighed. "Has Kyle ever seen you in anything other than your work outfit?"

"No."

Greer planted a hand on her hip. "If you're going to win him over, a little sex appeal won't hurt."

Nessa chuckled. "I have my own wardrobe I can pick from." Kind of.

Greer shrugged. "If you want to go hiking in the woods or crawling through a mine, sure, but you rarely show off your…"

"My what? Boobs and legs? Are you saying that I'm not feminine enough?"

"Not exactly, but they are your best attributes. While I love your ponytail, it lacks a certain kind of…oh, I don't know…sensuality." Greer leaned over, lifted Nessa's ponytail, and then let it drop. "I'm just saying that if you want Kyle Harper to desire you, consider dressing a little more…shall we say, provocatively."

Nessa huffed. "Next you're going to tell me to put on eyeliner and blush so I look like a stripper."

Greer laughed, and the light tinkling sound helped soothe her bruised ego. "I wear eyeliner, blush, and lipstick. Do I look like a stripper?"

"No, you always look elegant and well put together."

"See? Tonight. Five fifteen. My place."

Nessa knew when she was defeated. "Fine."

Perhaps it would take her mind off this whole sabotage thing if she let her sister play dress up. After one more hug, Nessa left.

The next order of business was to return Kyle's car since he'd need it once he returned from the hospital. The problem was that she didn't know where he lived. Her brother Logan might be able to find out though. Not only did he run the business end of the company, he was a computer expert. While he didn't like to snoop or do anything illegal, the man could find information on the web like no one else.

She called Logan who answered on the first ring. "Hey. I heard you were holding down the fort."

"I was until someone was injured at the mine a few hours ago."

"Who?" His tone turned almost cold.

"It's not one of our workers. It was Kyle Harper."

"The mining inspector?"

"Yes."

"Was he badly hurt?" he asked with sudden warmth.

"Kind of." She explained about the blow to the head and the subsequent concussion.

"Sounds painful."

"I want to return his car to his place, but I don't know where he lives."

"Give me a sec to check." Tapping sounds filtered through to her. "Got it. He lives over on Pindale and Wayne." He gave her the address.

"Thanks."

"I have to say, you sound overly worried about him."

Her pulse shot up. Nessa wasn't ready to blurt out that Kyle was her mate. The two of them needed to spend more time together before she told everyone.

"I just feel responsible for leaving him alone in the monitoring room." She wouldn't have left him in the first place if her hormones hadn't been going wild—and if she hadn't needed to make sure the skeleton crew was clear on their jobs. Knowing her, if she stayed in those close quarters, she might have done something stupid—like kiss him. Or worse, straddle him.

Who was she kidding? Every time she was close, she wanted to rip off his clothes and do him.

"Ah, huh."

"Thank you, Logan."

She smiled then disconnected. Her brother was too intuitive for his own good. It was partly what made him a good businessman. He could tell when someone was telling the truth and when he was lying. Clearly, he'd spotted her stretch of truth on why she wanted to help Kyle.

THIS WAS A bad idea. She never should have let Greer *dress* her. For starters, Nessa Caspian did not wear dresses. It was why she didn't even own one. It would be one thing if this had been a dinner date, but a trip to a hospital? She felt ridiculous. If she didn't possess excellent balance, she'd never have been able to walk in heels. Sandals were much more her style.

After Greer finished with her, Nessa didn't have time to go home, shower, and redress before visiting hours were over. Because she wanted time to think about what she was going to say to Kyle, she took her car to the hospital instead of flying. Since he had no idea how that man got the drop on him, she bet he'd be curious to know what she'd learned. His reaction when he found out that some magical beast had bested him would be less than positive.

She wouldn't be surprised if Kyle told her he would never come near the mine again. If Kyle hadn't been her mate, she would have been thrilled by this fact, but not anymore. It wasn't just because they were mates either. Everything about Kyle drew her in. No doubt about it, he'd hooked her.

Regardless of their mate status, she needed him to sign off on the fact that her family had not been at fault for any of the accidents. The insurance company was already breathing down their necks.

Nessa pressed the elevator button to Kyle's hospital floor, and it arrived too quickly. Once at his door, she knocked and then entered. Two heads turned. Oh, crap. One face glared at her, while the more important one gave her an appreciative look, helping to boost her confidence. Clearly, she was interrupting some important conversation.

"I, ah, can come back later," she said. Talk about uncomfortable. "I didn't know you had company."

"No, stay. This is my sister, Lily."

She should have guessed. Wasn't this just fantastic? Standing straighter, Nessa plastered on her best smile and held out her hand, but the handshake was not returned. Nessa hoped Lily would excuse herself, but she must not have trusted Nessa with her brother, so she remained seated. That was okay. Nessa would have to try harder to show both of them that she meant well.

Because there was only one chair in the room, Nessa had to stand. "I've studied the video of the incident."

Kyle pushed up on his elbows. "Were you able to identify him?"

"No." She glanced at Lily, who was still glaring at her. "The video shows you collapsing. That's all."

He shook his head. "I don't understand."

"I didn't either at first. Vic thought you'd just fainted, but we couldn't explain the blood to the back of your head since you landed on your face. After watching a few times, it became clear that an invisible being picked up a rock and smashed it over your head."

"Invisible being?" he asked.

"I bet it was a dragon shifter," Lily said. "Nelor could cloak himself when he became a dragon."

Nessa stepped closer. "Could Nelor become invisible in his human form?"

She shook her head. "No, or at least not that I knew of."

Nessa didn't know this Nelor so there'd be no reason for him to target her family. "Good to know. From what Vic and I could tell, this person was able to become invisible in his human form as well. That means he's a dragon shifter as well as a powerful dark lighter."

"Damn," Kyle exclaimed.

The image of the attack raced across her mind. Oh, shit. She'd meant to take the rock that had Kyle's blood on it to the police department, but after Greer told her she was such a tomboy, Nessa had totally forgotten about it. "I plan to ask the police to test the rock to see if there is any trace evidence on it."

"I appreciate that. You said you found the location of the explosives. Let me ask you this," Kyle said. "If you wanted to blow up your mine, where would you have placed them?"

Her initial reaction was to go on the defensive, but then she realized it was an excellent question. "Exactly where this person put them."

A small smile lifted his lips. "Then I'd say that narrows down the suspect pool even more. How many men or women are experts in demolition?"

Nessa looked down to the side then back up at him. "I couldn't say, but there have to be two or three people at each mining company who specialize in explosives."

"If you limit the number of mines to this province, what are we talking about? Ten or fifteen people max?"

She liked the way he thought. "I'd say even less than that."

"I've spoken to every mine owner already, but I'll ask them again to list the people who possess the skill. I'll pass that onto the cops."

"I suggest you ask them to only list dragon shifters." Goddess, she was adding fuel to Lily's fire.

"Have you figured out why this person conked me on the head?" Kyle asked. "I never saw his face."

"That's what I'm hoping the cops will find out." She chanced a glance at his sister again, but she still had a sour look on her face. "I need to get going. I've taken up enough of your time. Sorry to have interrupted."

"I'm glad you came," Kyle said.

"Me too."

His eyes turned softer, and as he scoped her out from head to toe, heat suffused her body. Nessa could tell some of her purple scales were starting to glow under her dress, so she smiled and waved as she hauled her flash dancing dragon ass out of there.

As soon as Nessa left, Kyle looked over at Lily. "You weren't very nice to her." Though Kyle should probably be thankful his sister hadn't been outright rude.

Her jaw dropped. "Nice? She's a dragon shifter. Did you forget what—"

"No, Lily. I never forget, but I've learned that not all dragon shifters are the same. Nessa is a great person."

She huffed. "You're thinking with your other head."

Heat flushed his face. His usually sweet sister never said anything like that. She must be upset. "Do I find her hot? Hell yeah, but I'm trying to stay objective. Trust me, I can't forget what she is."

"Your eyes tell a different story."

He lifted one shoulder. "Don't worry, I have no intention of dating her. Nessa is just interested in finding out who tried to kill either of us, more so than any human I've ever met. She's never done anything to indicate she's unscrupulous."

Lily shook her head. "You are a fool. She's trying to seduce you so that you'll reopen the mine. Ten bucks says she knows who tried to harm you. Hell, I bet she hired him to run you off the property."

That couldn't be true. "If that were the case, would she have brought me to the hospital?"

"Kyle, she set you up. She probably had you knocked out so she could swoop in and save you. Like a knight in shining armor. She wants you to think she's amazing."

He still didn't buy it. "I can't be that bad a judge of character."

"Seriously? What about Mary Lou or Janet? You thought each of them was the perfect woman." She tapped her chin. "Let me see. Mary Lou got pregnant with another man's baby, and she wanted you to pay for it. And Janet? She stole you blind."

"I was young and foolish."

Lily held up her hands. "Do what you want, but I will never believe Nessa cares for you. She clearly came here to catch your eye, so be leery of her motives."

"Don't forget it was Nessa who almost died in that last explosion."

"No one could have survived that. She must have known about it and protected herself somehow."

Her bitterness was eating such a huge hole in her heart that Lily might never recover. He hated that his sister would never know true happiness if she didn't change. "Until Nessa proves that she was behind any of these attacks, I'm going to believe she means well."

Lily stood. "You're an adult and will do what you want, but don't say I didn't warn you. I'll stop by tomorrow morning and drive you home if the doctor releases you."

"I appreciate that."

Once his sister left, Kyle's head pounded worse than before. He didn't want to believe anything Lily said, but she'd brought up some good points. The fact that Nessa had dressed up kind of implied that she was trying to use her wiles on him. But why? Did she think he'd open the mine just because he liked her? Hell, maybe he had been blinded by Nessa's beauty and strength. Kyle should probably keep his distance and gain some perspective.

Chapter Eight

NESSA COULDN'T WAIT to get out of the hospital. Her hormones had gone haywire the moment she stepped into the hospital room, and it hadn't helped seeing Kyle in a bed. She wanted to ask Greer or Declan to heal him, but she had the sense Kyle would think she was trying to manipulate him.

Even with the bandage on his head and pain shooting from his eyes, Kyle was sex on a stick. Goddess, she had it bad. If only there was something she could take to help calm her overactive imagination when she was around him, she would.

Lily shooting daggers at her helped dampen the feeling of lust somewhat, but Nessa's sympathy for Kyle kept swelling. It also hadn't helped knowing he'd been injured on Caspian property.

The only plus was that Kyle had ogled her when she'd walked in. He might not like that she was a dragon shifter, but he did seem to find her attractive.

Most likely Lily had seen Kyle check her out. Right now, she was probably trying to warn Kyle to stay away from her, reminding him that dragon shifters were evil.

If only Lily knew that she and Kyle were destined to be together, his sister might change her mind. Nessa, however, wasn't ready to spill those beans. While she'd give anything to get his sister on her side, the only way to do that was if the cops found the man who'd injured Kyle. To succeed, they'd need the rock.

After a quick drive back to her complex, Nessa rushed up to her condo to change and retrieve the small bit of explosive she'd discovered before flying over to the SinCas building to retrieve the rock from her locker. After a short flight, she landed on the roof. She transformed into her human form and took a quick elevator ride to the first floor. Once in the changing room, she jerked open her locker.

Her heart stopped.

The rock wasn't there! Her shirt with Kyle's blood on it was gone too. What the hell? Had it smelled and some janitor needed to investigate where the stench was coming from? That would explain the missing shirt, but why take the rock? She'd even wrapped it in a bag.

Before she let the panic set in, she raced down the corridor and took the elevator to the basement where the maintenance crew had their headquarters. Hopefully, they had an explanation.

Unfortunately, no one was around. Crap. When voices echoed down the hallway, relief soared through her. She followed the sound. Inside the room labeled *Shop* were two men working on a piece of metal, bending and twisting it. They both looked up at the same time and then straightened.

"Ms. Nessa. This is a surprise," said the dark-haired man.

They knew her name, but she only recognized the man with the scruffy beard. "Hey, Joe. I had a soiled shirt in my locker, as well as a paper bag that contained some evidence to a crime. Did either of you touch it by any chance?"

They both looked at each other. "No. It was in your locker, you say?"

"Yes."

"The monitors would catch it if anyone was in there."

She'd forgotten about that. Normally, she changed in the bathroom because of the cameras, but today, she'd been so worried about Kyle that she forgot they were running.

Ever since the cave-in, her brains had been scrambled. Once she thanked them, she rushed to the monitoring room located on the fourth floor. A woman by the name of Helena was hunched over the screen. She jerked when Nessa stepped in.

"Sorry," Nessa said. "I didn't mean to scare you."

"No problem." She smiled. "What can I do for you?"

"Can you run a tape for me?" Helena nodded. "Someone stole something out of my locker in the changing room."

Her eyebrows rose. "That's terrible. What time was this?"

She had to think. "Today, maybe around two o'clock?"

Nessa pulled up the chair next to Helena and watched her scroll through the feed. At 2:32, the locker handle just disappeared and then the door opened—all by itself.

"Did I just see that?" Nessa asked.

Helena's hands shook as she replayed the video. "If I believed in such things, I'd say it was a ghost."

Oh shit. It was him—the man who hurt Kyle. He'd followed her there and then cloaked himself in his human form. But how had she not sensed him?

She turned her attention back to the screen. Her shirt disappeared, and then the right half of the rock became invisible before the left half did. The door then closed.

"It was a ghost—or rather, it was a human who can imitate a ghost very well. Thank you, Helena. It's what I needed to see."

Nessa decided to walk home since it wasn't more than a few blocks to her condo, hoping the hustle and bustle of the city would clear her head. By the time Nessa finally entered her apartment building, she realized this was far bigger than she'd first imagined. With her evidence gone, she didn't know what Anderson Caspian could do. Regardless, she had to call him and confess what happened.

"Can you send me a copy of that video?" he asked.

"I sure can. I really am sorry. I think the cave-in did a number on my ability to concentrate." Being around Kyle didn't help either.

"You didn't mean to lose evidence."

"No, I definitely did not."

"I have a small piece of explosive I found half way down the shaft. I can tell it was one of ours. Do you want it?"

"Keep it for now, but don't lose it."

"I won't."

Next, Nessa called Helena and asked her to copy the video and send it off to her cousin.

"I'll do it right now," Helena said.

"Thanks." Crap. No one was any closer to finding Kyle's attacker—mostly because she couldn't keep her head in the game.

Once she reached the top floor of her condo building, one of the men her father had assigned to watch her place was leaning against the wall doing something on his phone. "Ms. Nessa."

"Has anyone been by?" she asked. She'd only been gone twenty minutes.

"Not since you left."

She smiled, leaned over to place her eye near the scanner, and waited for the door to open.

Once inside, Nessa poured a glass of wine, and then filled the tub with hot, soapy water, needing a relaxing soak. Even after staying in the heated water for half an hour, it only helped calm her a little. First of all, she couldn't get the image of Kyle's reclined body out of her mind. Had she not seen the live feed, Kyle might have bled to death. A small shiver raced up her spine at that terrible thought.

To her surprise, she was more worried about Kyle staying safe than the mine reopening. When her family returned from their humanitarian mission, they'd have to sit down with Kyle and go over all of the facts. They'd done that exercise after each of the first two incidents, but her dad said they'd come up empty handed. The only thing Nessa knew for sure was that a dragon shifter was involved—one that was part dark lighter.

She snapped her fingers. Maybe the Four Sisters knew someone who fit the bill.

Adrenaline pumping, Nessa told the guard where she was going, and then shot out of her apartment. She flew to their shop. Despite it being late, the front door was open and Magnolia was inside organizing some of the shelves.

Wearing a baggy black blouse over a long black skirt, she rushed over to Nessa as soon as she entered. "Am I happy to see you looking so well. I can't imagine what it must have been like being trapped under all that dirt. I admire your determination to reach the surface."

News did travel fast. Nessa half chuckled. "It was either climb up or possibly die down there."

Magnolia nodded. "What can I do for you?"

Nessa inhaled, not sure where to begin. It shouldn't matter. The white lighter probably knew what she wanted before she'd walked in. The Four Sisters had more magic in them than all of Tarradon combined.

"We had another attack at the mine." She explained about Kyle seeing someone near one of the warehouses. "When he went to investigate, someone smashed him over the head with a huge rock."

Magnolia's jaw slackened. "That's terrible. Is he okay?"

"More or less. I took him to the hospital where they patched him up. I'm hoping he gets to go home tomorrow. The strange part was that on the tape we couldn't see anything. Whoever hit him was invisible." Nessa then explained how the rock she'd found disappeared from her locker. "It was so strange. Unless multiple people are involved, I believe it was a dragon shifter who can remain invisible in his human form. Do you know of anyone who has that ability?"

"There are many who can disappear at will without being in animal form."

"Really?" How had she never heard about this type of person? "He would also have to be highly skilled in the use of explosives. Does that narrow it down?"

Magnolia placed a hand on Nessa's shoulder, and her heart rate jacked up. "If you're asking me to identify the man who wants to bring down the Caspian mines, I'm afraid I can't."

"You can't or you won't?"

She smiled. "Choose whatever word you like. My sisters and I have given an oath to not interfere in anything that might change the path Fate has set."

"But you helped my cousin's mate—Finn McKinnon—break

into the castle to free Kaleena."

Magnolia looked to the side. "My sister Acacia can be very impetuous at times, but remember she merely helped transform Finn to look like the guard for a short time. She didn't name names. The path Fate set for Finn and Kaleena wasn't changed. In fact, it actually aided in a small way."

Nessa hadn't thought of it in that way. "Kyle and I are mates, so I guess Fate wants me to work through this."

Magnolia smiled. "Yes."

"Would it be possible for you to give me something to hide my shifter signature?"

Kaleena's mate had said that Magnolia had given him the ability to appear as a dragon for a short period of time.

"Why would you want to do that, my dear?"

"I'm not exactly sure, but if that man ever comes near me, I'd like to be able to hide from him. The charges set at the mine were meant to kill me. Fate might have helped me escape." That might have been a little white lie since Nessa couldn't be positive the collapse was aimed at harming her.

"Hmm. I see no reason not to help, but note this will only work for a little while."

"Even if I can remain undetected for a minute, it could save my life."

As if she knew what Nessa was going to ask all along, Magnolia pulled out what looked like a highly polished clay stone from her top pocket. "If you need to hide, hold this tight in your palm for three seconds, and your scent will disappear." As soon as she handed the stone to Nessa, a tremendous weight lifted off her shoulders.

"Thank you."

"Go and be safe. This man wants to destroy your family and all that you hold dear."

Her stomach churned. Nessa held Kyle dear. "Why?"

"That's all I can say."

Nessa knew begging would do no good. She thanked Magnolia again and then left, not sure if she was more scared now than before.

Chapter Nine

T HE MORNING AFTER Nessa visited the Four Sisters Pottery Shop, she called the hospital to check on Kyle's progress. Admissions told her that he'd been dismissed about an hour ago. As much as Nessa wanted to head on over to his house to see if he needed anything, she figured Lily was keeping an eye on her brother and wouldn't welcome another intrusion by a dragon shifter.

Frustrated at not being able to help, Nessa decided to seek her father's advice about whether there was anything anyone could do to speed up the process of finding the person who had tried to kill her and Kyle.

Grindale was a ten-hour drive or a ninety-minute flight. Had she not been desperate, she would have waited until he returned to Edendale. Even though there were some dragon shifters who might want to harm her, she decided to chance the flight, promising herself to keep a keen eye on her surroundings. She probably should have asked the guard watching her condo to come with her, but he needed to make certain no one tried to get into her home.

All of her brothers and cousins were either at the cleanup site or at the mine, holding down the fort. If she remained vigilant, she'd be safe.

In the past, whenever she soared above Tarradon, Nessa loved nothing more than to get lost in the beauty of the place, but today she couldn't afford to. Once aloft, she flew as fast and as straight as she could to Grindale province. The dam rupture had happened in the town of Plux, not far from Drifsdown where her uncle's good friend, Gregor Kearn, lived. If she couldn't find her dad in the middle of the disaster, she bet Mr. Kearn would know where he was.

In a little under ninety minutes, Nessa arrived without incident. It didn't take any kind of internal GPS to find the horror unfolding below her. She recognized several of the dragons flying people to safety. The entire town of Plux appeared to have been nearly wiped out, and her heart ached. Only the tops of homes were exposed as the floodwaters continued to rush down the main streets. Oh, my. This was far worse than she had thought possible. While Nessa had important issues to discuss with her father, these people needed her more.

She landed near what looked like a makeshift tent city. She shifted and then rushed in to give aid. Before she could even ask if anyone had seen her siblings, cousins, or father, someone shouted for help. She hurried over to them. "What is it?" she asked.

"We need these water bottles delivered to the far side of the camp. Can you take them?" The young man asked with such sincerity, she couldn't turn him down. He was human and must have seen her fly in.

"Sure thing."

Shifting in this crowded space wasn't advisable, so she lifted two of the cases and walked them about five hundred feet to the other side of the camp where workers were handing out water to needy families. Her back was not happy with lugging so much weight, but for the next hour, Nessa transported the goods from one side to the other. The victims were filthy but surprisingly upbeat, and she never ceased to admire their spirit.

Nessa continued to help out the best she could, from setting up tents, locating loved ones, and delivering food. She did a few food flights into neighboring towns that hadn't been affected and collected what supplies she could.

Near the dam itself, she was thrilled to see other mine owners there, including Safford DeLeon. To be honest, she wouldn't have thought he'd ever be caught doing humanitarian work. She could still remember when he tried to lure some of the Caspian workers away from their site with promises of riches. A few had succumbed, but most had returned when they realized the man's safety practices were suspect. Fortunately, after the death of his wife, he'd become more cautious.

It was close to sunset when she found her brother Birk. He was covered in dirt, but from his strong movements, he hadn't tired.

His smile came out broad when he spotted her. "Nice to see you here, but who's watching the mine?"

"The skeleton crew is. I would have stayed behind, but I have to find Dad. There have been some developments that I need his advice on."

Birk sobered quickly. "What happened?"

She gave him the brief rundown. "After someone stole the rock that must have had incriminating evidence on it, I became worried that Kyle's incident might not be an isolated one. The scariest part is that this dragon shifter isn't normal. The ability to become invisible when in his human form means there is no end to the damage he could inflict."

Birk wrapped an arm around her shoulders. "We'll figure it out. Dad's at Gregor Kearn's estate. They've turned it into a shelter. I'll show you where it is."

"Thanks.

The flight from Plux to Drifsdown was like going from a catastrophe to lush green rolling hills. The castle was easy to spot mostly because of the large number of people milling about its vast acreage. They landed in the front driveway and entered through the open front door.

"Whoa," she said. "People are everywhere."

Mattresses were tucked side by side along one of the corridors, and families were huddled together as relief workers hustled between them.

Birk stopped one woman. "Have you see Laird Caspian?"

"The last time I saw him, he was on the back patio."

"Thanks."

The two of them wove their way through the crowd. Someone had turned on a rather loud stereo, playing upbeat music, and a few refugees were attempting to sing along. Once outside, they had to ask a few more people where they might find their dad.

Finally, someone pointed them in the right direction. She found their father talking to yet another mine owner, Wilson Snar. The fact he was here implied he probably hadn't had a hand in Kyle's attack.

Birk leaned over. "Snar has motive to want our mine to go out of business. His operation focuses solely on gold, and his success has been sporadic. Of all the mine owners, he'd have the most to lose if our gold mine panned out."

"I don't see him as a dark lighter."

"Neither do I, but I've been fooled before."

Nessa waved to their father to get his attention. "Hey, Dad."

He spun around and grinned. "Well, if this isn't a nice surprise." Her father turned to Birk. "How are the relief efforts progressing in Plux?"

Wilson placed a hand on her father's arm. "If you'll excuse me, I see more dragons are dropping off another group of casualties. We'll talk later."

"I'll be over shortly to help," her father said.

Wilson smiled and limped off.

It was quite a sight to see the dragons carrying the injured and setting them down safely. Once the relief team arrived to take care of them, the dragons returned to the air and headed back in the direction of Plux.

Their dad faced Birk. "You were about to tell me about the relief effort."

"It's bad there, but everyone is making good headway. We've been searching all of the homes and rescuing everyone we find. It just breaks my heart to see the devastation though. Declan has been a lifesaver—literally. He's healed so many people that he's beyond exhausted. I had to battle with him to take a break."

Her cousin was a hero. After all this talk of good deeds, Nessa wasn't sure she should mention what happened to Kyle, but she needed to know what her father thought. She placed a hand on his arm. "Something happened at the mine, and I need your help—or at least your opinion."

He looked around. "Sure. How about we step into the large tent over there? We'll have a little more privacy."

With the din of the rescue dampened, Nessa once more went over what had happened to Kyle, the stolen evidence, and what Magnolia had to say. "She knows more than she's saying."

Her father nodded. "That's always the case with those ladies. What I don't like is that Magnolia seems to believe that someone is targeting us. In light of what happened, do you have any ideas who it might be?"

"Kyle and I agree that whoever set the charges at the gold mine has to know as much about explosives as I do."

"Do you believe this expert is the mastermind?"

"I have no way of knowing."

Birk looked at their dad. "I'm worried that whoever it is might try something else. I think I should go back with Nessa to help out at the mine. I'm not sure how we can work our skeleton crew any more than they already are."

"I agree, but ask them to check in at different intervals when they are doing their rounds," their dad said. "No matter how many cameras we have, it may not be good enough if this man is able to cloak himself. He seems mighty dangerous." Her father placed his hands on her shoulders. "As for you, I don't want you in the air unless you're with someone. Usually one dragon won't attack two at once."

As much as Nessa didn't want to be so restricted, it was sound advice. "I won't. If no escort is available, I'll drive."

Her father nodded. "Good. You know, if you're so convinced this culprit is a fellow miner, maybe I can have a few men try to hire on at the other mines."

"To act as moles?" she asked.

"Yes. I know we're paying them wages, but I'm sure they wouldn't object to receiving a second paycheck."

"Do you actually think the other workers will talk about some disgruntled owner who wants to take us down?"

He shrugged. "That or maybe someone is aware which dragon shifter is capable of cloaking himself when in human form. It might even be better to send in humans who say they were spooked by what happened at our mine. They heard some ghost is responsible for the attacks. Someone might talk."

She liked her dad's imagination. "It can't hurt, but that could take months before we get a lead."

"You have a better way to catch this guy?"

If only she did. "No."

He hugged her. "I should be back in two or three days, but if anything else happens, call me any time of day or night, okay?"

"I will."

"I might be busy here, but you always come first, sweetheart. You know I want to stay on top of anything to do with the mine."

"I'm proud of all the work you and the rest of the men are doing. I know Grindale province appreciates it," she said.

"I'm sure they'd do the same if we needed their help."

After another round of hugs, she and Birk took off for home.

SOMEONE KNOCKED ON Kyle's door, and he clicked off the television. There hadn't been anything on the tube other than the chaos at the dam. Seeing all of the devastation and pain made his head ache even worse. At one point, he even thought he saw Nessa there, but he must have been hallucinating. Her brother had told her that because of what had happened, she needed to stay at the mine. On second thought, Nessa seemed like the impulsive type to do something like that.

"Coming," he called as he slowly eased off the sofa. He had to wait for his head to stop pounding before crossing the living room.

When he opened up and saw his sister standing there, it was as if someone had punched him in the gut. Her hair was messed, she sported a black eye, and the cut on her lip made him momentarily forget about his own issues. "Oh, shit, Lily. What happened?"

She shuffled past him, not making eye contact. "I am the stupidest woman alive."

He wrapped an arm around her shoulder and led her over to the sofa. "Sit here and let me get you something to drink."

"I could use a hot tea."

He was thinking of something stronger, but the caffeine would help his head too. "Tell me what happened."

"Nelor happened."

Fuck. His fists clenched as acid burned in his stomach. "Did the bastard come to your house? I thought he was still in jail for assaulting you."

"He just got out. And yes, he came to my house."

Double fuck. "I take it he broke down your door?" Kyle failed to keep the bitterness from his voice.

"I, ah, let him in. He told me he was very sorry about what he did and that during his incarceration, he'd realized how much he'd hurt me."

Kyle didn't believe a word of it, but apparently Lily did. "Then Nelor should have offered to pay for your medical bills." They'd been extensive, especially with all the skin graft operations that followed.

She looked up at him with teary eyes. "I know he hurt me, and I know you can never understand, but I actually miss him."

"Him? Or someone to be with you?"

Lily didn't answer him at first. "That makes me sound like some lonely pathetic person, but you don't know how hard it is for me. When I do have the courage to go out, if they see or feel the scars on my back, I get a look of pity or disgust and then never hear from them again. I'm tired of being rejected and alone."

Kyle dropped down next to her and hugged her. "Oh, Lily. Your time will come. Not every man is shallow. You are an incredibly beautiful and talented woman who has a lot to offer."

"You're my brother, and that makes you prejudiced."

"Am not. Prejudiced that is." He had questioned his own integrity a few times. If he'd met a scarred woman, how open would he be? Somehow, he didn't think he'd like the answer. "You'll find the right man someday, but that man is not Nelor Dobbins."

"I know." She hung her head.

"Did you call the cops at least?"

She nodded. "They said they'd search for him, and once they catch him, he'll be arrested for causing bodily harm."

"Since he was just released from a two-year sentence for the same thing, it sounds like he will be in for a long time."

"I hope."

"Rest while I fix that tea." He hustled into the kitchen, put the water on to boil, and dropped a tea bag into each of the two cups.

Kyle didn't want to lecture her on how Nelor almost killed her the last time and that she was damn lucky he hadn't done worse this time. His sister felt bad enough, but what had she been thinking? The man would never change. That dragon shifter was bad to the core.

He mentally sighed. The worst part about Nelor begging forgiveness was that his sister would harden her heart against all dragons even more. It was ironic that Lily would give the scum Nelor a second chance but not give Nessa the benefit of the doubt.

Not that Kyle planned on asking Nessa out when the mess with her mine was finished, but the woman intrigued him something fierce. Hell, during his recovery in the hospital, she'd had the starring role in his fantasies. Something about her fierce loyalty and determination to right all wrongs spoke to him. Okay, her body spoke to him too, but that alone was not enough to create a good relationship.

The teakettle whistled. Kyle poured the water and then carried the two cups of tea out to the living room. He placed them on the coffee table in front of him. "What stupid reason set Nelor off that he felt it was all right to use you as his personal punching bag?" He wasn't sure why he asked, but for some reason, he needed to know.

She shrugged. "He apologized for everything, and then said he wanted us to get back together."

"Seriously? After all this time?"

She nodded. "It's not like I ever visited him in prison. I don't know why he thought I'd say yes."

"You told him no, right?"

"I did." She huffed out a laugh. "Apparently that was not the right answer."

"I hope the cops catch him and lock him up for good."

"That would be wonderful."

If Nessa were here, he bet she could give Nelor a run for his money. "Until Nelor is caught, you should move in with me."

She leaned over and hugged him. "Thank you, but I'll be okay."

That was what she always said.

"Then how about taking some self-defense classes?"

She looked up at him with teary eyes "What good would that do? Even if I had a gun, I couldn't kill him."

Was that because her heart was too big or because the soft spot above a dragon's heart was a small area and hard to hit? "There's more to self-defense than learning to shoot. I just don't like you being alone."

She lifted her tea and took a sip of the steaming liquid but immediately placed it on the table. "I won't be careless again. I've learned my lesson."

"I hope so. I will be keeping an eye on you. I may even look into hiring someone to stand guard outside your place."

Lily rolled her eyes at him. "I told you I will be fine, Kyle."

"Lily, I am your brother; please let me do this. It would kill me if anything happened to you, sweetie."

"Fine. I would be lost without you too."

"And speaking of that, you'll stay here tonight. And no arguing." She smiled and then nodded. "Good. Now drink your tea."

Chapter Ten

ONCE BIRK ESCORTED Nessa to her condo, he stayed for a while to discuss a possible strategy on how to handle this new threat.

After they exhausted their options, Birk slapped his thighs and stood. "Are you sure you're going to be okay staying alone?"

Nessa might be unsettled by what had happened, but she'd deal. "I have a guard outside the door. If this person manages to get by him, he'd have to bust down the steel door to get to me. By that time, I could escape out the window." Without a balcony, it would be a bit tricky to jump out as a human and then shift into her dragon, but it could be done.

"Just checking. I'll discuss our new tactics with the men. I want to go over the security measures we currently have in place and what additional things we'll need to add in order to beef it up. We'll meet tomorrow morning at nine in the top floor conference room."

She forced a smile. "I'll be there."

Once he left, she headed to the bathroom to clean up. Too bad, she couldn't forget everything and just relax for once, but she kept going back to the motive behind Kyle's attack. Clearly, the person wanted something in the warehouse, only she couldn't figure out what it might be. Destroying the equipment seemed the most likely scenario, but then why not just blow up the building? That seemed to be his M.O.

Nessa ran the shower water, and once it warmed, she stood under the soothing flow. Pushing aside her situation, she focused on those poor flood victims. She almost felt guilty having a nice safe place to live while so many people in Plux were now homeless. Jobs had been lost, possessions ruined, and some had family members who'd died. She ached for them, especially since it would take them a long time to recover.

Good thing so many from around Tarradon had offered to help. Once the mess with the mine was over, she would figure out a way to help them rebuild what they'd lost.

After she finished washing, Nessa dressed in some comfy clothes and then fixed herself something quick to eat. She sat in front of the television, hoping to take her mind off the flood victims. No matter which show she put on though, it was interrupted with more videos of the catastrophe.

As she watched, her mind wandered back to Kyle like it did time and time again. With those thoughts came a stronger yearning to be by his side. Too bad, he probably didn't feel the same, which meant rushing him into a relationship would most likely result in him putting more distance between them instead of less.

Several times today she had debated calling him, but most likely he'd just tell her that he was fine.

No, a phone call was too impersonal. The only way to convince him she really cared was to visit. Nessa could only hope Lily wasn't spending the night there. That would be really awkward.

As much as Nessa felt safe flying the short distance between her condo and Kyle's, she'd promised her dad that she'd be cautious, so she drove. Twice though, she almost wrecked. Her mind had been on what she was going to say to him rather than on the traffic and the crazy pedestrians who didn't look when they crossed the street. Yikes.

When she finally pulled in front of his apartment, she cut the engine and remained in the car, trying to figure out the best way to accurately judge his mental state. Because he was a human, she thought it best not to tell him about her trip to the Four Sisters Pottery Shop since that might scare him more. On the other hand, she needed to warn him about another possible attack. He'd ask why she thought this, and she'd end up spilling the beans about what

Magnolia had told her. Damned if she did, and damned if she didn't.

Nessa would just have to wing it. As she eased out of the car, she could almost hear Greer chastise her for not dressing up. She hadn't in part because Nessa didn't want to appear to be something she wasn't.

After climbing two flights of stairs, she reached his apartment. Nessa raised her hand to knock but then stopped. What if he shut the door in her face? He might have been with Lily, the dragon hater, for most of the day. No telling his state of mind now.

Please don't let Lily answer the door, she pleaded to anyone who would listen.

It shouldn't matter. Nessa had come to warn him about the future danger. And that's what she was going to do. She knocked. And then waited. Then waited some more.

Finally, footsteps sounded. It was only nine at night, but in light of Kyle's head injury, he might have gone to bed early. Okay, now she'd be totally embarrassed if he had to get out of bed to answer her knock. The door eased open, and Kyle, thankfully, wasn't in his pajamas. He wore faded jeans, a body hugging white T-shirt, and was barefoot. Oh, my. The man sure could set her dragon on fire. Her scales had to be flickering, and she was pretty sure her eyes were turning purple.

Pant, pant. I want to jump his bones, her dragon shot back.

Dragon, behave, she pleaded. It didn't matter she wanted that too.

"Nessa? What are you doing here?" At least he sounded more surprised than angry.

"I'm sorry to come over so late, but I just got home from helping out in Plux." She hadn't meant to tell him that, as it would sound like bragging, but part of her wanted him to know she wasn't totally self-centered.

"I thought I saw you on TV. Come in."

She stepped inside, and as much as she tried to focus on the task at hand and not on her swelling lust, she failed. Her nails sharpened, and heat swamped her lower half. Damn it. Her pulse pounded, and her scales began to form over her skin. Not good at all.

With great concentration, she looked away from Kyle and studied his apartment, pleased he was alone. The interior space was small but cozy. The dark blue sofa that sat in the middle of the living room faced a wall with a television mounted on it. To the right and left of the TV were large picture windows, but the adjacent buildings blocked much of the city view. To the right of the sofa was a small dining room table, and to the left was a hallway that she suspected led to his bedroom.

"I really should have called first. I wasn't thinking."

"Don't worry about it. I was up. Come sit down. Can I get you some coffee or tea?"

She waved a hand. "Nothing. Thank you. I came to see if you were okay and to warn you about something."

He sat on the couch next to her, and her dragon started blowing heat. She couldn't blame her animal. With his messy hair and tight shirt, Kyle was sexy as sin. The only flaw to his perfection was that he looked totally stressed out.

"Warn me about what? Lily?" His voice came out thick with emotion.

"Lily?"

"Yes, she was attacked earlier this evening by her former boyfriend. He's a dragon shifter, and I thought—"

She finished his sentence. "That all dragon shifters know each other's business. I'm afraid there is no special hotline or mental connection that we share with each other. Besides, if this is the one who burned her, trust me, I stay away from assholes like that."

He looked away. "I'm sorry. I'm so upset I'm ready to spit." He twisted back toward her. "I just want to tear his head off, but I know that as a human, I don't stand a chance. The cops are out looking for him, but he seems like the type who's good at hiding. I convinced Lily to stay here tonight."

"She's here?" Nessa looked around.

"Don't worry. She's crashed in my spare room. I got her to take something for her pain, and it conked her out."

Hopefully, she would stay asleep because Nessa was pretty sure Miss Lily wouldn't be very happy to see her there. "What is his name?"

"Nelor Dobbins."

"I've never met him, but if I do, I'll keep a wide berth."

His shoulders slumped. He must be disappointed that she didn't insist on sending a team of dragons to destroy the man, but that wasn't how she—or any of the Guardians, for that matter—worked.

"You said you wanted to warn me about something?" he asked, suddenly acting distant.

"I know this will be hard to understand, but I believe you're still in danger. I visited a powerful woman today who confirmed it."

"By powerful, do you mean a white lighter?"

Delight rippled inside her that he knew about her kind. "Yes. I went to ask her if she knew of any human who had the ability to become invisible. She didn't, but she told me she believed you were still in danger."

He waved a dismissive hand. "Were you trying to find out who hit me?" This time he sounded angry. "That's the job for the police who, by the way, called me a while ago to ask questions about what happened. I couldn't tell them much though."

"Was it Detective Caspian?"

"It was. He told me he's your cousin."

She nodded. "Believe me, I'm not trying to do his job or yours. I visited this white lighter because I thought she might know of some dragon shifter who could become invisible in his human form. If I had learned a name, I would have told Anderson and let him deal with the criminal."

Kyle huffed. "Somehow I doubt you'd let it go so easily."

He seemed to know her quite well. "You might be right, but that's only because I care what happens to you." When he didn't react, Nessa felt like a fool. "You don't believe me, do you? Hell, you probably think I'm trying to manipulate you somehow, but I'm not."

He stared at her for quite some time. "You're wrong, Nessa. I do believe you. I know you care. In fact, I think you are one of the most caring people I've ever met."

His words were like the most soothing balm. "Really? I just figured you hated my kind as much as your sister did."

When he clasped her hand and squeezed it, pure pleasure tingled up and down her spine. "That might have been true before I met you." His voice softened, and his eyes turned darker. Oh, my.

She wanted to grab him and kiss him more than anything. But if she did, she'd never know for sure how deep his feelings ran for her. "Thank you for that."

He cleared his throat. "Let's um, get back to what you were saying. You think I'm in some kind of danger. Why? The guy who attacked me has to know I can't identify him. He has no reason to harm me."

"If he saw me take you to the hospital, that alone could make you a target, especially if he's trying to hurt me and those I care about." Her words came out passionate.

Kyle rubbed her hand, and dampness pooled between her legs. He couldn't know how much he affected her. "It's funny. Until recently, dragon shifters weren't high on my list of those people I liked, especially with what happened to Lily, but then I met you."

Her heart nearly stopped, and her skin burned at the intimate contact. "I appreciate that." *More than you can know.*

He let go of her hand and stabbed it through his hair. "Look. I know I've been hot and cold around you, and I want to apologize. I really think you are a wonderful person."

She waited for him to continue. Actually, Nessa wasn't able to form any words.

"It's my fault that we got off on the wrong foot," Kyle said.

"Uh-huh." Nessa fisted her hands, not wanting him to see how her nails had grown. Good thing she had on a long sleeve shirt to hide her pulsing purple scales.

"I haven't been there for you either during all this mess. Hell, someone—maybe the same person who attacked me—tried to kill you, and I kept telling myself to think of this as just another case. I should have been more sympathetic. For that, I'm sorry."

Wow. Her heart beat so fast, she wasn't sure she could keep from ravishing him. She wouldn't, partly because Lily was close by. "What are you saying, Kyle?"

His brows rose as he inhaled deeply. "That I find you attractive and care a lot about you too." He held up a hand. "But I think we shouldn't act on our feelings yet."

She so wanted to ask him why not, but Nessa would try to be patient. She was about to make some cute comment when Kyle rubbed his temples and grunted.

"Are you okay?" Nessa wanted to be the one to soothe his aches.

"I still have a headache that flares up now and again."

"Did the doctor say you should be alone? I mean, Lily might be here, but she's asleep."

He smiled. "He didn't say anything, but does that mean you're offering to nurse me?" He winked and then sobered. "Don't answer that. I need to focus on who is doing this to you—and me—and not on what I'd like to be doing. If my headache gets worse, I'll wake Lily."

Nessa couldn't help but wish she were the one staying and taking care of him. Her dragon nearly revealed herself when he said *doing* in an obviously sexual way. He wanted her!

Nessa needed to say something. "How about if I ask my sister to come over and try to cure that headache of yours?"

"Your sister?"

Nessa smiled. "Greer. She saved me after the mine explosion or rather she was the one who finished the job my dragon was too tired to do. She uses her magic to heal people."

"I'll tell you what. If it doesn't go away by tomorrow, I might take you up on it."

She smiled. "Deal. With all that you've been through, you

should probably go to bed."

Damn. Just saying the word *bed* had her thoughts shooting in the wrong direction.

"I will. I can't tell you how much I appreciate you stopping by and checking up on me. As for your warning, I promise I will be extra cautious."

Nessa ran a hand down his arm, and then had to swallow the urge to do more. "Perfect. Call me if you need anything."

"I don't have your number."

His voice was pure sex, forcing her to tamp down her desires once more. "I forgot about that," she said. He told her his number and she entered it into her phone. "I'll text you so you have mine." Okay, she needed to get out of there before she leaned over and kissed him. "I'll see myself out."

Chapter Eleven

NESSA HURRIED OUT of Kyle's apartment and rushed down the two flights of stairs. As she exited, she glanced upward, checking for dragon shifters. Yup. There they were, but the big question was whether they were waiting for her or not.

After sitting on the stair stoop for a bit to be sure none of the shifters were circling, she jogged to her car. Once inside her vehicle, she locked the doors and started the engine. Sure, a dragon could attack her in the car and rip off the metal door, but Nessa crossed her fingers that none would risk it with all the people coming and going around the apartment building. It might be late, but no one seemed to sleep in this town.

Nessa headed home. Just before she turned into her underground garage, she realized the car behind her had been following her for a while. Instead of entering the parking garage, she sped up and then took a sharp right turn followed by a quick left turn. When she exited on the street one block from the garage entrance, the car was gone. Okay, maybe her talk with Kyle had made her a bit paranoid. It also might have been a coincidence that the gray sedan was behind her during the whole drive home.

Nessa rounded the block, and when she didn't spot the car again, she went into the lot and up the ramp. Because the garage serviced more than just her building, the parking structure was three stories tall. To make doubly sure no one was lying in wait, she circled the first level and then drove up to the second. Few spaces were free, but she managed to squeeze in between two large vans.

The sound of tires squealing on the ramp below her caused her heart to jackhammer. Holy crap. What appeared to be the same gray car that had followed her rounded the corner and then slowed. She tightened her hands on the wheel. Two men were inside. Oh shit. She ducked her head. If she slipped out now, they'd see her for sure.

Think.

She could hide in the trunk. It was accessible by pulling down her back seat. When the car that had passed backed up, she had to do something.

Move!

She crawled over the front seat and climbed in the trunk then pulled up the back to secure her hiding place. Nessa then sneezed. Damn. And sneezed again. The trunk smelled of dust and potting soil. Even if they couldn't see her, they would hear her and definitely scent her dragon signature.

Nessa's rapid heartbeat prevented her from hearing where they were. What was wrong with her? She could set explosives, yet she couldn't remain still when a bunch of goons were looking for her? Sheesh.

Without thinking, she stuck her hand in her pocket for her phone, and her fingers touched the stone Magnolia had given her— the stone that would cloak her dragon signature. Perfect. Nessa clasped it and concentrated on eliminating her shifter scent. If the men did come near her car, they'd never know she was there. Her pulse slowed at that comforting thought.

The car stopped right behind her, and then two doors opened. Her pulse skyrocketed again. With her free hand, Nessa pulled her phone from her shirt pocket to text Birk, but her fingers were shaking so much. It took forever to text him to tell him she was in trouble. Thankfully, she remembered to silence it before she messaged him.

"Where the hell did she go?" one of the men asked the other. She didn't recognize his voice, but maybe it was a Caspian employee looking for her help. Right and the Royals would cut taxes starting tomorrow.

"She must have spotted us and gone upstairs. Come on."

Who were they? The car doors opened then closed, and the car drove off. While the coast was clear for the moment, Nessa didn't need to be wandering around the parking garage waiting for the men to return from her condo. She just hoped like hell they didn't harm the man guarding her place.

Her cell lit up a few seconds later. It was a return text from Birk.

Birk: *Where are you now?*

Me: *I'm in the trunk of my car on the second level. They went up to my condo. I think there are two of them.*

Birk: *Stay right where you are. I'll check it out.*

Me: *Okay.*

The tension in Nessa's body released somewhat knowing help was on the way. She wouldn't let down her guard though until her brother arrived. Each time a car drove up the ramp behind her, her blood pressure rose.

Being in a confined space reminded her of being trapped in the mine, making it hard not to climb out. For her safety though, she'd stay put. If Birk flew from his place to hers, it should only take a few minutes. After checking her phone every thirty seconds, she wondered what was taking him so long.

Four minutes. Then five. Then six. Where the hell was he? Had he checked her apartment first to make sure the men were gone?

Twelve minutes later, someone tapped on the trunk.

"Nessa, it's Birk."

Never so happy to hear someone's voice, she punched the seat-back, and it fell forward. She crawled out and then unlocked her door. A second later she was in her brother's arms. Logan stood next to him, and she gave him an equally tight hug. "Thanks for coming," she said to Logan. While he was an amazing fighter, he preferred handling business deals instead of racing around the countryside saving people—like Birk did.

"I had to. You were in trouble."

Another car pulled up behind them and rolled down the window. She recognized both men from the mine. They looked over at Birk. "Where do you want us?"

"Stay down here while I take Nessa to her condo."

"What about the two men who were here?" Ernie said.

"Sanchon said they showed up, but when they saw him, they turned around and left. I didn't get Nessa until I was sure they were gone."

"We'll make sure they don't return."

"Thanks." Birk wrapped an arm around Nessa's waist. "I bet you could use a drink."

She laughed. "Boy could I."

They escorted her upstairs, but even as they walked down the hallway to her condo, she remained on edge. Sanchon was standing watch at her door, and when he spotted them, he smiled.

"I'm glad to see you're okay," he said.

She was happy he was all right. "Thanks for chasing them off. Did you recognize either of them?" she asked. Birk gave her a dirty look. "What? It's not like I'm investigating."

Birk shook his head then returned his attention to her guard. "We now have two men downstairs to make sure they don't come back. When I leave here, I'll head to the mine and send someone over to relieve you."

"Appreciate it."

The three of them headed inside, and for the first time since she left Kyle's apartment, Nessa relaxed.

"I'll fix us all a drink," Logan said.

"Beer is in the fridge, and a bottle of whiskey is in the cupboard next to the sink."

The cupboard opened, glasses clinked, and the door shut. Logan returned and set three shots on the table in front of the sofa. She downed half her drink in one gulp.

"Ah, now that's smooth," Nessa said.

"What were you doing out so late?" Birk asked, his tone almost harsh. "I thought you were staying in for the night."

Had she told him that? "After I bathed, I began worrying about Kyle."

Logan swigged his drink. "I'll ask you again. What is it about this guy that has you so concerned?"

She couldn't hold it in any longer. "He's my mate."

Logan almost spit out his drink. "Seriously?"

She sat up straighter. "What's wrong with that?"

He wiped the look of surprise off his face. "Nothing. It's just that I thought you considered the mining inspector our enemy, especially since he indirectly works for the Royals."

"I did, but Kyle is different."

Logan shrugged. "Of all of us, I figured you'd be the type to give Fate the finger and say she was wrong."

"I can't deny how my body reacts to him." Her face heated just saying those words.

"Okay, then. Kyle is your mate. Good to know. So how is he doing?"

"With the exception of a major headache, he seems okay."

Birk leaned forward. "How does he feel about you? I thought I heard his sister isn't high on dragon shifters."

"She's not. Lily poisoned him against our kind, but he's coming around." She explained about Nelor and what he'd done to Lily.

Birk's hands clenched. "Geezus, that's horrible."

"I know."

Nessa hadn't taken more than a few sips of her drink when her cell glowed through her pants. She retrieved it from her pocket and turned the sound back on. "It's a text from Kyle."

Her fingers shook, partly out of excitement and partly from dread, fearing he'd had a setback. She swiped the screen and froze. She had to read it twice, wanting to make sure she understood what he was saying.

"You're pale," Logan said. "What does it say?"

"At Lily's. Need help. We've been—" She sucked in a deep breath. "That's all. The rest of the message didn't come through." Or at least she hoped that was all that happened.

"Or someone is there and smashed his phone." Birk jumped up. "We should check it out."

Birk was the consummate protector. "When I left Kyle's, Lily was asleep at his place. Why would they go back to her apartment?"

"You'll have to ask him. We should go to his sister's and check it out," Birk said with much urgency in his voice.

"I don't know where she lives."

"Where is your computer?" Logan asked.

"In my bedroom." She rushed in there and turned it on.

"What's her name again?"

"Lily Harper. She works at the Avonbelle Insurance Company."

It took less than five minutes for Logan to find her address. "Got it. Let's go."

Because there were three of them, they flew and were at Lily's apartment building in under a minute. They would have landed on the roof had it not been covered in air conditioning units. They found a park a half-mile away instead, landed, and then shifted. Running, they reached her place in less than three minutes. She lived on the first floor. The moment Nessa saw the damage to Lily's door, her heart nearly gave out.

Birk held up his hand. "I don't sense any shifters."

Both she and Logan shook their heads, indicating they didn't either. Birk pushed open the door, and when they stepped inside, Nessa's legs shook, and her heart dropped to her stomach. Chairs were turned over and what looked like had been a vase was in pieces. Lily was sprawled on the floor with blood all over her face. Kyle was face down in an odd position. Claw marks marred his arms and back. Birk ran to where Lily was laying, while Nessa shot over to Kyle.

She gently shook him. "Kyle, can you hear me?"

They may not be mated yet, but pain was rushing through her veins. He groaned, giving her hope he would survive. "Who did this to you? Was it Nelor?"

Kyle lifted a hand to his face and grunted. As much as Nessa wanted to hold him, it was safer for him to lie still.

Birk spoke to someone on the phone. "We need you now, Greer." He gave her the address. "Thank you. He's in Plux, but maybe he can get away." Birk pressed a few more buttons. "Declan. Thank goodness I got a hold of you." He explained about the extensive injuries. "I'm worried about this girl, Lily. We need you fast. Yes, I know you are in Plux, but—oh, that's great." Once more, he gave out Lily's address.

Thank goodness help was on the way. Nessa stood and went in search of some towels to clean the blood off their faces and to stem the flow on Kyle's arm and back. She wet a few then returned to the living room.

"I'll take one over to Lily," Logan said.

She held out a towel to him, but when Birk made an odd growl at Logan, she gave it directly to Birk instead. They both watched as he gently dragged the cloth over Lily's face. Something was going on. Birk was more of the warrior type than a nursemaid. It was Logan who was the gentler of the two.

And what was up with Birk growling at Logan wanting to help Lily? She couldn't think about it right now though. She was worried about Kyle and needed to be with him.

Nessa wrapped one of the towels around the wound on his arm and then tried to clean his face. He opened his eyes and pushed up on his elbow. "Why are you here?"

He was recovering from a concussion, so his confusion concerned her. "You texted me that you were in trouble. Don't you remember?"

He glanced down at the blood covering his hand. "Oh, fuck. I did. Thank God you're here. I see you brought help." He managed to sit up. "I need to check on Lily."

When Kyle tried to crawl toward her, Nessa stopped him. "Just lie still Kyle; you have been hurt pretty bad too. Birk is helping her."

Kyle blinked. "Oh, yeah. Birk. He's in charge of security at the mine."

She sighed with relief now that he seemed more aware of his surroundings. "Yes. Can you tell me what happened? Was it Nelor?" From the claw marks on Kyle's body, it was a shifter. The question was which one?

"No." Kyle looked over at his sister again and then back at her. "Is she going to be okay?"

"She will be. My sister Greer and our cousin, Declan, who's flying in from Plux, will be here soon to help. They'll be able to give her better care than at any hospital."

He dropped back down to the floor and winced. "If anything happens to her—"

"It won't," Birk said with such force even Nessa didn't question him.

She hadn't realized he'd been listening. "I thought Lily was spending the night at your place."

"She was, but after you left, she woke up and was quite agitated. Lily insisted I take her home. Not wanting to upset her, I did. I locked everything up for her and said I would call her when I got home to make sure she was all right. I was half way to my place when Lily called to say she heard footsteps outside her door. I think I told you that Nelor, her ex-boyfriend, had recently been released from prison and had come over to see Lily, and that visit ended in him hitting her."

"Yes, you did."

"Well, she thought he might have seen me leave and had returned. She was really scared."

"I'd be scared too."

"She was crying so hard. Shit. I knew I shouldn't have left her. Damn girl is so stubborn. I turned around and headed back to her apartment. I didn't see anyone outside her place or in the hallway. I wasn't here more than five minutes when someone knocked on the door. I told her not to answer it, and she didn't. But apparently, they heard me and broke it down."

"Them?"

"There were two of them."

This was worse than she thought. "Then what happened?"

"After they smashed their way in, they threatened me, saying I had to make sure your mine never reopened."

Her mind swam with questions. "Why come to Lily's place instead of yours?"

"I didn't think to ask them. This is all my fault. I should have insisted Lily remain at my place. She would have been safe there, damn it!"

Now Nessa felt bad for questioning him when he was obviously so upset. "Kyle, it wouldn't have mattered. It sounds like they would have gotten to you both one way or another. They obviously aren't amateurs as they got through what security Lily had too. Can you tell us what they looked like?"

"Fuck if I remember. They were huge and were able to turn their hands into claws." Kyle faced her. "Like the way you can."

"It's possible they were the same two men I heard come after me tonight," she said more to herself than to Kyle.

As if he forgot about his injuries, he grabbed her hand. "They came after you? Are you okay?"

She appreciated his concern. "Yes. I hid in the trunk of my car until Birk rescued me."

"I thought you were a tough dragon lady," he said with a half-smile.

Tough was a relative word. "Can I fight a dragon and win? Most likely, but two dragons? Probably not. When these two guys located my car, I was in the parking garage of my condo, hiding in the trunk. I couldn't have shifted even if I'd wanted to. If they'd remained in their human form, I would have been injured."

"I'm sorry, Nessa. I'd hug you, but I don't want to cover you in blood."

He was such a sweet man. "A virtual hug it is then."

A knock sounded on the door, interrupting their moment. Greer pushed it open and stepped inside. "Oh, my."

She was dressed in a crisp navy blue suit and three-inch blue and white heels. With her hair piled on top of her head and her makeup perfect, Greer was a vision of loveliness. She glanced between the two injured parties.

"Greer, I'm so glad you're here." Nessa said.

"Help, Lily first," Kyle said.

Her sister nodded. She kicked off her shoes and knelt in front of Birk. "Has she regained consciousness at all?"

"I don't think so," Birk said with more worry than she'd heard in his voice in a long time.

Greer placed her fingertips on Lily's forehead and dragged them across her cheeks to her throat. Her sister closed her eyes as she began to hum.

"What is she doing?" Kyle whispered.

"Greer uses magic to close the wounds and heal the skin."

"That's incredible."

Birk held Lily's head steady while Greer did her work. When Lily moaned, Kyle grabbed Nessa's hand and squeezed, but she doubted he was even aware he was doing it. Lily finally opened her eyes and looked around. Fear and distrust radiated off her body.

"It's okay, Lily," Kyle said. "They are here to help."

Kyle's sister tried to push up to a sitting position, but when her arms collapsed, Birk stopped her from hitting the floor. Once he propped her up against his chest, Lily's gaze focused on Nessa, and her lips thinned. "What are *you* doing here?"

Chapter Twelve

S EEING LILY WAKE up brought Kyle great relief. He would have crawled over to his sister, but Greer instilled confidence in him.

Lily's question about why Nessa was in her house held quite a lot of animosity, but it was also tinged with curiosity. "I called Nessa. I feared those men might come back, and if they had, I wasn't in any shape to defend you."

Lily sucked in a big breath and hiccupped. Birk picked up the wet towel and wiped away some of the blood on her face. "You're healing nicely," he said softly.

Her brows scrunched, and then she grunted. "Then why do I hurt so much?"

Greer placed a hand on Lily's arm. "I promise the pain will go away shortly."

Lily glanced up at Greer then over at Kyle. "Maybe you can help my brother."

"I'll try." Greer looked up at Birk. "What about Declan? Is he coming?"

"He's on his way."

"Good," she said.

Greer rose, and when she moved over to Kyle, Nessa scooted out of the way. If her brother hadn't been watching, he would have asked Nessa to stay by his side. Just being next to her brought comfort. No doubt about it, Nessa Caspian had gotten under his skin. Hell, every time he was near her, he couldn't help but want her. When the attraction had grown to this heightened point of need, he didn't know—but it had.

Greer placed her hands on his face, and when she touched an open wound, he winced.

"Close your eyes," Greer said. "Try to absorb my healing energy."

The moment he did, Nessa returned to his side and held his hand. Her touch helped him relax. Seconds later, the pounding headache subsided, and the stinging on his arms and back lessened, though he wasn't certain which of the sisters was giving him more relief.

Kyle opened his eyes, and both Greer and Nessa smiled down at him.

"How do you feel?" Nessa asked.

It took him a moment to assess his condition. "I can't believe it. My headache is finally gone for the first time in days."

Nessa smiled. "Greer is amazing."

No, you are amazing, Nessa.

Kyle looked down at his arms and then touched his face. The wounds had dried up and were healing. "Thank you, Greer. I never would have believed it was possible if I hadn't just experienced it."

"You're welcome. The wounds on your back will heal as well," Greer said.

Nessa squeezed his hand. "We probably should get out of here. Those men might come back."

"Why would they? They delivered their message—loud and clear."

"Perhaps, but I like to be cautious." She pressed her lips together. "I'm very sorry you had to go through this."

"Thank you. I'm more worried about Lily right now," he whispered. He would handle whatever came his way, but his sister was innocent. "She has nothing to do with this."

Nessa rubbed his arm, and his thoughts scattered. "In a way, she does. I'm betting the attackers want her to suggest to the injured workers that they sue us for everything we're worth. Avonbelle insurance might say everything is our fault. If we lost in court, it could do some serious damage to our reputation."

Lily spoke up, sounding a lot stronger. "My company is not like that. Besides, I'm just one of many workers who make recommendations. People review my case files. I can recommend all I want, but Avonbelle Insurance would only spend the money to fight your family if they thought they could win."

Kyle loved hearing his sister's passion. The fact she wasn't spewing hate was a good sign that she might be softening toward dragon shifters.

Birk looked down at Lily and then at Kyle. "I'll make sure nothing happens to her."

Kyle didn't like the possessive look in the man's eye. Nelor had acted like that at one time and look what happened. Kyle sat up straighter. "I can take care of my sister."

The moment he said it, he realized he might not be able to. Those men had barged in and shoved him like he weighed nothing. Sure, he got in a few good swings, but when the men's claws came out, he was smart enough to know he couldn't fight them both.

One of the men started tearing up the place, and Lily nearly lost it. She screamed at them to stop, but the men ignored her. It was then that she charged one of them. He swung a fist and connected with her face, and she'd dropped like a stone. The second man then lifted her off the floor and shook her.

To protect Lily, Kyle had jumped on the man's back and tried to pry him off his sister. Sadly, his act of aggression only made things worse. That was when one of them clawed him.

With his memory becoming clearer, he told Nessa what had occurred. "After that, everything is a blur. I remember them giving me another warning about never reopening your mine and then they left. I texted you but then passed out before I could finish my message."

"Thank goodness you contacted me."

Birk sat up straighter. "Declan is here. He must have flown in at super speed."

Right now, Kyle was thankful for all the help they could get. Lily's face was white, and despite her recent outburst, her breathing was becoming shallower. His sister must be weak, or she would have never let Birk hold her. Or did she yearn for the comfort?

While Greer had worked a miracle in rousing his sister from the depths of unconsciousness, Lily had a long way to go before she was restored to health. He, on the other hand, was improving with each minute.

Someone knocked, and then another giant of a man entered. Birk motioned him over to Lily. She looked up at him and seemed to shrink back against Birk. That wasn't the reaction Kyle wanted. His poor sister. Being surrounded by so many dragon shifters had to be traumatic for her.

"Hi, Lily. I'm Declan. I'm sorry it took me so long to arrive, but I was helping out in Plux." Her brows pinched. "Where the dam broke. Did you hear about that?"

"Yes." Her voice came out weak.

"I know that Greer helped you, but I might be able to restore your health completely. May I try?"

Kyle was thankful this huge man came off as non-threatening.

She looked up at Birk, who nodded. "Okay."

Kyle hadn't expected she'd seek Birk's opinion, but he was pleased she had. Declan knelt in front of Lily. Unlike Greer, he merely held his hands inches above her body without touching her. Slowly, the lines of pain in Lily's face softened, and right before his eyes, the wounds closed up completely, and Lily's labored breathing slowed.

Kyle looked over at Nessa, who was smiling. "Declan is amazing," he said keeping his voice low.

"He is," Nessa said, her voice filled with pride.

"Do you think he can heal the scars on her back?"

She shook her head. "The wounds need to be fresh."

"Oh."

Lily touched where her face had been injured and smiled. She then looked up at Declan. "I can't believe it. Thank you."

Declan leaned back on his heels and then rose. "My pleasure."

Birk slid Lily off his lap. He stood and helped her up. "I think both of you should come to our shelter. You'll be safe there."

Shelter? For some reason, Kyle didn't want to be taken care of anymore. It might have been his wounded pride talking, but he and his sister had been a team for a long time. "I appreciate the offer, but we'll head on over to my place. I'll hire some bodyguards to keep watch."

"They better be dragon shifters, because no one else can protect you," Birk said.

Nessa placed a hand on his arm. "Please reconsider. It's not a prison, but rather a safe place. Both of you can go to work. One of us will even escort you there to ensure they don't harm either of you again."

Kyle wondered if it would be Nessa by his side. If that were the case, he'd gladly stay at her safe house. He looked over at Lily who was worrying her bottom lip. She must be considering it. "I'll go if Lily is willing."

Lily actually looked up at Birk. "Maybe for a little while."

Thank you, Lily.

"Are there showers in the shelter?" Lily asked Birk.

He looked as if he were fighting a smile. "It has all the comforts of home. Why don't you pack and then you can see for yourself?"

Lily faced Kyle. "What about you?"

Before he could answer, Nessa spoke up. "I can go with Kyle back to his place so he can grab a few things too."

Kyle didn't want to leave Lily with all these men. "Greer, can you stay with her?"

"Definitely."

Declan walked over to them. "I'll fly overhead to make sure these men don't follow you back to the safe house."

"Thank you." Nessa spun to face Kyle. "We'll need to drive your car, since I flew here."

"No problem."

Kyle assured his sister she was in good hands before he and Nessa left. Declan followed them out. When they reached his car, parked out front, Declan said goodbye and headed in the direction of the park.

"Where is he going?" Kyle asked.

"The streets are too narrow for him to take off. The park down the street has more space."

"Ah."

Nessa held out her hand. "Mind if I drive? You did suffer a second concussion."

As much as he didn't like giving up the control, she was right. His vision was still a bit blurry. He probably shouldn't have driven Lily home in the first place, but she'd been insistent. He stuck his hands in his jeans pocket and withdrew the key. "Be my guest, but please drive carefully. Most of the accidents around here seem to be with dragon shifter drivers."

She laughed, and the sound bolstered his spirits. "That's true. I admit I'm better at flying, but I promise to take care."

"Thanks." He touched her arm. "I appreciate all you did tonight, and I also appreciate you retrieving my car from the mine. I never thanked you for that either."

She smiled. "I figured you would need it."

They both climbed in, and Nessa started the engine. The drive to his place only took a few minutes.

Once inside his apartment, she placed the car keys on the coffee table. Something had been eating away at him during the drive over. "Do you think it's possible those men followed me to Lily's?"

"I wouldn't rule anything out, but don't start blaming yourself. If one or both cloaked themselves, you wouldn't have seen anything even if you'd been looking."

He liked how she tried to make him feel better.

"Thanks. I'll only be a minute." Only then did he realize he didn't know how long this protection service would last. "Any idea how long Lily and I will be in your safe house?"

"No way to say, but pack light. You can always come back for more, though we do have laundry service there."

She made it sound like a hotel. "Got it."

Kyle tossed some essentials in his case, still amazed at how much his body had healed. He then returned to the living room with his duffel in hand. "You know, Declan and Greer should go into business as healers. They'd make a mint."

Nessa chuckled. "I agree, but it tires them out. Declan has been working non-stop over in Plux helping the flood victims there. I'm surprised he was able to fly as fast as he did, let alone heal Lily."

Kyle knew that Declan was a relief worker, but he hadn't realized the extent of his help. He'd bet the two men who'd attacked him and his sister would never take the time to help with any relief effort. He hoped Lily realized that.

Kyle lifted his bag. "I'm ready."

Once more, he let Nessa drive. For some reason, he'd expected them to head to the Caspian mine, but she drove past the turn off.

"If you're wondering, we're going to the Sinclair mine, but I have a favor to ask you first."

"Anything." He meant it too.

"This is a safe house that both families use, and as such, no one must know about it." She glanced over at him.

"I give you my word that I won't divulge where it is."

She tossed him a brief smile, and his cock hardened. Without thinking, Kyle reached over, and when he squeezed her leg, heat shot through his hand. It was almost as if she'd sent a bolt of electricity straight through him. He jerked away.

"What's wrong?" she asked.

Well, crap.

Chapter Thirteen

KYLE HADN'T MEANT to react so strongly to the sexual current charging through him, but it had taken him by surprise. "Nothing. I just didn't want to distract you while you were driving."

Lame. Very lame. Fortunately, Nessa didn't say anything, but from the slight upward turn of those sexy lips, she obviously knew that wasn't the real reason.

Nessa pulled into the Sinclair Gem mine, but he didn't spot anything that looked like a safe house. Kyle glanced around for Lily's car and didn't see that either, forcing him to tamp down his worry. He trusted Nessa though. "I see we beat my sister here."

"Birk probably parked her car underground."

This was becoming stranger by the minute. "I don't see any garage entrance."

Nessa pulled to a stop in front of a rock wall. "I'll show you. Wait here. I need to open the door."

He would have asked what door, but he'd come to realize that of late, nothing was as it seemed. She took something from her pocket and waved her hand over the stone. The rock glowed, and then a garage door opened. "Well, I'll be damned," he mumbled to himself.

Nessa returned and slid into the front seat. "Cool, huh?"

"Totally. How did you do that?"

She smiled, and once more his libido shot up. "It's called magic."

Magic seemed to rule everything the dragons did. Nessa drove into the underground parking garage, and when he spotted Lily's car, relief shot through him. After sliding into a lined spot, Nessa cut off the engine and hopped out. While Kyle retrieved his duffel, Nessa did some hand waving stuff, and the door closed.

"Right this way," she said.

"What is this place? It's a lot more than a safe house." Kyle couldn't drink it all in. While he had inspected this mine last year, he had no idea something like this existed.

"The Sinclairs and Caspians need a place they can go when things get, shall we say, rough. It's equipped with a lot of bedrooms and has a huge kitchen—including a gourmet chef—along with many meeting rooms. The monitoring rooms here would put the one we have at our mine to shame. This is a truly state of the art building."

"So I can see." The fact Nessa was willing to let him and Lily see their secret hiding place warmed him. It meant she trusted him. Evil dragon shifters would never do that.

Nessa's upbeat attitude continued to amaze him, and his gut decided once and for all that she was a good person. And a sexy one. Okay, and yes, someone he could see himself with long term.

NESSA COULDN'T HELP but smile at Kyle's large eyes. If he was impressed with the parking garage, he'd be thrilled with what else they had, and she couldn't wait to show him. She wasn't sure where Birk had stashed Lily, but she bet he gave her the suite—the one with a comfy sitting lounge area and the large soaking tub. From the way Birk reacted to Lily, something was going on between them. If Fate had paired her with Kyle, it was possible that Fate had decided siblings should stay together. It wouldn't be hard to believe that Birk and Lily were meant for each other. How her brother could convince her she should be with a dragon, Nessa didn't know.

"I'm not sure where Lily is staying, but she has to be somewhere down this hallway," Nessa said. "The last three rooms are reserved for guests." She tapped on the first door, and when no one answered, she pushed it open. It was empty. "You can stay in here."

Kyle stepped inside and set down his duffel. "Wow." He turned around and had a big smile on his face. "This is amazing."

"Thanks. My father and uncle designed it. I think you'll find it has everything you need. If you think this is great though, wait until you try our food. We have an amazing chef." Which reminded her that she needed to let him know that there would be guests here for a while.

"Seriously?"

"Yes. Let's find Lily. I'm sure she is anxious to see you."

Just as Nessa turned to leave, Kyle stopped her. He tucked a stray piece of hair behind her ear and let his finger stroke down her cheek. Then Kyle leaned in close and, ever so lightly, brushed his lips across hers. "You constantly amaze me, Nessa Caspian. Thank you for everything you and your family are doing to help Lily and me."

Her heart nearly burst out of her chest. If she weren't careful, her purple scales would show through her skin. As it was, her body was already radiating an excessive amount of heat. "You are very welcome. I'm quite impressed with you too."

"Good to know." He winked, and her knees weakened, something that had never happened before.

Good goddess, what this man could do to her! She was the one who handled explosives and was never scared of anything—except for spending the rest of her life alone because she'd botched up this whole mating thing.

"Nessa?" he asked.

She jerked her attention back to him. "Ah, yes. We need to find Lily."

Happy to have something to do, she stepped next door and knocked. When Birk answered, she quirked a brow. Nessa would have thought Lily would have booted him out before this. "Everything okay?"

"Yes. Lily is next door. I'm staying here so I can keep an eye on her."

Was that so? Birk shared a room with Logan whenever they

stayed in this bunker, and that room was down the hall. Where he was now was reserved for guests, and he knew as well as anyone that no one could get into this complex, so there was no need to be so close. Unless…Nessa kept that thought to herself.

"I imagine she'd like to see Kyle." Nessa stepped next door, knocked, and then faced him. "I'll let you two chat."

"Are you staying here?" Kyle asked.

More heat poured into her at the excitement in his tone. "Yes."

"But you didn't pack anything."

"We always have stuff here. Since we never know when we'll need refuge, we keep spare clothes in the rooms we use."

Before he could ask her any more questions, Lily opened the door and was in Kyle's arms in a moment. While endearing, Nessa worried about Lily's influence on him. After all, she was very anti dragon shifter.

Kyle glanced back at Nessa and mouthed *thank you*. The wink that followed had her heart pounding. First, he'd squeezed her leg in the car and then he'd tucked a strand of hair behind her ear—all signs that he was an independent thinker when it came to her kind. Then there was that small but amazing kiss. Yes. Nessa was beginning to think there was hope for them after all. The way his beautifully expressive eyes sparkled when he looked at her confirmed it as well.

"I'm going to say goodnight to you both," Nessa said, wishing she were the one in Kyle's arms right now. "I'll be down the hall— four rooms away on this side—if either of you need me. Birk is just next door too."

"Thanks," Kyle said, his voice soft and sexy.

Lily nodded then looked away as if she just couldn't bring herself to change her mind about dragons.

Nessa headed to her room, wishing she had the courage to drag Kyle away from his sister and into her bed. It was becoming increasingly more difficult for her not to touch him. Before Kyle came into her life, she thought nothing of spending her nights alone.

Hell, she preferred it. Now that those deep feelings had been released, Nessa wasn't sure she'd ever be able to rein them in again.

After undressing, she stepped into the shower. As she ran the wet soap over her body, she closed her eyes and imagined Kyle was in there with her. He'd be standing behind her, snatch the soap from her fingers, and insist on washing her until her skin glowed. Little did he know that she didn't need any water to make her body shine. Just being near him would do that.

Nessa ducked her head under the shower and reveled in the heat. She spun around to face her imaginary mate. He'd grin and then drag the tip of the soap over her nipples, hardening them to points. Unable to stand there and do nothing, she would grab his huge cock and tug on it. He'd moan and then slam his body against hers.

The kiss would be a nibble here and a nibble there until her nails sharpened, and her scales pulsed so hard that she'd have to dip her tongue into his mouth and devour him. He'd taste of mint or maybe cinnamon. While she was losing herself in his sensuality, he'd slip a finger into her pussy, and the spikes of need would cause her to cry out and then beg him to take her. Her eyes would glow purple, and his would deepen to the color of navy blue.

She'd run her hands over his firm ass and then drop to her knees and suck on his cock while the water sluiced over their bodies.

Nessa's groan, and her resulting climax, jerked her back to reality. Well, damn. Two of her fingers were inside her pussy, and her other hand—not Kyle's—was pinching her nipple. Nessa never stimulated herself—more proof she was losing her mind.

Clearly, something had to give, and soon, or she might march into his room, strip off her clothes, and jump into bed with him.

That image helped calm her but only for a moment. The chance of Kyle rejecting her still existed.

But he kissed you, her dragon reminded her.

He did at that, though way too briefly. Needing to mentally move back to reality, she washed her hair and rinsed off. After she stepped out of the shower, Nessa stood in front of the mirror and slowly dragged the towel over her body, wondering what Kyle would honestly think of her shape. She had tits, but they weren't very big, and her hips were too slim. Damn. Most men told her she needed to gain weight.

Once she finished towel drying her hair and body, she slipped on a pair of panties and a T-shirt. She then slid under the crisp covers. After that sensual daydream in the shower, she probably wouldn't be able to sleep though.

Reading might take her mind off the hot Kyle Harper. She licked her lips, remembering the light brush of his mouth. Wouldn't it be great if Kyle were waiting for her to make the first move?

Or wasn't he ready to be with a shifter?

The kiss! The kiss! It wasn't just to say thank you, her dragon said. *He was testing to see if you wanted him.*

Was that true? Uncertainty sucked.

Nessa picked up the e-reader she and Greer kept in the drawer. They both loved romances, so it was stocked full. Nessa mostly stuck to romantic suspense and some thrillers, whereas Greer liked the more sappy contemporaries with an occasional shifter story thrown in. The ones written by people from Earth were funny though. Nessa appreciated their imagination, but too often she wanted to tell them they had it all wrong.

Nessa snuggled in bed, and just as she was about to start reading, someone tapped on her door. It was Kyle. She could feel it. Her hands almost morphed into talons, and she had to force her body to stop the shift.

"Coming." She threw off the covers and scrambled to find a pair of pants. Her fingers were about to tug on the dresser drawer when she stopped. Why not show him what he would be missing?

Not wanting to go overboard and actually flaunt herself, Nessa stood behind the door and opened up. "Kyle!"

"I'm sorry. Were you in bed?"

"I was just reading."

"Do you mind if I come in?"

Nessa smiled and swung the door open for him to enter. *Not. At. All.*

Chapter Fourteen

W HEN KYLE ENTERED Nessa's room, the sight of her long naked legs had his cock so hard he was sure she could tell exactly what he was thinking. Adjusting himself in front of her, however, wouldn't be cool, so he angled to the side to minimize his exposure.

He just couldn't take his eyes off her. The fact she wasn't shooing him out implied she might not mind being partially undressed in front of him. Other than when she'd visited him in the hospital, all he'd seen her wear were khaki pants and a rather baggy shirt with the SinCas logo on the pocket.

Now, she looked totally different. Her wet hair had soaked part of her pretty purple t-shirt, outlining her breasts. Lucky for him, the material was thin enough to show her protruding nipples.

Looking away wasn't an option. His libido was soaring too high, but he needed to be cautious. She might have thought the earlier kiss was just a thank you, and if he tried again, she might just smack him. Although with the way her eyes had changed to that gorgeous purple color, she might not.

"Come on in," she said with a sassy smile. Nessa sauntered over to the bed and stood next to it.

His blood heated at the implication. "I just wanted to say thank you for all you've done. When I texted you, I wasn't sure you'd rush over." That sounded weak, but Kyle spent most of his time working—not on developing pick-up lines for gorgeous women.

"Of course I would! It was because of the problems at the Caspian mines that landed you in trouble in the first place. I'm the one who should be sorry you got tangled up in this mess."

He shook his head. "It's my job." *Just shut up.*

She smiled, and all thoughts left his mind—all thoughts other than delving into that sweet mouth of hers. Her lips moved, but he didn't hear a word. Her expressive eyes sparkled and moved in a sensual rhythm that mesmerized him. And then there was her mouth. He slowly parted his lips, imagining what it would be like to kiss her.

Nessa placed a hand on his chest. "Kyle?"

He refocused. "Yes?"

"You're staring."

Tell her why. "That's because you are so beautiful."

Her face turned a pretty shade of red. "Thank you."

"Why do you always act so surprised when I give you a compliment?" He hadn't meant for his words to have an edge to them. They just came out that way. While he could understand his sister's low self-esteem after what that bastard Nelor did to her, Nessa was strong and seemed to know what she wanted in life.

She shrugged. "I don't think of myself that way."

"You should." Nessa bit down on her lip and then leaned forward. His pulse soared, and he turned his head, fearing he might do something she didn't like, though deep inside he believed she wanted him as much as he wanted her. "I'm sorry."

"Sorry about what?"

"For sucking at this," he said.

"Sucking at what?"

She probably wouldn't stop asking questions, which meant he just needed to spit it out. Kyle hadn't felt this inadequate since his first date in high school after he had turned sixteen. "I really like you, Nessa. No. I more than like you. I'm highly attracted to you. I know that we kind of work on opposite sides of the fence so to speak but—"

Nessa held up a hand. "How about stopping there? Just so you know, I like you too, and I want you—as in all of you."

His pulse jackhammered. He figured she was attracted to him, but had no idea she wanted to be intimate.

Her eyes shone that glorious purple, which he'd heard indicated she was turned on. "You are such a good person, Nessa."

She smiled and dragged her gaze from his face down to his cock then back again. "Is that so? How good?"

Oh, God, was she actually coming on to him? Why was he even questioning it? The only way to find out what she truly meant was to really kiss her to test her reaction.

"This good." He grabbed the back of her head and brought his lips to hers.

When she didn't resist, he wrapped his arms around her waist, his erection pressing right below her belly button. Her lemony scent infused every cell of his body, and all he could think of was having her. Their lips melted together, and the kiss was everything he'd dreamed of—intense, passionate, and full of their unleashed desire for each other.

Nessa snatched the hem of his shirt and lifted it. As much as he didn't want to break contact, he wanted to be naked with her more. Raising his arms, he let her pull his shirt over his head. Nessa then tossed his shirt on the floor. Instead of resuming the kiss, she raked her gaze up and down his chest.

"Nice pecs," she said, dragging a finger from his sternum down to the waistband of his jeans. "And those abs are fine. Very fine indeed." The smile that followed gave him all the confidence he needed.

Kyle refused to comment that he had another body part that was even more impressive. Hopefully, in time, she'd see it.

"Turn around is fair play," he said as he slipped his hands under her shirt and cupped her very naked breasts. His palms heated, and his fingers itched to pluck those delicate nipples. Images of him sucking on them raced through his mind, making his cock even more rigid.

Kyle massaged her heated skin and held his breath, waiting to see if she'd complain. When she smiled instead, an explosion of need raced through him so great, he feared he'd come right then. Kyle never expected her skin would be so soft or his reaction would be this violent—but it was.

"I take it you like them?" She suddenly acted way more confident than when he'd first walked in.

"I'm not sure."

Her smile turned into a frown. "What do you mean?"

Teasing her was such a high. "A man can't make that kind of judgment based on feel alone. I have so many more senses. Like sight. And well…taste."

"What are you going to do about it?" Nessa chuckled, and the sound made him harder than any rock she'd probably ever blasted through.

He loved a woman who could challenge him back. "What do you think I'm going to do?"

Before she answered, he lifted her top off and tossed it on the floor next to his shirt. Lowering her to the bed, and then pressing her onto her back, he slipped next to her and feasted on her beautiful breasts. He sucked one nipple while he massaged the other. He probably should have started with kissing and then worked his way downward, but the air was so charged that his body wanted no such thing. She wasn't objecting, so game on.

Nessa slid a hand between their bodies and grabbed his crotch. Holy hell. His need escalated from zero to one hundred in under a second, but he had to let her decide how fast to take things. From the way she was squeezing him though, she was as desperate as he was.

Kyle looked up at her. "You taste so good."

She laughed, and the tingling sound altered something in him. "There are more areas than my chest that might intrigue you."

Oh, yes there were, and he wanted to explore every inch of her. Kyle crawled on top and devoured her lips once more. When she opened her mouth and touched her tongue to his, his zipper imprinted itself on his dick, and if he didn't free the bad boy soon, he'd be in big trouble.

Hold on. Just a little bit longer.

Her mouth tasted like sweet nectar. As they explored each other fully, Nessa dueled and fought for position. It was as if their taste became the air they breathed. Their chests heaved, and he had to cup her face in order to fully savor her.

A moment later, she broke the kiss. Her lips were swollen, her purple eyes shone brightly, and her face was slightly flushed. Nessa Caspian never looked more beautiful.

"It's my turn to taste you," she said, her voice so soft, he barely heard her.

"Isn't that what we've been doing?" he asked with total innocence.

She reached between them and undid the button on his jeans. "Yes, but now I want to taste you *completely*." Nessa smiled. "If you last that long, that is."

Considering the huge bulge in his pants, she rightfully assumed he wanted to make love to her. "I say try it and see."

To speed up the process, Kyle slipped off the bed, ditched his boots, and shucked his pants, never taking his gaze off her. His heart was doing a rapid tattoo, and his endorphins were shooting through him at breakneck speed. Only then did he see her scales pulse purple under her skin. As much as he wanted to ask her about them, he didn't want her to think he was put off by them. Far from it—being around Nessa made him wish he could light up too.

When she pushed up on her elbows, her gaze followed his. "I see you're studying my scales. What do you think?"

"They're awesome," he blurted. It was the truth.

Her laugh came out light, like tiny bells. "They're kind of like my sex thermometer."

"Sex thermometer? I'm intrigued."

Nessa ran a finger down his arm. "You see, when a dragon is highly excited, she begins to glow the color of her secondary scales. My dragon is black with purple scales. Others might be black with pink or tan ones. I imagine those would be harder to notice."

He straddled her and grinned, thrilled that he'd turned her on. "Did I tell you purple is my favorite color?"

Her eyes widened. "Why no, you never mentioned it." She batted her eyes. "And my eyes match."

"Not always though."

"When I'm excited they do—which is most of the time when I'm around you."

"I have wondered about that." He leaned closer. "I also wonder if your purple skin tastes as good as it looks." Kyle had never delivered such slick lines before, but with Nessa, it came naturally.

Because it was fun to see what turned her on, he slid down to taste her tits once more. Nessa seemed to thrive on him sucking hard on a nipple and then biting the tip. The problem was the more she moaned, the harder he got. Even though he might come prematurely, Kyle had to drink in her deliciousness. He kissed his way down her body.

"I thought I was going to suck on your cock," Nessa said.

"In a moment. I'm liking this too much to stop."

"Mmm."

Kyle's focus never left her beautiful purple eyes as he pushed her legs open then ran his hands down the inside of her thighs. He gave her a sexy wink then looked down as he opened her folds with his thumbs. Fresh from her shower, he took a long tantalizing lick, and a hint of lemon soap left a trace on his tongue. He inhaled and groaned. Divine.

She clasped his shoulders and dug her very sharp nails into his skin. Not waiting another minute, he licked and nibbled around her clit, savoring her distinctive flavor. Bucking her hips, she pressed harder on his shoulders. "I can't last much longer."

That might save him the frustration of losing it first. "Come as often as you want, I won't stop you. Just know I am not removing myself from this spot till I have had my fill."

"Grr. Be careful. You don't want me to shift on you."

She must be kidding. Her dragon would never fit in the room. "Please don't. Not when I have something else in mind."

"What would that be?" The joy in her voice filled him with hope.

"How about entering into a joint venture?" He waggled his eyebrows at her.

She laughed. "Now you're talking my language."

Kyle pumped a mental fist. He'd never engaged in banter during sex, but it was so easy with Nessa. Communicating like this fueled his desires as well as helped him gauge her urgency.

Wanting to enjoy the feast before him, he slipped two fingers into her opening and searched for that perfect spot. He swept the tips around until he found what he was looking for. He then pressed up into that spongy area and rubbed his middle finger back and forth. At the same time, he tormented her clit with his tongue and lips. Suddenly, her whole body tensed. Bingo.

She clutched his shoulders, dropped back her head, and moaned. "You knew just where to touch me."

Lucky guess, though it was possible dragons were more sensitive than humans. Kyle continued to pleasure her with his fingers and lick her clit, thrilled shifters were anatomically the same as everyone else.

Nessa dug her nails into him. "I need you, Kyle Harper."

Oh, fuck. He didn't have a condom. "I forgot protection."

With her lids half closed, she lifted her head. "It's okay. It's safe."

"Are you on the pill—or whatever the dragon equivalent is?"

"Yes, so hurry."

Kyle appreciated that she trusted he was clean—which he was. For the last few years, his encounters had been few. Maybe Fate had known he needed to wait for someone as special as Nessa Caspian.

While having her mouth on his cock would be total nirvana, he needed to join with her more.

Learning how Nessa bravely had fought for her life and then cared for others fit perfectly with his beliefs of honesty and integrity. His need for her had bloomed from there.

"You're glowing again," he said, enjoying how her body was so responsive to his touch.

"You have that effect on me."

Using his elbows to move forward, he crawled upward until their bodies were aligned. When she looked at him with such passion, he had to kiss her again. This time they explored more slowly and definitely more seductively. It was as if they were testing each other to see how well they fit together. In his mind, Nessa was perfection. She had enough confidence to be herself. He also liked the fact she didn't need to dress up to show how incredible she looked. Even in her work clothes, the woman exuded sex appeal—though he had to admit he liked her naked best.

Nessa finally broke off the kiss, and when she wrapped her legs around his waist, his cock slipped into her slick entrance, and a smile lit up her face.

Kyle delved in, and when she drew him in even deeper, every nerve in his body exploded with intense need. The more she pulsed and glowed, the higher he soared. She had to be using some kind of magic on him because nothing had ever felt this good in his life.

"Oh, Nessa." When Kyle drove into her again, he almost came.

Wanting this moment to last, he closed his eyes, blocking out her beautiful face—a face that would drive him to do anything just to be with her. He probably should be thinking about what this was going to do to his relationship with his sister, but making love with Nessa eclipsed all things.

Tightening her grip around his waist, Nessa grabbed his head. The vise, coupled with her rapid breathing, implied she was as close to the edge as he was. Kyle inhaled. Everything about this woman bewitched him.

With each thrust of his hips, his climax built. Her body gave off waves of heat that matched the building temperature in his body. Needing as much contact with her as possible, Kyle dipped his head and kissed her hard. He'd become desperate for her. It might not be smart to fall for a woman whose family owned a mine, but there was nothing he could do about it now. She'd drawn him in like the proverbial moth to a very hot flame.

As Nessa lifted her hips to meet him thrust for thrust, their sweat slickened bodies slapped together, and their lustful moans came out louder. He never wanted this to end, but as he struggled to hang on, she scored her nails down his back and then dug them into his ass. Her tight pussy clenched hard around him as she started to climax, and her deep purple eyes filled with flecks of gold and crimson, creating a kaleidoscope of incredible beauty. Everything was happening at once, and Kyle lost his ability to stop. His rhythm stuttered as he gave it all to her. With one final push, the fire in his balls released, and he came harder than he ever had before.

When she buried her head against his chest, Kyle rolled to the side and dragged her on top.

"That was even better than I imagined it," she said, her body going totally limp on top of him.

"Me too." Kyle breathed in her scent, a combination of lemon and salt, and his body calmed. He probably fell asleep with her in his arms, because when she jerked, adrenaline filled him, along with another wave of desire.

Nessa lifted her head. "I guess we should clean up."

Before he could move, she slipped off him and headed into the bathroom. After returning with a wet towel, she cleaned him up, and once more, her touch ignited him. How was this possible? Hell, his cock was still stiff. That proved it. Nessa was a magical witch of some kind.

"Did you put a spell on me?" He had to ask.

"A spell? I do have some magical powers, but putting spells on people is not in my wheelhouse. You'll need to check out some other white lighters for that—unless you have something sinister in mind. Then a dark lighter can do your bidding." She winked, and he grinned.

Kyle had no idea where this relationship was headed, but he sure as hell would enjoy the ride.

Chapter Fifteen

KYLE LEANED CLOSE to Nessa at the large conference table, his scent making her hormones soar. Because Nessa was told her attraction would continue to grow, she worried she wouldn't be able to keep her dragon in check for much longer.

Now she was almost glad Kyle insisted on returning to his bedroom last night, but it wasn't until after they'd had another round of fantastic, earth-shattering sex. He'd left because he said he didn't want her to tire of him. Ha! That would never happen.

Even though she'd been exhausted after that, Nessa didn't sleep a wink. Her body wouldn't stop zinging from the intense pleasure that kept pounding throughout her body. Kyle told her a minute ago that he too had stayed up the rest of the night reliving their amazing experience.

"I still think Lily should be here," Kyle said under his breath, his delicious scent once more infiltrating every one of her pores.

"Why is that?" She wasn't able to think clearly.

"Lily represents Avonbelle Insurance. They are just as interested in learning whether this was negligence or sabotage as we are."

He might be right, but Nessa wanted to enjoy being with Kyle without Lily shooting daggers at her. "We both know it was sabotage," she said softly. "We just need to prove it—or rather, *you* need to prove it. In the end, the insurance company will have to pay the workers who were injured—not us. Once you narrow down the suspect pool, you can provide your sister with all of the findings. Besides, Lily needs to rest, not work."

He held up his palms. "You have a point. Lily is strong, but she's been through a lot recently."

That was an understatement. Actually, Nessa did admire his sister's fortitude.

The door opened to the conference room and Birk joined Logan and them at the table. Even though Birk probably wanted to make sure Lily remained safe, he was head of security and needed to be in on this discussion. Declan would have been able to add a lot of insight, but he'd wanted to return to the people in Plux. Nessa totally understood.

The large monitor on the wall mirrored her computer. Once everything was ready, she slid her computer over to Kyle. "I helped Kyle create this spreadsheet that will list the possible suspects and their motives."

He straightened the computer. "We need to give each suspect a rating on the likelihood of pulling off these crimes. The only thing we know for sure is that our man, or woman, is a dragon shifter with magical powers of invisibility in human form. Secondly, from what I can tell, this person knows his way around explosives."

"Who is your first suspect?" Logan asked.

"The first is Safford DeLeon, but that's not to say I believe he's the most likely suspect."

Birk harrumphed. "I'm not so sure. The man is a mean mother-fucker. As owner of the Vulcan Metals Extraction company, he would suffer financially if we were to mine all the gold Nessa claims is down there."

Kyle typed something into the spreadsheet. "I'm adding a column to indicate whether we believe the man is the planning type since these accidents seem to be premeditated. Safford DeLeon's bookkeeping is impeccable. I can't vouch for whether he's honest, but he keeps excellent records. A man like that would be a planner."

"As a mine owner, he would also know about explosives," Nessa added.

The group nodded. "If we're putting down Safford DeLeon, we have to add Wilson Snar," Birk said. "He's a dragon shifter, and his primary metal is gold. He'd have the most to lose if we had found the mother lode."

"Which I did, by the way," Nessa added. "We'll all need to pressure Dad into digging a new tunnel at some point. He's under the impression that finding such wealth would bring us more bad luck."

"I think he'll listen to reason once things calm down," Logan said.

"I hope so."

"I just entered Snar's name," Kyle commented. "He's not as detailed or as organized as DeLeon, but he is a worthy suspect nonetheless. I don't recall my source, but I've heard his wife puts a lot of pressure on him to bring in the money. She's rather attractive and has Wilson wrapped around her little finger. She might have urged Wilson to sabotage Caspian Mining."

Nessa wasn't so sure about Snar. "We should note that both he and DeLeon were in Plux for the relief effort, though it's possible one of them could have flown back here, attacked you, and returned to help. They could even be co-conspirators."

"Interesting. They might be using the relief effort to establish their alibi," Kyle said.

She shrugged. "It's something to consider."

The group discussed both men in more detail. In the end, they remained on the list.

"Speaking of your attack, does anyone know if Anderson learned anything?" Logan asked.

Once more, guilt attacked her. If she hadn't stored the bloodied rock in the locker, the invisible thief wouldn't have gotten his hands on it, and Anderson might have a suspect by now.

Kyle nodded. "I called your cousin this morning to see if he'd learned anything more. He hasn't. Apparently, ghosts are hard to find." Logan laughed. "I filled him in on what I've learned since then, so maybe he'll get a lead."

"Let's hope," Birk said. "Who else do we need to add to the list?"

Nessa couldn't help but add her two cents. "My favorite. The Royals. Mind you, not them per se, but someone they hired."

Kyle leaned back in his seat. "This is where Nessa and I disagree."

She twisted toward him. "Their power is extensive, and they have the financial ability to hire someone who is an expert in explosives and who has magical talents."

Kyle held up his hand. "If you say so. I'll have to leave the magic stuff to you all."

"None of us know for sure. That's the problem," Logan chimed in.

"Their motive would be revenge for the death of their son, Prince Rathan," Birk said.

Kyle typed in the information.

"Any one else?" Logan asked looking around.

"Darnax Pinter, your former foreman." Kyle added his name.

"He has an alibi," Nessa said.

"I know, but people lie."

"Very true." Kyle winked at her repeated words, and her body swelled with more lust. Sheesh.

"Would anyone like to add anyone else?" Kyle asked.

No one said anything.

"Good. Then I'll have my team check out the two mine owners," Kyle said. "Tom Delaney will be particularly effective speaking with the two mine owners since he worked for both of them before he came to work for me. I can have Dennis Taylor check out Darnax Pinter again."

"Great job, Kyle," Birk said, and Nessa beamed.

Kyle had an analytical mind that she appreciated. She also appreciated the way he seemed to adore her tits—and her lips—and her pussy.

Thank goddess this meeting was about to end. Sitting next to him and pretending nothing had happened between them last night had been so hard.

Birk and Logan pushed back their chairs. "It would be great if we could have some leads by the time Dad gets back to town."

"I'll do my best," Kyle said.

AFTER NESSA FOLLOWED Kyle to work the next day to make sure no one attacked him, she headed over to the SinCas building. As much as she tried, Nessa couldn't hold back her excitement any longer. Making love with Kyle had been mind-blowing, thrilling, and oh so sensual. If she ever had a doubt that the two of them belonged together—which she didn't anymore—the compatibility in bed would have erased it. Even as she entered the building, her dragon was still going crazy with need. Assuming her horny animal didn't make her seek out Kyle sooner, Nessa planned to meet him for lunch.

When she entered the ground floor jewelry store, Greer was dealing with a customer so Nessa studied what was in the cases. While she'd seen the pieces of jewelry many times, their beauty never failed to impress her. She wasn't one to wear earrings, necklaces, or rings, but now she realized it was because she had no desire to look good for a man. Ever since meeting Kyle, her attitude had changed.

Ten minutes later, Greer's customer left, and her sister came over to her. "How are Kyle and Lilly doing? I imagine both are still rather traumatized from the attack."

"Kyle's injuries are basically a thing of the past, but I really haven't spent much time with Lily to know about her wounds. Understandably, she has issues with our kind, so I haven't gone out of my way to friend her." She held up a hand. "I do plan to make time however." After all, she was her mate's sister.

"I'm glad both are doing better," Greer said. Nessa appreciated that her sister didn't lecture her on making nice with Lily right away. "By the way, did you notice the way Birk wouldn't leave Lily's side?" Greer wiggled her eyebrows.

"I know, right? I agree our brother is highly protective, but he's acting a bit strange even for him."

Greer grinned. "Do you think Lily is his mate?"

Nessa loved how the two of them thought so much alike. "It's a definite possibility. Even if it's true, I don't think Birk will make a move until all of this is over."

"I agree. I am so excited for you and Birk, assuming Lily is his mate."

Poor Greer. She was so gracious and kind. She had yet to find the perfect man for her. "Thanks. I stopped over because I wanted to tell you…" *How do I say it without making you feel bad that you've not found your mate?*

"Tell me what?"

There was no way Nessa could ever hide something this important from her. *Here goes.* "I made love with Kyle last night, and it was the most wonderful experience of my life."

Greer squealed. "Tell me more."

For the next few minutes, Nessa told her how Kyle had come into her room last night, acting a bit hesitant.

"Maybe he didn't realize how much you liked him. You aren't the most open person."

So now not only was Nessa a tomboy, she wasn't very expressive? If she didn't know that Greer loved her, Nessa might develop a complex. "Trust me—I let him know I was interested rather quickly. From there, the fireworks happened." A customer came in, cutting short their sister time. "Ugh. I'll let you get back to work, but we'll chat later."

Greer grinned. "I can't wait to hear more."

KYLE WAS EXPERIENCING some guilt. He was at work while poor Lily had to be cooped up in the Sinclair compound. Lily had insisted on returning to work today, but Birk said it was still too dangerous to go out. He did agree to take her to the office tomorrow, but only if he could wait there for her. Kyle hadn't had a chance to ask her about her reaction to that suggestion.

He also didn't understand Birk's desire, or rather need, to watch over Lily, but he was thankful for the man's diligence. The Caspians, including Nessa, took protecting others seriously. It was one of their wonderful traits.

Right now, he couldn't dwell on how awesome she was or how fantastic their lovemaking had been. If he did, he would accomplish nothing. Rather, he needed to focus on his men investigating the mine owners as well as verifying the previous Caspian foreman's alibi. Before he and Nessa could move on, finding who had sabotaged the mine had to be his primary concern.

Kyle asked his secretary to contact Dennis Taylor and Tom Delaney since he needed to speak with them. While he waited for his second-in-command and his assistant to arrive, Kyle reread the alibi of the Caspian Mines' previous foreman—an unhappy man who was very vocal about wanting more money and more benefits. On the surface, his alibi seemed solid, but as Nessa had said, people were known to lie.

Fifteen minutes later, both Dennis and Tom arrived. "You wanted to see us, boss?" Dennis asked.

"Have a seat." They both pulled up chairs. "We have some possible suspects in the Caspian Mine explosion."

Tom glanced over at Dennis. "Who?"

"Three suspects actually." He didn't bother mentioning the Royals since he wasn't able to investigate them. If none of these three suspects panned out, then he'd look at the Royals more closely.

Kyle started with the reasons why both of the other metal mine owners might be guilty and why they could be innocent. "Tom, I'd like you to interview each of them to see where they were at the time of the explosion, and then check their alibis again. Both of the men might still be in Plux helping out with the flooding over there, though it's possible they've returned."

"Sure. Anything else?"

"Yes. The guilty party is a dragon shifter who can become invisible in his human form."

Tom whistled. "He sounds dangerous."

"Yes, which is why you need to be very careful. Try to interview each of them inside a building. If you are indoors, they won't be able to shift in the small space. But be careful not to arouse too much suspicion. Riling them could prove deadly."

Tom nodded. "Don't worry. I've worked for both Snar and DeLeon. I think both men will be upfront with me."

Tom might be more naïve than Kyle. "They will be unless one of them is trying to take down the Caspian Mines. Remember that Wilson Snar is heavily invested in gold, so he has the most to lose if the Caspians find the mother lode."

"Got it."

"What do you want me to do?" Dennis asked.

"Talk to Darnax Pinter again," Kyle said. "I know he has an alibi, but check it out more thoroughly. I'm not even sure if the man's working right now. Rumor has it he started to drink rather heavily after he was fired."

"I'll dig deep, boss."

"Great. Get going and let me know what you two find out. We're all counting on you."

Both men shoved back their chairs and charged out of his office.

Because the Caspian mine wasn't the only one he needed to supervise, Kyle took care of other issues for the next few hours, reviewing complaints and looking for compliance violations.

It was close to noon when he heard Nessa's voice in the outer office, and his body reacted quickly and strongly. He stood and had to adjust himself before stepping into the outer office. As hard as he tried, the moment he spotted her, he failed to keep the smile off his face.

Chapter Sixteen

"HEY." KYLE SMILED at Nessa before turning to Michelle, his secretary. Even though Nessa was still wearing her khaki mining outfit, he couldn't help but picture her deliciously naked body. Kyle cleared his throat. "Michelle, this is Nessa Caspian."

Michelle swallowed a smile. "We've met a few times."

Really? Eventually, he'd ask how these two knew each other, but right now, if he didn't kiss Nessa, his physical needs would embarrass him. He motioned her to step into his office, and the moment he closed the door, he pinned Nessa against the wall and made love to her mouth.

Her hands roamed up and down his back, and her kiss came out strong and desperate. Both of their bodies heaved with unbridled lust as they tried to absorb each other's essence. In need of air, he leaned back.

When Kyle dragged his hands down over her luxuriously long hair, the soft texture ignited something inside him. "Oh, Nessa, I can't stop thinking about you."

She grinned. "If you were a shifter, you'd know it is ten times worse for me."

That was good news—kind of. But ten times worse? How was that possible? He hoped she wasn't suffering too much. "If I thought Michelle couldn't hear us, I'd clear off my desk and make love to you here."

She dragged a hand down his chest, and then grabbed his crotch. "How about we pick up something to eat and go somewhere more secluded?"

He liked the sound of that. "Where do you have in mind?"

"It's a special place I've only heard of, but it might give us some answers."

Answers? Hadn't they been discussing having another round of wild sex? "Where is this special place?" He hoped she wasn't planning on interfering with his investigation.

"It's in the middle of the realm where the four provinces meet. It's said to be the most magical spot in all of Tarradon. I thought we might find this oracle I've heard about."

He failed to hide his disappointment. He wanted some secluded cove where they could make love. He needed to taste her, touch her, and take her hard. "So, you're hoping this oracle will tell you who attacked us?" Or whether they would live happily ever after?

"Yes." She dragged a finger down his chest. "The best part is that the area is supposed to be quite isolated. That means no one would hear us…should we decide to continue our exploration." She cupped his balls and squeezed.

Yes! Joy speared him so much that he picked her up and spun her around. "I say let's go."

The trip sounded like a long one, so he told Michelle he'd be gone for the rest of the day. She gave him a coy smile as if she could guess what he was up to. "Have fun," she said.

"It's business, Michelle." She pressed her lips together, suppressing a smile. "If Dennis or Tom come back, tell them I'll meet with them tomorrow."

"Will do."

He would have suggested they call if they learned anything, but he wasn't sure if there would be cell service where they were going. Isolated meant isolated.

As soon as they left the building, Kyle wrapped his arm around Nessa's waist, and when she relaxed into his side, his cock surged. Even her luscious lemony scent poured heat into his veins.

She looked up and smiled. "Hungry?"

"For you."

She reached across him and punched him lightly in the stomach. "I wasn't talking about sex, silly. What kind of food do you want?"

This might be the first conversation they'd had that wasn't about finding the invisible dragon shifter, and he was enjoying it. "I'm flexible."

"For speed, let's go to Pepe's."

He appreciated that her need was as strong as his. "It's one of my favorite places."

"Perfect."

They walked the three blocks to the restaurant, and for the first time in a long while, there was some pep to his step. Kyle hadn't realized how much not having someone in his life had affected his outlook. Nessa gave him a sense of well-being and happiness. "Tell me more about this magical place."

"Have you heard of the eternal flame of Tarradon?"

"I've heard of it, but I've never seen it."

"Me neither, but I want to go there."

Now he was confused. "I thought you said we were headed to some magical spot."

"We are."

"In school, we were taught that the eternal flame was built to show the solidarity between the four provinces—a peace offering between them, if you will. I never heard anything about it being magic."

"My dad must have told me then."

"I've never really believed in fortune tellers, but I'm game." Plus, it would be awesome to spend some quality time with Nessa.

They entered Pepe's. The fairly long line gave Kyle some time to decide what to order. He opted for a Terraburger and a liquid gold tea while Nessa went with a Pollo salad and iced metal cola. Wisely, they didn't discuss their destination since there was no telling who was listening or who might be interested in their plans. If only he could tell a shifter from a non-shifter, he'd be a lot more relaxed.

Fifteen minutes later, they'd received and chowed down their meal.

"Ready?" she asked.

"Yes. Do you want me to drive?"

She laughed. "It's probably a six or seven hour trip. How about I fly us?"

Kyle might have acted brave a long time ago when she suggested she fly him to the mine, but after watching a few of the dragons dip and soar overhead, he wasn't sure how he'd like being suspended over the vast realm. "Do I have a choice?"

"Not if you want to be alone with me." Nessa held up her palms. "But if you're afraid, just say the word."

The woman knew how to punch his buttons. "You drive a hard bargain, lady." He leaned over and kissed her quick. "I don't think I've mentioned it, but I've piloted an airplane before."

"Are you kidding me?"

Her pride made him stick out his chest a little. "I even thought about becoming a pilot full-time, but it is a dangerous profession, what with your kind buzzing around."

She shook her head. "We're careful. Okay, usually we're careful. I am always on the lookout for others. To make this flight as enjoyable as possible—or less scary—I promise to fly very conservatively."

He doubted that. Nessa was rather wild. "Won't you tire holding onto me for so long?"

She cupped his face and kissed him like tomorrow might never happen. "Do you trust me?"

"Totally," Kyle said without giving it another thought.

"My grip will never give out—at least not when I'm holding you. And just so you know, if you scream, it's okay. I won't think any less of you." She winked.

He didn't believe that for a moment. "You've crossed the line. I won't scream." Damn. Now she'd take that as a challenge. "I meant I will try not to panic, assuming you don't execute some crazy dive."

She arched an eyebrow. "I told you I'd be good."

"Okay then. I'm game."

They headed back to the SinCas building since she said it was easier to take off from there. Given the distance they had to travel, Kyle couldn't chicken out now.

"Stand over by the door," she said once they reached the roof. "I need room to shift."

He'd seen how large she was when the men had carried her out from the mine. For his safety, he moved far out of the way. The biggest downer about the whole trip would be their inability to communicate during the hour flight.

One second, this trim woman was standing in front of him, and the next, she was a glorious animal, shimmering in the sunlight. Purple scales interspersed with the black ones, created a stunning animal. Nessa spread her wings and lifted a claw. He guessed that was his clue to climb on board.

Inhaling, he straightened his shoulders and strode toward her. Just as he reached out to grab hold of her very long talons, she scooped him up, his face toward the ground. Oh boy. While he couldn't judge her expression as she grabbed hold, she was probably laughing. He swore he'd acted rather macho and quite self-confident, but considering her extensive talents, she could probably tell his heart was beating hard.

All of his bravado disappeared the moment she took off, because the ground disappeared beneath him a hell of a lot faster than he'd anticipated. Kyle had to work not to tense his body—or vomit. Nessa probably could tell if he was scared, and he wanted to make her proud.

Cows became dots, and roads turned into thin ribbons. Once he realized he could actually breathe and that Nessa wasn't going to drop him, he started to enjoy himself. The fact his feet were dangling was a bit disconcerting, but her grip was tight enough to keep him from feeling as if he might fall. Kyle really wanted to watch Nessa flap her wings, but twisting in her grasp might not be smart.

True to her word, she flew level. Only when he became totally entranced in the landscape did she change altitude. Somehow, she must have sensed he was okay with the trip, or she wouldn't have tried any maneuvers.

To his surprise, Kyle was actually disappointed when they landed, and she set him down. Whoa. His feet had gone to sleep.

She returned to her human form. "Well? Did my flying skills live up to the hype?" He shifted from leg to leg. "Oh, no. I forgot to lift your feet when I flew. Your feet are asleep, aren't they?" She hissed in a breath.

"Yes, but give me a sec. The feeling is coming back." Kyle waited before taking a step. "It's all good now. The flight was great. It was like flying in a plane. Surprisingly, I wasn't cold despite being so high up."

"Heat radiates off my body and keeps you nice and toasty." She never ceased to amaze him. "Ready to find this special spot?"

"Lead the way."

NESSA WAS IMPRESSED with Kyle. She had carried a few humans before, and most had panicked, wiggled, or yelled. Kyle's muscles were rather bunched at first, but it didn't take long for him to relax. The fact he trusted her that much gave her such pleasure.

"Do you know how far it is to the eternal flame?" he asked once they found the trailhead.

"Nope." Actually, she'd seen the faint flicker of flames when she was overhead, but why spoil the adventure for him?

"What are you going to ask these magic people?" Kyle asked.

"I'm not sure. Hell, it's only rumored that shamans live there. I'm not expecting some man or woman to step from behind a tree wearing a long robe, waiting to answer our questions about the universe."

"If you don't really believe there are any soothsayers at the flame, what evidence is there to support the idea that there is magic in this part of the realm either?" he asked.

"That's a good question. None of my relatives have found any kind of oracle or fortune teller, but it doesn't mean others haven't. I have heard rumors of fairies flying around."

He pressed his lips together. "Fairies?"

"You know those really small creatures with wings."

"I know what those mythical fairies are supposed to look like. How small do you think these fairies really are?"

She enjoyed that Kyle was playing along. His humorous side appealed to her—a lot. "I never asked for details since I didn't really believe they existed. Until I meet one, I'll reserve judgment. Dragons are usually bigger than a human, so I'm guessing fairies will be much smaller."

He smiled. "Good point. How about we act like tourists and find this eternal flame first and then see what happens? Afterward, we can enjoy the peace and quiet of the surrounding woods."

She looped an arm through his. "Now you're talking."

In less than twenty minutes, the fairly dense forest path that was to take them to the eternal flame dead-ended at a rock face.

Kyle turned to Nessa. "I don't know what I expected, but it wasn't this."

Protruding from the rock face were four five-inch diameter metal pipes spewing water into a fountain basin. Off to the side sat the eternal flame, which was on top of a concrete pad in the shape of a circular bowl ten feet in diameter. From the center shot a flame. Mesmerized, they approached.

Engraved in the metal sphere were pledges from each of the four provinces, Avonbelle, Grindale, Hearndon, and Thedia that vowed to unite instead of fight.

Kyle ran his hand around the edge. "I never thought I'd see this."

She loved the awe in his voice. "Even though it isn't far for any dragon to come here, I never have."

They chatted a bit about what it must have taken to bring the realm together. The past had been fraught with battles. After reminiscing about bravery for a bit and finding no one there to answer her questions, they stepped over to the fountain that never seemed to overflow. Nessa bent down and studied it. "I don't see any drainage system."

Kyle looked too. "Me neither."

What she did see were several coins at the bottom as well as four names engraved on the stone ledge surrounding the fountain: SolRa, LunRa, EstrelRa, and TerraRa. Nessa wasn't sure what any of it meant, but it sounded ancient.

"I see you're curious about the fountain," said a melodious voice behind them. "If you toss a coin in, your wish will come true."

Nessa and Kyle jerked around. In front of them stood a beautiful, blonde woman who was quite tiny—less than five feet in height. She wasn't a shifter, but her size implied something else. "Really?"

Kyle pressed a coin into Nessa's palm. "Go ahead. Try it," he said.

What should she wish for? That Kyle would fall madly in love with her or that whoever was out to harm her would be caught?

Believing that with time Kyle would fall for her, she tossed in the coin wishing for her second option.

Nodding toward those names engraved around the rim, Nessa asked the woman, "Do you know what the names mean?"

"I do," responded the blonde. "For thousands of years, many here have worshipped different gods. SolRa is the god of the sun, LunRa is the god of the moon, AstraRa is the god of the stars, and TerraRa, as you know, is the god of our Tarradon."

"What about the eternal flame?" Kyle asked. "How long has it been lit? And does it ever go out?"

The woman smiled. "No, it never goes out, but that's only because a few of us watch over it and make sure it never extinguishes. We have no idea what evil would descend if it did."

Chills rippled across Nessa's chest. No one ever mentioned that possibility existed. "I never thought about that."

"Most don't." The woman held out her hand. "I'm Fay Forrester by the way."

"Nessa Caspian. Nice to meet you." Not that she wanted anyone to treat her differently, but most people she'd run into knew the Caspian name. When Fay didn't react, Nessa figured her family's path and this woman's had never crossed.

Kyle shook her hand too. "Kyle Harper."

"Did you come to ask the flame a question?" Fay asked, acting as if that was the reason why anyone would be there.

"Not the flame per se," Nessa said. "I was hoping to find the oracle."

The tiny woman smiled. "I've never met any fortune teller, prophet, or oracle as you say, but the flame often provides answers if you look deeply into it."

Nessa was not a superstitious person, so she would feel rather silly staring at a flame and talking to it. Kyle moved closer to the flame, his gaze fixed in one spot.

"We were hoping to learn something about a shifter who has the ability to become invisible when in his human form. Have you ever run into anyone like that?"

"I can't say I have."

Nessa tried not to show her disappointment. "Do you know of anyone who might know if such a person exists?"

Fay rubbed her chin. "Hmm. There are some very smart people around here, but I think I would have heard of someone like that. Have you tried Cargonia? Or the Earth realm? I've heard they have some unique characters."

"I get the sense he's from here."

Fay shrugged. "Well, I hope you find what you're looking for. Are you sure this person is a dragon shifter? Over the years, I've learned that not everyone is who he appears to be."

Nessa wasn't in the mood to tell this caretaker about all the crap that had happened to Kyle and the mine. "Oh, he's a dragon shifter all right. Of that I am sure." He wouldn't have been able to set the charges if he'd had nothing to stand on, nor would he have been able to follow her to the roof of the SinCas building if he couldn't fly. Then again, a dark lighter might have been able to put a spell on a person that would enable him to do this. Stranger things had happened.

"I wish you luck."

Before Nessa could thank her, the small woman sprouted wings, shrunk to about six inches in size, and then flew away. She then disappeared. In her place were hundreds of fireflies. Wow. Fay was right. People aren't always who or what they appear to be. "Kyle, did you see that?"

He broke his gaze from watching the flame. "See what?"

Hadn't he been paying attention? "Did you see how that woman just sprouted wings and flew away?"

"She's a dragon shifter too?"

"No! She was a fairy who was maybe a half foot tall."

"I'm sorry. The flame transfixed me. I was in my own world. You really saw a fairy?"

"Yes."

He moved next to Nessa and cupped her shoulders. "Tell me exactly what happened."

"This woman, Fay, was a real live fairy. You met her. She looked like a regular woman, right?"

"Yes."

"When your back was turned, I asked her about our invisible shifter, but she said she didn't know anyone like that. That's when she sprouted wings, shrunk, and flew away."

He glanced around as if he expected to find her hiding behind a tree.

"She warned me about people who weren't who they seemed. Maybe she was trying to warn me about the type of person who was trying to harm my family."

"So now you think some tiny fairy is out to get your family and not a dragon shifter?"

When Kyle said it like that it did sound ridiculous. "No, not a fairy, but…I don't know what to think anymore."

Kyle stilled as he looked behind her. Nessa turned around and sucked in a breath at the beauty unfolding in the forest. "Oh, my. Fireflies."

"I thought they only came out at night."

"So did I."

They stood there, enjoying the scene before them, and for a moment, Nessa almost forgot about the odd creature, Fay. In all of Nessa's one hundred plus years, she'd never known humans could grow wings. Live and learn. Or wasn't this fairy human at all?

"Nessa?" Kyle asked.

She jerked her attention back to the present. "Yes?"

"What do you think about exploring more of the forest?" Kyle wrapped an arm around her waist and kissed the top of her head.

Her impulses shot to high alert. She grabbed his hand. "Absolutely. We definitely need to find a place a bit more secluded though."

Kyle grinned. "You read my mind."

They followed a dirt path deeper into the forest. For the first twenty minutes, the fireflies darted in and around the path. It was almost as if they were keeping watch. Eventually, the fireflies disappeared. While Nessa found the whole experience with Fay and the fireflies odd, she didn't want to dwell on it. She had more important things to think about—like seducing Kyle.

Mate, mate, her dragon chimed in.

Not yet. I want to make sure he wants me forever first.

He does. I can tell.

Nessa almost laughed out loud. She shut off her internal chatter and concentrated on Kyle and her surroundings. Birds were chirping, furry sardons were scurrying up the trees, and the heavenly scent of the frenlen trees filled the air. As they moved farther into the forest, the rustling of water echoed in the wind, and joy spread through her.

"I hear a stream to the west," she said. "Let's head that way." *So I can strip you naked and make love to you like I've been dreaming about.*

"Sounds great." Kyle moved out of the way so she could lead.

She loved how Kyle didn't have to be the one in control all the time. It was such a nice change from her ex-boyfriend, Landry Madison, the dragon-shifting ass who always had to be in charge. What she'd ever found appealing about him, she didn't know. Oh, yeah, he knew everything about mining.

Nessa forcibly kicked that memory out of her head and followed her nose toward the clean water. They had to trek uphill for a bit, but when they crested the ridge the view below thrilled her. Trees, pasture, and water jacked up her endorphins, though not nearly as much as being with Kyle.

He stepped next to her. "It's beautiful."

"It sure is." A small patch of grass bordered the gurgling stream, and a hundred feet down the river was a three-foot waterfall that screamed of peace and passion. "Let's go."

Nessa charged down the hill laughing, loving the thrill of her feet almost going too fast for her body. By the time they reached the bottom, her young spirit had emerged. After a quick glance over her shoulder at Kyle, she shucked her shoes and rushed into the six-inch deep stream. The cold was a bit of a shock, but soon, it became refreshing. Too bad it wasn't deep enough to submerge herself.

Just as Kyle joined her, she bent over, scooped up a handful of water, and tossed it in his face.

His mouth dropped open, and then he squinted his eyes. "You've really crossed the line this time, young lady. That is an act of war."

"Is that so?" she countered, enjoying the fact he didn't consider her old even though she was three times his age.

The next thing she knew, Nessa was on her back in the cold stream. Goose bumps rippled up her body as the water nearly encompassed her waist. The rest of her muscles froze for a moment before her instincts kicked in. If he wanted to fight, she'd play along.

Nessa partially shifted, extending her claws—claws that could shoot fire out the tips. She aimed toward the water, turning it warm.

Kyle smiled and nodded in clear appreciation of her talent. "You are clever, I'll grant you that."

She returned her claws to their human form. "Never forget it." Without warning, she jumped up and plastered her still cold front against him.

"Hey!" he shouted as he grabbed her shoulders, trying to keep her wet body away from him.

She laughed. "Next time you'll be more careful."

"I'll show you careful." Kyle dipped his head, and when he kissed her, every ounce of chill disappeared.

Nessa melted into him, and as the two of them became one, all sounds disappeared. Without breaking contact, Kyle carried her to a patch of grass alongside the stream.

After kneeling with her in his arms, he broke the kiss. "I can't even put into words what I want to do to you."

She tried to feign innocence—something that was hard for her. "Are you sure you don't need me to participate?"

It seemed to take him a moment to understand. "I stand correct-ed. I meant to say what I want to do *with* you, not *to* you, though both apply."

"Tell me."

"I'd rather show you."

Kyle stretched her out on the grass then joined her. After a few heady kisses, he dragged her on top of his chest. With his hard cock wedged deliciously between her legs, her body exploded with shards of lustful bliss. Even with her clothes on, her purple scales glowed through her thin top.

Kyle's eyes widened. "I don't think I'll ever get used to seeing a bit of your dragon expose herself."

"It will only happen when I'm with you."

"Then let me see more."

In a hurry to get this party going, Nessa drew her knees up and straddled him. She then lifted off her wet top, but had to struggle a bit to ditch her sports bra. From the dreamy way he was looking at her, he was very much enjoying the show.

Kyle traced a finger along her ribcage and then lifted it to her breast. When he swirled the tip around her nipple, she radiated heat. "Don't take too long," she said.

"We have a few hours of daylight left."

Who was he kidding? "You can last that long?"

His cheeky grin ignited every cell inside her. "Not really, but it sounded like the macho thing to say."

Kyle's honesty was so refreshing. Without wasting more time, she slipped downward and unhooked the button on his jeans. What she wouldn't give to have the magical ability to strip a person naked with the flick of a hand, but she wouldn't complain about what she could do.

Once she lowered his zipper, his cock pressed through his briefs. She slipped her hand underneath the material and grabbed hold. Kyle lifted his hips and tugged his jeans downward, taking his briefs with him. Damn, they should have undressed before they started, because now she was absolutely crazy with need.

Nessa slipped off to the side to help him finish undressing. Before she removed his shirt though, she rose to her knees, bent over, and grabbed his thick cock.

"Oh, hell yeah." Kyle clutched her shoulder and squeezed. His chest rose, and then he let out a grunt as she drew him deep into her mouth. Her own dragon started to pant, and with each stroke of her tongue, her purple scales turned even brighter as her heat grew more intense. She shouldn't have teased him about lasting a long time. During their trip through the forest, her need for him had grown immensely. Never had Nessa experienced something this wild or needy before. It might be a good reason not to mate with him right away since the need worsened afterward.

Kyle's grip tightened, and she let up on the pressure. Swirling her tongue around the tip, his panting breaths increased. Then a tinge of cum shot out, and she pulled back.

"You were smart to stop. Any longer and this would have been over before we really got started," he said with eyes glazed over from his desire. Kyle sat up and undid the snap and zipper on her pants.

While she liked his hands on her, she needed to be naked quickly. Only then could they truly explore each other to the fullest. Between the two of them, she was undressed in seconds. After she slipped off his shirt, Nessa climbed back on, wanting, or rather needing, to take the lead. "Are you ready?" she asked.

He grinned, and his eyes sparkled. "More than I can say."

Chapter Seventeen

NESSA HAD NEVER been with anyone this passionate before. When she'd first met Kyle, he'd been uptight and closed off. Now, he could joke one second and be vulnerable the next. The combination was intriguing and sexy as hell.

Nessa leaned over, and Kyle took advantage of her new position by nabbing one nipple between his teeth and cupping the other breast. The dual stimulation almost made her lose it. With an expert touch, he teased and tormented her at the same time, making her blood pressure shoot so high her talons started to grow.

Be careful, or I might escape, her dragon warned.

You better not. Nessa had to block out the ecstasy thrumming through her veins in order to keep her dragon at bay.

She wiggled her pussy, letting her juices flow over his cock, and her scent ripped through the air.

"Nessa. I need you. Ride me, please."

"Then hold on tight as this could get wild."

Lifting up on her knees, she reached between them and guided his cock straight into her. At the first contact, her inner walls contracted and spikes of need impaled her. Her breath lodged in her throat, and when she completely dropped down onto him, waves of pleasure nearly toppled her.

Kyle grabbed her waist, withdrew, and drove up into her. Holy realms. Sparks flew, and waves of delight swamped her. It was so damn hard not to explode.

Wanting more, Nessa dipped her head and kissed him. When their tongues collided, she was sure her wings would sprout. Even the green grass below glowed purple from her body radiating her own light. With each swipe of their tongues, their hips matched the heady rhythm. They had started out fast, then slowed for a bit, and finally picked up the pace again.

With her breasts pressed against his chest, his hands grabbed her ass, and she delved her fingers into his hair. It was total sensory overload. Love speared her, but she wasn't ready to tell him about her feelings—at least not right now. Their lives were already too much out of control.

On the next thrust, Kyle's grip on her ass bordered on painful. He lifted his head and looked her in the eye. "I'm about to burst," he panted.

"Me too."

As if someone punched a hole in their dam, their passion exploded. He pummeled into her and kissed her even harder, and it was as if Nessa needed him in order to breathe.

She finally raised her head and gulped in air. Their bodies were in such perfect sync that they reached their peak at the same time. Her climax came fast and furiously, and her sight dimmed while her hearing shut off for a moment. Kyle's cock expanded and then exploded, stretching her wide and taking her to a new place.

It seemed like forever before their pulsing stopped and reality returned. Out of energy, Nessa dropped onto his chest and begged her muscles to regain their strength.

The sweet odor of the grass calmed her, and the babbling brook created the perfect reason for not moving.

Finally, it was Kyle who nudged her. "As much as I'd like to stay here, we need to clean up. It's getting dark."

How was that possible? Hadn't they just arrived? Maybe this magic forest had altered time.

Kyle helped her off him and then guided her to her feet. Once they took a quick dip in the water to clean up, they redressed. Nessa then moved to the edge of the stream where she'd have enough room to shift. "Ready for your ride back?" she asked.

"I'm looking forward to it."

This time she believed him. In a flash, she was in her dragon form. After wrapping Kyle safely in her talons and making sure to support his legs this time, she took flight.

Nessa hadn't given a second thought to flying by herself on the way to the eternal flame, but now that it was growing dark, a hint of fear trickled through her. Fighting someone with Kyle in her grasp could cost both of them their lives. She hadn't thought ahead. Damn.

To lessen the chance of anything happening to her precious cargo, she flew lower to the ground than usual. She also searched the skies constantly for any sign of another dragon shifter. Hopefully, she'd be able to sense any. She'd failed to detect their attacker when he'd followed her to the SinCas building and then stolen the rock used to harm Kyle. That scared her.

Kyle had become her world, and she couldn't let any more harm come to him.

After a rather tense hour-long flight, they arrived in town unharmed. Once she landed on top of the SinCas building, she set Kyle down and let the security of the building encase her. She'd been careless this time, and Nessa wouldn't make that mistake again.

He leaned against the wall and rubbed his torso.

"Is something wrong?" she asked once she'd shifted into her human form.

"It's nothing."

"Something is wrong. Tell me." She didn't need any magic to see that.

"Your grip was a bit intense."

Oh, shit. "I am so sorry. I was worried about flying alone. I must not have been paying attention to how tightly I was holding you." Nessa should have listened to her brothers and not been in the air by herself, but her need to find answers cut short her ability to think.

"That's okay. Maybe we should postpone any more flights until things settle down," he said.

She appreciated his concern. "I agree." Nessa smiled, trying to erase her unease. "How about I take you to dinner as a thank you for putting up with me?"

"Only if you let me pay."

"Done." She smiled, appreciating how readily Kyle was to forgive.

As they headed into the middle of town to find food, what sounded like fists smacking flesh echoed down one of the alleys. Nessa's first instinct was to make sure some innocent person wasn't being attacked. While her dragon persona wouldn't come out in the narrow confines of the alley, a few sprays of fire often stopped the fisticuffs. "Wait here," she told Kyle.

Nessa took off at a run. Instead of staying put though, Kyle followed. She inwardly smiled at his manly attitude. Halfway down the alley, she spotted one man beating another. She might have let them continue had one of them not been Safford DeLeon, the mine owner Kyle was investigating. What the hell? The victim didn't seem to have the strength to fight back. In another few punches, the mine owner might kill the man.

Before she had the chance to interrupt the brawl, Kyle charged past her and grabbed Safford's arm.

Jerking out of Kyle's grasp, DeLeon shouted, "What the fuck are you doing here?"

As much as Nessa wanted to interfere, she decided to wait and see how Kyle handled the hothead.

"Trying to save you from a murder wrap, you jackass."

That seemed to stop DeLeon in his tracks. He abruptly shoved the victim away from him. "Jerk isn't worth it anyway."

The man DeLeon had hit rose to his feet. Bloodied lip and bruised face, he turned around and staggered off. Nessa rushed after him to see if he needed help. "Hey, wait up," she called. "Are you okay?"

"Yeah." He touched his lip and spat.

"You should go to the cops and report this."

He shook his head. "I work for him—or rather I did work for him. I quit, and DeLeon got mad."

She doubted that was all that had occurred. Nessa checked out his face. His lip would heal. "You still should report it."

The man nodded. "I just might. If you'll excuse me, ma'am, I need to clean up."

Once she saw him exit the alley, she returned to Kyle. "Where's DeLeon?" she asked.

"He huffed off. When I asked what the altercation was about, he said the guy was spreading rumors about his company and then quit."

"So he just hit him?"

"Apparently," Kyle said. "I told him he needed to show a bit of restraint. I also asked him about the accidents at your mine. He swore to me he had nothing to do with any of it."

"It's not like I expected him to confess."

Kyle slid an arm around Nessa's waist. "Neither did I, but DeLeon looked surprised. I don't know. There was something about his demeanor that made me think he was telling the truth."

"It's possible. Only one of the four people we suspect will actually be guilty."

"I'll talk to Tom tomorrow to see if he knows what really set DeLeon off. You ready to chow?"

"Yes." Nessa rubbed his arm. "Thank you for helping me."

"Well, I wasn't going to let you tangle with that guy alone."

She could have handled DeLeon. "You might be right. So what are you in the mood to eat?"

"Can I have you?"

She punched him lightly. "We are not having sex in an alley."

Kyle snapped his fingers. "Damn. Okay, how about sirloin steak and onion rings for dinner and then sex for dessert?"

She laughed. "You are incorrigible." Just the way she liked him.

Because it was between the early crowd and the late night eaters, they scored a table at the Highlanders' Steak Restaurant. Wanting to forget the altercation between DeLeon and his former employee, she ordered a bottle of red wine.

Once the waiter brought their glasses and the bottle, they ordered their meal, and Nessa leaned back and sipped the pleasantly dry drink. "You know, for all that we've done together, I really don't know that much about you," she said.

He tucked in his chin. "Sure you do. You've seen me in action."

Nessa waved a hand. "Other than knowing where you work and that you have a sister, your past is a blank to me."

"My life isn't that interesting."

"It is to me."

Kyle sipped his wine. "Okay. I'll tell you since I don't want any secrets between us."

Nessa smiled. "Me neither."

"Where to start? My mom was a very hard working woman who grew up dirt poor. When she was seventeen, a dashing man with big dreams swept her off her feet. She believed he was the answer to her prayers. My dad appeared to have it all—a nice car, a good job, and best of all, he didn't hit her."

"I hear a *but* coming."

"When I was about three, Mom got pregnant again with Lily. I think the pressure was too much for him. He started to drink and spend too much time at the racetrack. Long story short, he left us when Lily turned one."

"I can't imagine what it would be like to grow up without a dad."

Kyle polished off the rest of his glass, but he didn't pour another. "It was hardest on my mom. To make ends meet, she took a cleaning job on top of working at the food store. When that became too much, she turned to drugs."

Her heart broke. "How sad. What about you? How did you handle not having a dad or a mom who wasn't…reliable?"

"I didn't know any better. When we were young, my aunt watched us during the day, but by the time I was twelve, I found my way into the streets."

His voice had lowered, and she could guess what happened next. "Did you hang out with the rough crowd?"

Kyle reached across the table and squeezed her hand. "Rough crowd? I take it that's a euphemism for thugs and gangs, right?"

She didn't want to believe it. "I guess, but if you were involved in illegal activities, how did you turn yourself around?"

He leaned back and said nothing for a moment. It was almost as if he was debating whether to tell her. "My best friend at the time got mixed up with a group that loved to steal from the rich. Only they didn't give the money to the poor. They kept it for themselves. Richie was their flunky and did whatever they told him to do. I wasn't there, but one time, they stole from the wrong people—shifters. Since we humans can't tell a shifter from a human, it ended in disaster. I don't blame the panther who attacked Richie, but I was angry that he killed my friend."

"I'm sorry."

"Me too. Up until then, I didn't think about consequences. After that, I pulled away from those *friends* and threw myself into work."

Her heart ached for him. "What about Lily during that time? How did she cope?"

He blew out a breath. "Lily was always shy but she had a good heart. During the time I was sowing my wild oats, she continued working hard at school. I'm guessing she didn't want to end up like our mom. To say the least, Lily and I butted heads a lot. My biggest regret was not recognizing that my sister needed me more than anything when she was growing up. I just wasn't there for her."

"I think you've made it up to her."

His chin quivered. "I hope so." Kyle managed to paste on a smile. "Enough about my sordid past—time for you to share."

She knew she shouldn't have started this soul baring experience. "I was the fourth of six kids."

He whistled. "I can't imagine taking care of that many children."

"My mom didn't work outside of the home. She loved having

and taking care of us."

"If my mom hadn't needed to work, she would have enjoyed raising more too. Of course, she'd have needed a great husband who stayed and loved her," Kyle said.

"Where is she now?"

His expression turned dark. "She passed away three years ago."

"I'm sorry." That seemed to be her refrain.

"Her life was hard." He leaned forward. "I don't think I've met your mom or all of your siblings yet."

"You've met most of them. Griffin, who you haven't met, is the eldest. He's the even-tempered one of the group, which might be why he's head of sales. His job takes him all over the realm. Next there's Logan, Birk, me, Greer, and finally Camden. He works in the SinCas lab, experimenting with cutting the gems, as well as combining metals into new compounds."

"What an amazing family."

"Thank you." She smiled. "There's something else I need to tell you."

His brows rose. "You sound serious."

"I am." She inhaled and then let out a long breath, trying to figure out the best way to do this. "I'm not sure how it works in the human world, but in my world, Fate lets us know who we are best suited for."

"You mean fated mates."

Her heart beat hard. "Yes." He'd grown up in Tarradon, so it shouldn't have surprised her that he was aware of them. "A shifter knows when he or she finds their mate because of the incredible draw between them."

"Like instant lust?" Kyle looked around.

"Yes. Have you ever experienced something like that?" she asked.

"From the moment I saw you, I knew there was something special between us—a bond if you will."

Nessa couldn't believe what he was saying. "Me too!"

His brows rose. "That's hard for me to believe. You were a little pissy toward me when we first met."

She chuckled but was unable to tell if he was teasing her or not. "Seriously? You had just shut down our mine! Besides, I'd nearly been buried alive and wasn't in my right mind." She didn't need to be coy. "Truth was, even before I saw you, when you were in the hallway talking with Birk, this wave of lust washed over me. It didn't take me long before I knew you were my mate." She sucked in a breath, waiting for his response.

Kyle grinned, and relief rushed through her. "Well, I'll be damned. I wish you'd told me sooner."

Nessa laughed. "I thought you would freak. I mean, mating is a lifetime commitment. It's not something you can walk away from."

"I know."

"Do you also know that if we mate, you'll become an evil dragon?"

"I don't think all dragons are evil. At least I don't anymore."

"What about Lily?"

"Nessa, Lily will have to deal. I don't want to hurt her, but I think she'll come around to my way of thinking eventually."

Nessa wanted to slip over to Kyle's side of the table and kiss him silly, but she would refrain for now. She'd do that just as soon as they finished eating and had some privacy.

Chapter Eighteen

T HE NEXT AFTERNOON, Kyle found himself staring out his office window, reliving their wonderful day: seeing the eternal flame and then making love with Nessa on the bank of the secluded cove— and again at her condo. It was something he'd never forget. Getting to spend time with her when it wasn't work related had been better than he could ever have imagined.

The conversation at dinner still blew his mind when she'd told him they were fated mates! Actual mates! It was surreal, yet wonderful. As much as he wanted to tell Lily, he knew he needed to postpone that conversation.

Nessa never said when this mating would occur, but she acted as if she wanted to wait. Maybe it was to make sure he was willing to spend the rest of his life with her.

A knock sounded on his office door, jarring him out of his pleasant memories. Kyle spun around. The door opened, and a grinning Tom Delaney stepped in. "I found him."

It took Kyle a second to realign his thoughts. "Found who?"

"The man who sabotaged the Caspian mines, of course."

Adrenaline flooded his senses. "Who is he?"

"Safford DeLeon."

That was too easy. "Are you sure? Are you saying the man copped to murder and destruction of property?" When Kyle had asked DeLeon last night about the recent mine explosion, he hadn't acted guilty at all.

"Not in so many words." Tom held up a hand, pulled up a chair, and sat down. Kyle leaned a hip on his desk. "I couldn't locate him yesterday, but early this morning I caught him on the way into his office. I asked him quite a few questions about where he was at the time of the Caspian mine explosion and drilled him about what he did after that."

So DeLeon's outburst last night hadn't been a result of Tom's accusatory questions since they occurred this morning. Interesting. "Did you ask if he attacked me?"

"Hell, no. I was subtle—more or less."

"I hope so." So far Tom hadn't said anything to convince Kyle of DeLeon's guilt. "Where did he say he was during the time their newest mine collapsed?"

"He claimed he was at his mine. No one seems to know exactly when the charges were set, so that makes it difficult to have an alibi."

"Very true."

"After that he flew to Grindale province to help with the disaster there."

That implied DeLeon wasn't the one to hit him on the head or steal the evidence from the SinCas building unless he snuck back. "I take it you didn't believe him?" Kyle asked.

Tom waved a hand. "Hell no. The guy has shifty eyes and lies any chance he gets. Remember, I used to work for him."

"Then what?" There had to be more.

Tom's face lit up. "I waited for him to leave, and when he did, I followed him."

Tom was resourceful. "Where did he go?"

"He has a cabin about thirty miles north east of here. He drove, so I followed him."

"Did he disappear on you or something?" Kyle was half joking, partly because he wasn't all that convinced this hotheaded mine owner was guilty. Financially, his mines were doing a lot better than Wilson Snar's were.

"As a matter of fact, he did."

Kyle's heart plummeted to his stomach. "Are you shitting me? He actually disappeared?" Kyle studied Tom's body language to make sure he wasn't making it up. The man exuded confidence.

Tom crossed his arms. "I swear. I followed him for quite a while, but when he turned off onto a dirt road, I kept going. I parked and hiked in. It wasn't hard to find his cabin. It was the only one there." Now, Kyle was intrigued. "When I arrived, he was in the cabin, but I must have made some noise because he rushed outside—or at least the front door opened. I actually didn't see him."

"How do you know he wasn't airing out the cabin?"

"Because his footsteps made noise on the ground—as in twigs snapped, and leaves crunched." Tom held up a hand. "Then he opened his car door—all while being invisible."

Kyle tried not to jump to conclusions. "Why would he cloak himself like that? Did he think a burglar was hiding inside his car, and he wanted to get the drop on him?"

Tom shrugged. "It's not like I asked him. I figured he suspected someone was outside, and he wanted to be able to sneak up on him. Listen, he's still at the cabin. You've got to see it for yourself."

"Why? I believe you."

Something strange crossed Tom's face, and he jumped up from his seat. "I want to catch it on camera. I would have done it before, but I left my cell in my vehicle."

The idea of seeing DeLeon move about while in his invisible state would go a long way to proving he was guilty. It was the kind of proof he would need for the police. "Okay, but I want Nessa to come with us. If he catches us snooping around, he might try to harm us. Neither you nor I can fight a dragon."

Tom's lips pressed into a thin line. "She can't come. He'd sense her presence. Dragons can always tell when another dragon is nearby."

He was right. Damn. Now Kyle wasn't sure what to do. If Safford DeLeon was guilty, he wanted the man punished. "Okay, but under no circumstances do we confront him."

The tension in Tom's shoulders relaxed. "You don't have to tell me. I've seen what a dragon can do to a human body. I promise we'll stay out of sight. We'll go in, check it out, and leave."

Kyle thought this was a waste of his time, but Tom seemed determined to show him. "Fine."

Once they stepped out of his office, Kyle told Michelle about his plans. "Safford DeLeon has a cabin about thirty miles north of here. Tom and I are going to check it out. I shouldn't be gone long, but if Lily calls, tell her I'm on assignment, but don't say you know where I'm headed. I don't want her to worry."

"Got it, boss."

Once outside, Tom asked if Kyle could drive. "My engine was misfiring something fierce on the way back from the cabin."

"Sure, no problem."

They piled into Kyle's car. The drive to DeLeon's cabin took about forty-five minutes. They parked where Tom had stopped before and hiked in the rest of the way. Through the trees, a cabin appeared—small and rather isolated.

"Good. His car is still here," Tom whispered.

At least this wasn't a total waste of his time. "Where's a good vantage point to watch from?" Kyle asked.

"That's hard to say, but I think we should hunker down before we reach his place. I want to keep his car in sight in case he comes outside again."

That worked for him. They found a spot behind a large tree and settled in for the wait. "How are we going to get him to step outside in his invisible state? He has no reason to do it on his own."

"I suppose I could throw a rock at his window and force him to come out."

"As a dragon shifter, he has no reason to hide."

"Well, that's what happened the last time," Tom said.

Kyle wasn't convinced, but he didn't want to call Tom a liar. Less than fifteen minutes later, Tom stood. "I'm going to work my way around to the other side to see if he's even in there. He could have gone fishing or something."

They were near Lake Vista, so it made sense he might come out here for some relaxation. After DeLeon's outburst last night, perhaps he needed something to help him calm down. "Be careful."

Worried that Tom would try to force DeLeon out of his cabin, Kyle kept a close eye on him. If he did get into trouble, Kyle would call Nessa and her brothers for help. He had to hand it to Tom though. The man was light on his feet, darting from one tree to the next, stopping and assessing the situation at random intervals.

Within three minutes, he'd reached the other side of the house and was out of sight. Except for the rustling of the leaves and the scurrying of small animals, Kyle didn't hear or see anything. Unfortunately, no doors opened by themselves, but just in case something did happen, he had his cell ready to record it.

Ten minutes later, Kyle wondered what was taking Tom so long. He debated moving closer to the cabin, but he didn't trust his own ability to move about without being seen or heard. If he could be certain Tom's phone wouldn't chime, he'd sent him a text, suggesting it was time they leave. The probability that DeLeon would waste the energy to become invisible when he didn't suspect someone was there to do him harm was slim.

Just as Kyle was about to move closer, something cut off his air. His heart pounded so hard it was as if he was having a heart attack. He struggled to get up, but something was holding him down. He grabbed at his throat. His chest tightened, and he couldn't breathe. It was his last thought before he blacked out.

IT WAS FIVE-THIRTY, and Nessa wondered if Kyle planned to have dinner with her. She'd called him a few times, but each time the call went to voicemail. She would have contacted his secretary, Michelle, but she didn't have the woman's number. Just in case Kyle was holed up in his office, Nessa decided to walk over there and check.

When she arrived, the front door was locked and no lights were on. Okay, if he wasn't at his office, where was he? Lily might know, so Nessa dialed Birk who was probably only a few feet from her.

"Hey, sis."

"Birk, I'm looking for Kyle. He's not at his office, and he's not answering his phone. Could you ask Lily if she's heard from him?"

"Sure." His voice muffled as if he'd placed a hand over his phone. A moment later, he returned. "No. He hasn't called her either."

"Does she know Kyle's secretary's number?"

More mumbling. Birk gave her the number. "Let me know if something's wrong."

His worried tone wasn't comforting. "Sure."

Inhaling, she called Michelle, who answered right away.

"Hi, this is Nessa. I've been trying to reach Kyle, and I was wondering if you knew where he was?"

"He left maybe an hour and a half ago with Tom Delaney. They were headed to Safford DeLeon's cabin about thirty miles north of town. I just locked up the office and am headed home."

That didn't sound good. "Why were they going there?"

"I don't know."

"Do you know the address of this place?" She didn't need to bother Logan again if Michelle had it at her fingertips.

"I don't. Sorry."

"Thanks." Nessa called Logan and explained the situation.

"You sound worried."

"I am." She told him about DeLeon nearly beating up a guy last night in the alley and how Kyle had stopped him. "All I can think of is that Kyle found out more and went to confront him."

"I'll look it up in the property directory. Give me a sec." Keys clacked loudly. "Got it. The property doesn't have an exact address, but it's near Lake Vista." He gave her the best directions he could.

"Thanks."

"You aren't going alone are you?"

She didn't like to lie. "It's not far."

"I don't care. I'm coming with you."

"You don't need to."

"This is not up for debate. Meet me on top of the SinCas roof in five."

Nessa didn't like it, but she understood the need for caution. "Fine."

Nessa hoofed it back to the SinCas building and then took the elevator to the top where Logan was waiting for her.

"What's the plan?" he asked.

"We fly over the cabin. If everything looks good, we leave."

Logan shook his head. "Like I believe that."

He knew her too well. "I'm hoping I'll spot Kyle's car on the road headed back to town."

"You said he was with Tom. He could have driven."

"Let's hope not, since I have no clue what kind of vehicle he has."

They shifted and took off. While thirty miles wasn't far, they constantly changed altitudes to take advantage of the best air currents. She kept her eye on the road, but she never spotted Kyle's car.

Even with Logan by her side, finding the cabin was more difficult than she'd expected. The trees blocked many of the roads. It was only when she saw Kyle's car parked on the side of the road that she dropped to the ground. Immediately, the stench of fire registered. What the hell?

Needing a better vantage point, she shot upward again and headed straight toward the smoky area. Logan followed. When she saw flames, her heart pounded way too fast, and she landed so hard, her legs nearly collapsed.

Needing to call out to Kyle, she shifted back into her human form. "Kyle," she shouted and then spun around. "Where are you?"

Was he trapped inside? Or was Safford DeLeon? Or possibly Tom?

"We need to check inside," Logan shouted over the loud crackle of the fire.

The blood was beating in her head, making it difficult to hear anyone calling for help. Had DeLeon spotted Kyle and Tom, and believing they were on to him, set his cabin on fire with them trapped inside?

Where are you, Kyle? she mentally called out, even though he couldn't hear her.

The blaze licked the sides of the building, sending off a wall of heat. "I'll try to go in through the front door," Logan shouted as he took off for the front.

Nessa peered into the side window. No! No! No! Her vision faded, and her legs weakened. Kyle was inside, tied to the post that supported the roof, his chin on his chest. A band squeezed her heart so hard, it took effort to breathe. Before she could decide what to do, part of the roof collapsed and landed in front of Kyle's feet. Oh, shit. He would be engulfed in flames in seconds. She had to do something.

Logan rushed back to her. "The front door is on fire. I can't get through."

Shit. "Kyle's in there. We have to save him."

If she returned to her shifter form, the only way to get in was to rip off the rest of the roof. If she did that though, the pole would fall, taking Kyle down with it. With no time left to think, she partially shifted her hands into claws and smashed the side window.

Ignoring the jagged shards, Logan and Nessa ripped the opening wider. "I'm coming, Kyle." Her voice shook.

"I'm going first," Logan said.

They didn't have time to argue. "I'm right behind you."

He slipped a leg inside, and as he approached Kyle, more of the ceiling fell and nearly crushed her brother. Fear she'd lose both of them. Moving faster than she ever had in her life, she dove through the window. In the process, the sharp glass cut her thigh, but adrenaline blocked much of the ache.

The heat from the fire stung her eyes and nearly choked her. If she hadn't had dragon blood coursing through her, she doubted she would have survived staying in the cabin more than a minute. Kyle's body was limp, and she prayed he was still alive.

He isn't dead, is he? she asked her dragon who would surely be able to tell.

I don't know.

Nessa darted around the fire, but a blast of oxygen from the open window flared the flames, blocking her access to him. Fuck. Logan was battling a wall of flames himself trying to reach Kyle. Inhaling, she forced a partial shift, covering her body in dragon scales, and then charged right through the flames. Had it not been for her excellent eyesight, she might not have seen him through the smoke. She rushed behind him, and with her claws extended, cut through the rope tying his hands. Her eyes burned even worse than before, and her lungs struggled to draw in some much needed oxygen.

Logan had partially shifted as well. When he reached Kyle, he undid the rope around her mate's ankles.

We need to get him out of here, her dragon begged. *You have at most thirty seconds before the fire kills him.*

Logan jumped up and stomped out the flames that were catching Kyle's pants on fire while Nessa dragged him back a few feet. Just then, the roof creaked and groaned as the pole fell and the roof lifted off. The beam crashed next to them, missing Kyle by only inches.

When she looked up to see the damage, she spotted a huge black-scaled dragon overhead. Oh, shit. It was a Royal. Those evil bastards were always out to destroy her and her family. It didn't seem to matter to them that the queen and her mom were sisters—albeit somewhat estranged.

Nessa's anger nearly felled her at the injustice of it all. Before she had the chance to shift, the animal above turned into the most beautiful shade of aquamarine and shot out a torrent of water that swept her away from Kyle. She choked on the liquid and had to spit it out in order to clear her throat.

Seconds later, she realized the influx of water had actually put out the flames. When Nessa glanced upward again, the dragon was gone, and a million questions filled her head. Who was that water-spitting dragon, and how had he known that someone was inside the cabin?

It didn't matter right now. She crawled to Kyle, praying he was alive, but Logan reached him first and lifted up his limp body.

"We need to get him out of here," Logan said.

All Nessa could do was nod. She shook her head to clear the fog from her brain. "Kyle, can you hear me?"

He didn't answer. As Logan carried Kyle toward the door, she searched the cabin for Tom or some evidence of him, but she didn't see anything that resembled a body—charred or alive.

Logan smashed down the burned-out front door with his foot, rushed outside, and then set Kyle down.

Nessa dropped to her knees beside him. "Kyle? Please answer me." She looked up at Logan. "He needs Declan."

"Fly him back to the mine. I'll contact Declan as well as the medical doctor on call." When she didn't move, Logan shouted again. "Go! I'll be right behind you."

Her instincts finally kicked in. "Thank you."

She shifted, and with Kyle held gently in her claws, she flew toward the Sinclair mine where the doctor could tend to his wounds. Once above the trees, she searched the area for their savior but spotted no one. What kind of being was that? Never in her life had she heard of any kind of dragon capable of shooting water from its mouth.

Right now though, she needed to focus on the man in her arms: the man she loved. Sure they'd started out as adversaries, but once she saw his essence, she knew they would be perfect together.

Through her claws, she could feel his heat and his life force returning, giving her the strength to fly faster. *Stay with me, Kyle.*

In record time, Nessa reached the Sinclair mine. She landed, set him down, and shifted.

Logan landed a few seconds behind her. "I'll carry him inside. Declan is on his way."

Chapter Nineteen

S EVERAL WORKERS WERE rushing about. She'd forgotten that the Sinclair mine was in full working production.

"Excuse me," Logan said he carried Kyle through the door.

Nessa followed alongside as Logan headed to the infirmary.

The on-call doctor was waiting for them. Not that she believed he could truly heal Kyle, but the burns needed to be cleaned and bandaged as soon as possible. Humans were so susceptible to infection.

"If you two will wait outside, I'll get to work on him," the doctor said.

Logan and Nessa stepped into the hallway. The image of the water dragon still stunned her. "Have you ever seen anything like that dragon before?" she asked.

"I didn't see anything. One minute, we were fighting a losing battle with the flames, and the next I'm doused with so much water, I lost my footing."

Before they could speculate where he had come from, Greer barreled toward them, her sister's face twisted in torment. "Declan called me. I came as soon as I could. Tell me how this happened?" she asked as she placed a hand on Nessa's back.

Logan hugged Greer and then Nessa. "If you're okay, I'm going to wait outside for Declan."

"I'm fine. Yes, go wait for him please." As soon as he left, Nessa faced Greer. "When I couldn't get a hold of Kyle after work, I began to worry." She explained that she called his secretary Michelle who'd told her that Kyle and his assistant Tom had gone to Safford

DeLeon's cabin up north.

"Why did Kyle go there?"

"I don't know. When I called Logan to see if he could find the address, he insisted on coming with me. When we arrived, I smelled smoke." She explained about seeing the cabin on fire and finding Kyle inside tied to a post.

Greer clamped a hand over her mouth. "Oh, no. Was Tom in the building too?"

"I didn't see him. The fire was so intense that we had to break a window to get inside."

"Then how did you get out without burning Kyle further?" she asked.

"A water dragon saved us."

"What the heck is a water dragon?"

"Trust me, I thought I was imagining things too, but his scales changed from black to blue, and the next thing I knew, the cabin was full of water."

"So, this mystery dragon saved Kyle, you, and Logan?"

"Yes." She grabbed Greer's arm. "I was so scared. The flames had reached Kyle's legs, but Logan managed to extinguish them." The thought of Kyle dying made her gag.

Through the infirmary door, Kyle groaned, cutting short that terrible memory. "Maybe I should go to him," Nessa said.

"Let the doctor work on him. When Declan arrives, the two of us will do our magic."

Nessa sniffled. "Thank you. Kyle's been through so much. If these attacks don't stop, he could end up dead."

"What did Kyle's assistant say about it?"

Oh, crap. Her brain hadn't been working. "I haven't called him. I was so worried about Kyle. I figured he left before the fire started or he would have called for help, right?"

"I guess so."

Nessa pulled out her phone and called Michelle again. When she answered, Nessa told her what happened.

"That's horrible. How is Kyle?"

"He's being treated as we speak. Listen, I need to find Tom Delaney. Can you give me his number?"

"Sure." Michelle gave her the information.

"I'll give you an update when I know more."

Next, Nessa called Tom Delaney, but his cell beeped, indicating she should leave a message. Damn. "Tom, this is Nessa Caspian. Michelle told me you were with Kyle this afternoon. I found him in DeLeon's burning cabin. Can you tell me what—" The beep sounded and more frustration tore through her. She faced her sister. "Whatever."

"Do the police have any ideas?" Greer asked.

"Oh, shit. I have officially lost it. I didn't even report the crime yet, and I don't think Logan did either. I'll give Anderson a call. He should be able to find Tom and then talk to DeLeon." Nessa dialed her cousin's number.

"Detective Caspian."

"Anderson, it's Nessa." She gave him a rundown of what happened. She even included the arrival of her savior.

"I have to say that's a new one on me. How is Mr. Harper?"

"We don't know yet. The doctor is working on him."

"You said he was with Tom Delaney. Have you spoken with him?" Anderson asked.

"No. I called, but his cell went to voicemail."

"You take care of Kyle, and I'll send my men out to the cabin and follow up with both Mr. Delaney and Mr. DeLeon."

Knowing someone was helping was a huge relief. "Thank you so much."

"We'll get to the bottom of this, I promise."

Nessa disconnected then stuffed her phone back in her pocket. Greer placed a hand on Nessa's back. "Let's go to the safe house kitchen and get something to drink."

"That sounds wonderful. I am parched."

Thankfully, the kitchen was empty, so they sat at the small table in the corner.

Her sister brought over a glass of ice water. "Drink this. Does Lily know what happened?"

"No. I need to call Birk and have him tell her."

"I know it's overwhelming, but you'll get through it. I'm going to see if Declan's here, so we can heal Kyle," Greer said, and then left Nessa alone.

She didn't want to say that Logan would have come and gotten her, but if Greer needed to look for Declan, Nessa wouldn't stop her. As soon as her sister left, Nessa grabbed her cellphone. Once she got a hold of Birk, Nessa told him everything.

"I'm at Lily's office now, so it might be best to wait and tell her after Declan has done his magic. I don't need her thinking something like that could happen to her too."

He had a good point. "I'll let you decide what is best."

"Good luck."

AFTER AN EXCRUCIATING hour of waiting to hear about Kyle, Declan and Greer finally walked into the kitchen.

Nessa jumped up from the table. "How is he?"

Both her sister and cousin smiled. "The doctor cleaned the burns," Declan said, "but he wasn't able to do much more than give Kyle something for the pain. That's when we took over. I healed the burns, while Greer was able to clean out his lungs."

Sometimes her cousin could be so stingy with information. "So, how is he?"

Declan placed a hand on her shoulder. "He'll be good as new in a day or two."

Her heart soared. Nessa hugged him and Greer. "I can't thank you both enough."

"Greer mentioned you think Sanford DeLeon is behind this?"

"He's the most likely suspect, but Anderson is now handling it."

"Good."

"I really need to see Kyle."

"He's a bit groggy. The healing process takes a lot out of a person," Declan warned her.

"I won't stay too long." She stood on her tiptoes and kissed his cheek. "You are the best."

"Do you want me to come with you?" Greer asked.

"For now, I'd like to be alone with him."

"I understand. Call me if you need anything."

Nessa hugged her sister once more then rushed into Kyle's recovery room. His eyes were closed, and his breathing appeared a bit ragged. Hopefully, he wasn't in a lot of pain now that Declan and Greer had worked on him.

She sat on the side of the bed and held his hand. As much as she understood his need to rest, Nessa wanted to know how he ended up in the cabin. "Kyle? Can you hear me?"

He groaned then opened his eyes. It seemed to take him a minute before his conscious thought returned. "Nessa?"

She chuckled. "Yes. It's me. How are you feeling?"

He tried to sit up, but she placed a hand on his shoulder. "Don't try to move."

Kyle looked around. "How did I get here?"

"It's a long story. What do you remember?"

He licked his lips, and she poured him a glass of water and handed it to him. He downed the whole thing. "Tom said he followed Safford DeLeon to his cabin and saw him disappear right before his eyes."

Excitement rushed through her. "Then DeLeon is guilty. Do you know why he targeted us?"

"I don't know. I never saw him to ask."

"If you didn't see him, how did you end up tied to a pole in his cabin?"

"Tom had gone around to the other side of the cabin to look inside when, all of a sudden, I started to choke and thought I might be having a heart attack. I reached up to my throat and felt a hand. I'm thinking now that DeLeon was strangling me while in his invisible form."

"That makes sense."

"When I finally came to, the cabin was on fire, and I was tied to a post. All I kept thinking was that I was going to die without telling you that I loved you." He squeezed her hand.

Her heart pounded at those wonderful words, and tears leaked out. "You do?" Or was that fear talking? "I love you too, but you have to stop almost dying. I can't take it anymore."

A small smile lifted his lips. "I'll try. Hopefully, when DeLeon is in jail, both of us will be safe."

"I called Anderson, and he's looking for him now. Did you see what happened to Tom? We didn't find him in the cabin or anywhere outside. I called his cell, but it went to voicemail."

"No." His mouth pinched. "I hope he didn't go after DeLeon."

"I hope so too. Right now, you need to rest and not worry about a thing."

This time Kyle managed to sit up. "I'm actually feeling a lot better."

"I'm glad, but it will take time for Declan's and Greer's magic to fully work."

His eyes opened wide. "They both cured me?" She nodded. "I must have been in really bad shape."

"You were." Poor Kyle had been through so much. "Are you hungry or thirsty?" she asked.

Kyle's eyes rolled upward. "Both."

She smiled. He must be on the mend.

NESSA HAD INSISTED Kyle do nothing for the rest of the day, but by the next morning, he almost felt like his old self. Okay, not quite himself. He was still furious for not hearing anyone sneak up behind him at DeLeon's cabin. All Kyle could think of was going back to the scene to see if his memory of the event had sharpened. At the very least, he needed closure.

When he brought the idea up to Nessa, he thought she'd tell him to stay away, but she actually agreed. Naturally, she insisted on going with him in case DeLeon was there gloating over what he'd done. He doubted it as the police would hopefully have someone watching the place.

Nessa snapped her fingers. "I told Birk about what happened, but I never spoke with Lily. Did you call her yet?"

"No, I didn't want her to worry."

Nessa huffed. "You need to let her know."

She was right, but he dreaded the conversation. Kyle located his phone and made the call. No surprise, Lily was understandably upset. "Are you saying that you were caught in a burning building, but that Nessa and Logan saved you?"

"Yes, but I'm fine. Really. Declan made sure of it."

"Kyle, I'm scared."

He sank back onto the bed. He wished there was something he could do or say to make things better. "Birk is there, right?"

"Yes."

"Until we catch this guy, will you do me a favor?"

"What?" she asked.

"Do as he says? Birk will keep you safe."

She didn't answer for a second. "Fine, but are you sure you're okay?"

He loved his sister. "I'm positive. Nessa and I are going to run down a clue. Be good, okay?"

"I'll try."

He disconnected and blew out a breath. He faced Nessa. "I guess that went as well as expected."

"I'm glad she knows."

"Me too."

Darn. He dragged out his cell again. "I want to see if Tom is okay. Hopefully, he picks up this time. I need him to fill in a few gaps."

"Kyle? Is that you?"

"In the flesh."

"Oh shit, man. I saw DeLeon drag you inside the cabin. How the hell did you escape?"

Seriously? He witnessed what happened? He wanted to ask why Tom didn't try to stop DeLeon or call for help, but he'd question him later. "Nessa found me and got me out. How did you get away?"

"It was the craziest thing. When I saw that DeLeon had you, I tried to call for help, but I couldn't get any reception, so I ran down the driveway. I hadn't gone very far when out of nowhere something slammed into my head. I dropped like a stone. When I came to, the cabin was on fire and DeLeon was gone."

"That motherfucker. I wonder why he didn't try to kill you."

"I don't know. I'm telling you, I was so scared. I looked inside the cabin and shit, man, when I saw you in there, I freaked. I tried to get inside, but the front door was locked. I attempted to smash it in, but it wouldn't budge. There was nothing I could do. I'm just glad Nessa got to you in time."

He could have broken the window and climbed in like Nessa did. "Me too. How did you get home?" Nessa said she'd spotted Kyle's car still parked where he'd left it.

"I found the keys to DeLeon's car under the mat. I was surprised he didn't drive back, but I guess he just wanted to get the hell out of there."

"I wonder why he didn't fly to his cabin in the first place."

"Maybe he had a lot of supplies." Tom chuckled. "When I see the ass, I'll ask him. Hopefully, he'll be behind bars when that happens."

"I hear ya. Just watch your back until we catch the bastard."

"Will do. I'm glad you're okay."

His answers seemed rather pat. "When you got back to town, did you call for help?"

"Hell yeah I did. The fire department said they'd send a truck out right away."

"I guess they arrived after Nessa got me out."

"They must have."

"I left you a few messages, but you didn't answer." That wasn't like him.

"My battery was dead. I guess I forgot to charge it."

Uh-huh.

Kyle disconnected and told Nessa what Tom said. "Now, I really want to check it out for myself," Kyle said.

"I'm ready."

Chapter Twenty

BECAUSE NESSA HAD agreed to keep a low profile and not take to the skies, they drove to DeLeon's cabin. But instead of parking next to where Kyle had left his car, she shot down the driveway. He sure as hell hoped DeLeon wasn't there, but if he was, Nessa assured him she could handle the jerk.

When they arrived, a police car, along with one with the fire inspector's insignia blazoned on the side was parked in the driveway. Seeing them reduced the tension in his shoulders, but only for a moment.

The cabin's devastation made his chest squeeze tight again. How had he lived through that? The walls had collapsed, and the place was a heap of wet wood.

Nessa stared at the burned out shell too. "I can't believe Logan and I found you in time."

Kyle reached out and rubbed her leg. "I guess Fate had a hand in that too."

Her smile came out weak, but at least his comment gave her some cheer. "I'd like to think so."

They both slipped out of the car. "Let's see if Anderson has learned anything. He's talking with Josh Gerrard, the fire inspector," Nessa said.

"I know Josh."

They walked up to the two men, and Kyle shook both of their hands.

"It's good to see you're up and about, Kyle," Anderson said.

"Thanks to Greer and Declan, I healed quickly." He glanced

from one to the other. "Did you learn anything about the fire?"

"Only that no accelerant was used," Josh said.

Nessa slipped her arm around Kyle's waist. "Meaning a dragon shifter set the fire."

"That would be my guess. We're looking for evidence now. Let me ask you, how did you put out the fire? There's water everywhere, but we didn't see a spigot."

"Anderson didn't tell you?" He shook his head. "I know this is hard to believe, but a dragon flew overhead and dumped water from the sky."

Kyle almost laughed at his shocked expression. Josh asked Nessa if she was sure she wasn't hallucinating, but she never varied her story.

"Okay," Josh said. "A water dragon it is."

"I was able to get a hold of my assistant, Tom Delaney, the man who was with me and the one who called in the fire," Kyle said.

Both Anderson and Josh shook their heads. "We didn't get any call about a fire," Josh said.

"Maybe he meant he called the A.P.P."

Anderson scrubbed a hand down his chin. "I don't recall, but I'll check my records when I get back. What did he say happened?"

Kyle then ran through what Tom had said went down.

"I'm betting he was so scared that he just ran. Otherwise, he would have broken the window and tried to get in. I'll speak with him and see what he says," Anderson said.

"Thanks."

"Did you come here now to see if the scene would refresh your memory?" her cousin asked.

The man was smart. "I did."

"Let me know if you remember anything," Anderson said.

"Did you talk to DeLeon yet?" Nessa asked her cousin.

"Yes, but he claimed he hasn't been to the cabin in a few weeks. One of my men is checking his alibi now."

Josh held up a finger. "My arson team should be able to determine if the cabin was stocked with food as Tom suggested. If it isn't, it would imply DeLeon might be telling the truth."

Nessa squeezed Kyle's waist. "You said you wanted to show me the spot where someone choked you?"

"Yes."

They thanked Anderson and Josh and then walked back down the driveway. "I was behind that tree." Kyle led her to it and stood there a minute. "I was hoping something would come back to me, but nothing does."

"The next thing you remember is waking up to the fire and smoke?" she asked.

"Yes." Kyle looked around the area. "I don't see any kind of struggle either. Damn. I don't know if we'll ever find out who did this."

She rubbed his arm. "Anderson is the best. He'll figure it out. Ready to head back?" she asked. "I'll make it worth your while." Nessa winked, and Kyle fell more in love with her.

NESSA AND KYLE drove back in separate cars. During the trip, Nessa tried to sort through everything Kyle had told her, but there weren't any red flags, as those on Earth would say. DeLeon seemed to be the culprit. She might never learn his real motive for coming after her family, but she suspected it could be jealousy or maybe something someone had said to him. Most likely she'd have to learn to live with the fact that her family would always be targets. Many of the cases she and the Guardians dealt with ended with more questions than answers.

Once she arrived at the Sinclair safe house, Kyle pulled up next to her. They both got out.

"I've been thinking," Nessa said. "Not that I don't enjoy the safety of this place, but now that Lily knows you were almost killed, I might not get you to myself for a while." Nessa dragged a finger down his chest, and his eyes seemed to glow—or as much as a human's eyes could shine.

He wiggled his brows. "What are you saying?"

She loved that he could be flirtatious after all that had happened. "That I want you to myself."

"Is that so? Just exactly how much of me do you want?" He winked, and her heart soared.

"I want all of you. As in I want to mate with you. Now." She held her breath, waiting for him to process what she'd said. Because he'd told her he loved her, he should be fine with it—or so she hoped.

Kyle cupped her face and then smiled. "I was wondering when you would decide it was time. I would love nothing more than to join with you. Forever."

Yes! She loved that he'd become such a romantic. "I take it you're okay with being a dragon shifter?"

He chuckled. "Absolutely, though Lily might struggle with it a bit."

Nessa bet that once Birk showed his sister how great a guy he was, she'd change her mind rather quickly. "I think with time, she'll come to see the benefits of having a shifter brother." Nessa leaned closer. "So, your place or mine?" She gave him her sexiest look.

"Hell, I'd say we make love right here, but I don't want to embarrass your family."

She hugged him then glanced up at the sky. "If it didn't look like it might rain, I'd suggest another outdoor experience, but a bed is softer and dryer."

"I'd rather go to your place."

"Works for me."

"Since I'm so desperate, and driving will take too long, I think it's safe to fly the short distance home."

"You sure?" Kyle asked.

"DeLeon is probably at work. Even if he isn't, he wouldn't dare try something once we're over the city. It would draw too much attention."

He lifted a shoulder. "I'm game."

Nessa shifted, and then reached out to lift him up, but Kyle held up a hand. "I probably should have asked before, but can I ride on your back?"

Her fearless future mate was something else. Since she couldn't answer him, she lowered her head and dropped close to the ground. As if Kyle had ridden a dragon for years, he grabbed her wing and swung himself up onto her back. He was able to straddle her just fine, but then seemed to struggle a bit, trying to decide how to hold on. Once he found a good grip around some scales on her neck, she lifted up, shot out a small amount of fire to show off, and then flew toward the top of her condo building.

The flight might have only lasted a few minutes, but it seemed to take forever since she couldn't wait to hear his reaction regarding this new experience. Once she landed on her roof, she dropped low to the ground and waited for Kyle to slide off. The moment she saw his smiling face, she was thrilled she'd been able to give him that much joy.

Nessa quickly shifted back. "I take it you liked it?"

"I admit it was a bit scary at times, especially when you had to bank to land, but it was quite the experience. If you want to get into a different line of work, you could make a mint giving rides to humans."

She laughed. "I'd never be able to live with myself if they died of fright and let go."

Kyle wrapped an arm around her waist. "You do have a point."

"Ready to see my place?"

"I'm more than ready." He winked.

Now that they were about to mate, Nessa was actually nervous, despite having made love with him several times. From the rooftop, she led Kyle down one flight of stairs to her condo. As they drew near, her dragon snuffed and clawed at her insides. Nessa's scales pulsed under her skin rather brightly, and her nails and teeth sharpened. If she didn't calm down, she feared she might shift.

Once at the front door of her condo, Nessa nodded to the guard and then centered her eye over the scanner. If Kyle moved in with her, she'd have to add him to the list of people who were allowed access.

"That eye scanner is quite high tech," he said.

"It definitely is good security." When the lock clicked, she pushed open the door and held her breath as he stepped in.

Her lifestyle had intimidated a few men she'd dated. They seemed uncomfortable that she lived in such an expensive place.

Kyle said nothing as he walked through the foyer, into the living room, and past the sofa to the massive picture window that overlooked the city. "This is amazing."

She sidled up next to him. "It gives me a sense of peace to live this high up."

"I can see why. It's serene." He turned around.

"Just so you know, my mother insisted I hire a designer. It's not my personality to have things match and blend." Where she lived wasn't a big deal to her, but since it seemed to be important to her mother, Nessa had given in.

"Well, I really like it."

The band of anxiety squeezing her chest disappeared. "Thank you. Care for a drink?" Actually, she was the one who needed some fortification.

Her whole life, Nessa had been so sure of herself. Now that she was about to change her life forever, she was a bit tentative.

"What do you have?" he asked.

"I'll check." Nessa walked over to the sideboard and picked up a few bottles. "How about a Dinjan wine? It's a bit fruity, but it packs quite a punch."

"Sounds good."

She poured two glasses. As she walked toward him, her pulse rose, and her body heated. The thought of making Kyle hers forever jacked up her hormones to the point where she had to have him sooner rather than later.

He removed one of the glasses from her fingers and tossed back half of it. "Smooth."

She was worried he wouldn't like it. Oh, hell. Why was she nervous? Kyle was always considerate and a wonderful lover.

Nessa sipped her wine and then set it on the table. "Would you do me a favor?" she asked.

"Of course."

"Watch but don't touch."

His brows creased. "Watch what?"

The hint of uncertainty in his voice bolstered her courage. "Watch me undress. I want this to be special."

"Every time I'm with you is special. You should know that."

Could Kyle be any better? "I know, but doing something romantic is hard for me."

He held up his hands. "I understand. Do you want me to sit on the sofa while you do your thing?"

He was making her want him even more. "That would be awesome."

Nessa stepped over to the wall and ran a hand over the music selection button. She picked a melody that was soft and slow, hoping to entice Kyle even more. After kicking off her shoes, she slid her pants off but left her panties on. She'd let Kyle take care of those.

When she finally looked over at him, he had his hand on his crotch, and all thoughts of taking a long time disappeared. Nessa undid one shirt button at a time, and after each one, she moved closer to him. His hooded bedroom eyes made her want to rush, but she forced herself to slow down and enjoy the moment. She pushed the next one through the hole and then the next. When the shirt finally opened, she eased the material off her shoulders.

"You are magnificent," Kyle said. He licked his lips, and she almost straddled him on the sofa.

Without a word, she reached behind her back and unhooked her bra. As slowly as she could, Nessa lowered the straps and then let the black lace hit the floor.

Kyle reached forward and grabbed it. He then lifted the material to his nose, inhaled, and moaned. "I love the way you smell."

"I love your smell more."

His eyes sparkled. "How about coming over here and showing me?"

"In a moment." Nessa had never performed a strip tease, but watching Kyle turned her on so much. She didn't need an imagination about what to do next. She licked her thumb and index finger and then twirled her right nipple and then the left.

Kyle placed her bra on the seat next to him and jumped up. "I can't stand it anymore."

A second later, she was pressed against his chest. His mouth descended onto hers, and need flooded her senses. She slipped her hands around his neck and hugged him closer, loving the feel of his hard pecs on her breasts. Still wearing pants, he rubbed his rock hard bulge against her belly, and heat pooled between her legs.

She broke the kiss. "I need you. Now."

Kyle smiled and knelt in front of her, causing the glow of her purple scales to intensify just under her skin. He first ran his index finger over the lighted scales, and then kissed each colorful spot. With every touch, heat suffused her, and it took all of her control to stand there and let him do his thing. Mating with Kyle would change his life forever too, and she wanted to give him all the time he needed to adjust to the idea.

"You are so beautiful," he said as he dragged his hands up and down her legs, his soft touch sending sparks of need straight through her.

His kisses went higher and higher until his mouth captured the area between her legs. With her panties still on, the wetness provided a new sensation that was different yet quite exciting.

He clasped the waistband and slowly lowered her black panties past her hips and then down her thighs. *Hurry*, she urged, even though she understood he couldn't read her thoughts—yet.

When they reached her ankles, she stepped out of them and kicked her panties to the side. Her pussy was already spasming, and her scent was perfuming the air.

As much as Nessa wanted to urge him on, she wouldn't rush him, but it sure as hell took all of her control not to beg him to drive his cock into her.

"I can't wait to taste you," Kyle said.

Nessa moaned. "I don't know how much more I can hold on. It's been so long." Two days at least.

He looked up and grinned. "I feel the same way."

With a gleam in his eye, he leaned over and licked her slit. The onslaught of glorious bliss was too much. "Maybe we should take this to the bedroom." Nessa wanted to explore Kyle to the fullest and being on the bed would help.

He stood, pressed his chest to hers once more, and kissed her hard. Okay, that wasn't going to tame her dragon any time soon, but she wouldn't stop him for anything. Melting further into him, Nessa slowly explored what he had to offer. Their tangled tongues moved faster and faster, heating her core. If they kept this up, Nessa wouldn't last—or make it to the bedroom. Being naked and having Kyle still fully dressed both frustrated and excited her.

She reached between them and unhooked his jeans. Unable to stop herself, she slid her hand down his pants and grabbed his cock. Whoa. If she thought she was hot, Kyle was on fire.

"I need you to let go," he commanded.

She did. A second later, he lifted her up into his arms. "I can't wait any longer either. Which way to your bedroom?"

Nessa wrapped her arms around his neck. "Down the hall. First door on the left."

With their gazes locked, he carried her there. "I am so ready for you, Nessa."

His soft and sexy words erased all doubt in her mind. Fate had tossed them together, and she couldn't be happier. Once inside her room, Kyle set her down a foot from the bed.

Not able to keep from touching him, she tugged on the waist-band of his pants. "I want you."

"And you will get me just as soon as I have a little fun with you first," he said.

A moment later, she was flat on her back on the bed. Stars swam in front of her eyes, and her breath seemed difficult to find. Kyle was about to crawl on top when she stopped him. "If you don't get naked right now, I'll go crazy."

He sat back and grinned. "Yes, ma'am." Staying where he was, he finished tugging off his pants and briefs. She sat up and had the delightful chore of lifting his shirt over his head.

Nessa scanned his body to make sure there was no evidence of the fire. "You're perfect," she said.

"I have a few dragon shifters to thank for that."

"Is that so?" He nodded. "Maybe you should start by thanking me."

"Oh, I plan to show you a large amount of appreciation," he said then grinned.

Nessa giggled, something she rarely did. Kyle brought out long forgotten qualities she'd left behind years ago.

She grabbed his hard cock, leaned over, and sucked on it hard. He clasped her hair and moaned. The faster she stroked him, the harder he tugged.

"Nessa, I won't last if you keep that up."

She squeezed his cock once more and grinned.

In a flash, Kyle crawled back onto the bed and pressed Nessa onto her back. With his gaze never leaving her face, he climbed on top of her.

Her dragon clawed her insides something fierce, and when he kissed her, it was as if some other entity took over her body. Her usual purple scales pulsed several different shades, something that had never happened before. It was almost as if her dragon wanted Kyle to see all of her magic.

The kiss turned more desperate, and her hands roamed over his magnificent body. She wrapped her legs around his waist and pressed her pussy against his cock.

"Nessa, Nessa."

"Yes!"

As if it needed to find its home, he drove his cock into her, sending her even higher. From that moment on, she no longer had any control over her body. The first few thrusts were easy, but once they resumed kissing, it was as if they believed it was their last moment on Tarradon. Their speed increased, as did their joy.

Had she not needed to mate, she never would have broken off the kiss. Knowing the time was near, her teeth sharpened. Nessa then dragged her lips to his neck. He grabbed her hips to hold her still and hammered into her. Nessa lost it. Without hesitation, she sunk her teeth into the soft spot between the neck and his collarbone, and Kyle let out a yell just as his hot cum seared her.

Her own climax came so hard and strong that she became enflamed from the inside out. Clutching his cock tight to keep him inside her for as long as possible, she softened her kisses.

Cracking open an eye, she noticed all of her purple dragon scales had turned a brilliant white, signifying the mating process was complete. She returned to the spot where she'd bit him and gently licked away any evidence of the wound.

Exhausted, she relaxed back onto the bed. Kyle rolled off to the side and pulled her close. "I can't even describe how that made me feel."

"It was wonderful, wasn't it?"

"It was more than wonderful. I feel... I don't know. Stronger. More enlightened maybe."

She laughed. "I'm not sure about the enlightened part, but you will be a lot stronger."

"I can't wait to test out that theory."

Chapter Twenty-One

KYLE PRESSED HIS phone closer to his ear. "Are you sure?"

"Positive," Dennis said. "I spoke with several of DeLeon's men, some of whom I've been friends with for years. One of the men would like nothing more than to pin something on his arrogant boss, but he said he himself was in a meeting with DeLeon the whole time you and Tom were at the cabin. If you didn't see him there, maybe someone else could have learned you were headed that way," Dennis said.

"No. Only Michelle knew, and I trust her completely. I know the cops are going to ask around about DeLeon's alibi, but I trust you more. Thanks for checking."

Shit. Kyle and Nessa had discussed the possibility that it wasn't DeLeon, but pinning her foreman's death and the rest of the incidents on him seemed so clean cut.

The only other possible suspect was the water dragon who remained a mystery. But why set them up only to save them? Without knowing this dragon's identity, they might never figure it out.

Nessa touched Kyle's arm as soon as he disconnected. "What did he say?"

He gave her the rundown. "Tom swears he saw DeLeon at the cabin at some point. If DeLeon didn't knock me out, who did?"

"Are you sure Tom spotted DeLeon *after* you were knocked out?"

"I think so, though he might have imagined the invisible man."

"Sounds plausible."

"What do you want to do now?" he asked.

Nessa grinned. "How about you learn to fly like the dragon you are?"

There was no reason to be afraid of soaring hundreds if not thousands of feet into the air, but taking off under his own power was foreign to him. "What if I can't fly?"

Nessa leaned close. "Then I'll have to keep biting you until you do."

He grinned. "It's a deal. What about I take off from the ground level this first time instead of from on top of the roof? I'd hate to die on my first leap."

She chuckled. "I think that is an excellent idea. If you want some privacy, we can go to the edge of the Caspian property near where we dug the gold mine. No one will be there."

"I'd like that."

Because both of their cars were at the mine, Nessa flew them there. When they arrived, the place looked like a ghost town since only a few men were standing guard at the entrance.

From there, it didn't take them long to reach the collapsed mine. "I can't believe you crawled out of that," he said.

"It's all in the past. Come on, fly boy."

He braced himself for this new adventure. "Okay, so all I have to do is think like a dragon and imagine myself flying, and poof, I'm a fifteen foot tall giant?"

She sucked in her cheek. "That sounds right. I'll be with you, so you have nothing to worry about. First is the shifting part. Remember how you can read my thoughts if I direct them your way?"

Shortly after they'd mated, she'd used telepathy on him. He'd been freaked out at first but soon began to enjoy it. "Yes."

"Once we are in our animal form, I'll talk you through it. Just flap your wings, and you should take off."

That sounded easy enough. "How high am I able to go?"

She pressed her lips together. "That's a bit tricky to say. It mostly depends on the direction and strength of the air currents. I've known how to ride them from an early age. I suggest you follow me for a while until you learn to judge how the air changes."

"Are you sure it's safe for you to be flying? After all, your nemesis is still out there."

"He wouldn't dare attack two dragons." She held up a hand. "Don't worry. He can't tell you've never fought before."

That worked for him. Once in the large open space, Kyle faced her. "I'm ready."

"I'm so excited for you. You are in for a real treat. Okay, just close your eyes and concentrate. Take all the time you need."

He appreciated she wasn't putting any pressure on him. Shutting his eyes, he focused on what Nessa looked like as a dragon and tried to picture his shape changing to match hers. As soon as the image formed, a pain greater than any he'd ever experienced ripped through him. As much as he wanted to open his eyes and watch his transformation, he decided against it. Then as quickly as the stretching began, it stopped.

"You did it!" He heard her sweet, feminine voice inside his head.

He opened his eyes, and his heart squeezed. *"Holy crap! I'm huge."*

"You are also magnificent. Check out those green scales."

Relief shot through him. He'd thought he'd be purple like Nessa. Not that he had a problem with purple, but he didn't want to look like that purple dinosaur he'd seen a few times that were transmitted over Earth's children's TV stations. *"Cool."*

"Ready to fly?" she telepathed.

"As I'll ever be." Kyle couldn't wait to try out his new body.

"Flap your wings and follow me."

She hadn't steered him wrong yet, so he lifted his wings. He expected the twenty-foot span to weigh a ton, but it didn't. Feeling almost invincible, he flapped his wings faster, and he lifted off the ground.

A quick shot of panic grabbed him when he witnessed the ground dropping below him, but he inhaled deeply and pushed aside the quick shot of fear. Once he realized he wasn't going to crash, he pretended he was behind the yoke of an airplane. To his delight, the principles of flying a plane and just plain flying were similar.

"How are you doing?" Nessa telepathed.

"It's awesome."

He loved it when her laugh reached him. For the next hour or so, he followed her, learning how his massive body reacted to surrounding winds. He expected to be cold the higher he rose, but his scales must have protected him.

"Ready for a dive?" Nessa asked.

Was he? *"Bring it on."*

She laughed again. *"I'm going to head down and then pull up. You don't have to go as fast as I do though."*

Like hell he wouldn't. Nessa dipped her head, and Kyle followed. The adrenaline rush energized him as he sped toward the terrafirma. Nessa changed direction quite far above the ground, but Kyle wanted to see how close he could come and not crash. If he misjudged the distance, the consequences could be dire.

"Kyle?" Nessa telepathed.

"I know what I'm doing." A second later, he changed direction and reached her.

"Don't do that again. You scared me," she responded.

He didn't sense any anxiety rolling off her, so her comment didn't hold a lot of weight. *"Now that I can fly, when do I learn to fight?"*

"Soon."

They spent another hour darting around each other. While Nessa probably thought she was fooling him into thinking they were just playing around, Kyle could tell that each of her maneuvers was meant to test his capabilities.

"Had enough?" she telepathed.

He wanted to say he could fly forever, but Kyle had to be honest. He was exhausted. *"For today."*

"Try cloaking yourself."

Was she kidding? *"How?"*

She shot out a spray of fire. *"You figure it out."* Nessa did a loop around him and then disappeared. He might not be able to see her, but he could sense where she was. It was as if she left a scent trail, or maybe it was a heat trail that he could detect.

If all he had to do was think about becoming a dragon before turning into one, why not think about being invisible? Kyle closed his eyes and pictured a protective shield forming around his body.

"Watch out!" came Nessa's warning.

Kyle opened his eyes only to find the ground racing toward him. Oh, shit. At the last second he avoided crashing, but his heart beat so fast he thought it might burst. Vowing not to lose concentration again, he soared upward.

Not one to give up, he tried to block out the sound of the wind and the flapping of his wings, and think only about pulling an invisible shield over himself. As if he willed it, he disappeared.

"You did it! Meet me where we took off."

Nessa suddenly reappeared, and Kyle's wings showed up too. He hadn't planned that. Keeping the shield active required more focus than he realized.

A minute later, Nessa landed, and Kyle dropped down next to her. She shifted into her human form and smiled at him.

"Just tell yourself that you want to change form," she urged.

One second he was this fifteen-foot tall animal, and the next, he was standing beside her as a human. Joy spread throughout him at the sheer thrill of it all. He picked her up and swung her around. Nessa laughed once more, and the sound was the most beautiful thing he'd ever heard.

"That was incredible," he said.

"Being a dragon isn't all fun, you know. With power comes responsibility."

He chuckled. "Can't I just enjoy the high for another hour? I need to learn how to fight first, remember?" He'd seen a few dragons do battle, and it looked much like the street fighting he'd been involved in growing up.

Nessa wrapped an arm around his waist. "Absolutely. How about we clean up and then celebrate at the Highlanders' Steakhouse?"

"You're on."

NESSA WAS SO proud of Kyle. She'd trained with the best of them, and it was clear that he had a natural ability in the air. Sure, his talents were raw, but once her cousin Thane, who trained all of the Sinclairs and Caspians, took him under his wing for a few weeks, he'd make a formidable adversary. It didn't hurt that new dragons were infused with extra magic and strength.

Kyle parked a block away from the restaurant and cut the engine. He slipped out and came over to her side to open her door. "Ma'am."

She laughed, something she found herself doing more than ever of late. Being in love had a way of making her see joy in everything, from the flowers to the birds to the bright blue sky. The hard part was being so close to Kyle and not asking him to stop at some deserted spot by the side of the road and make love with him. Mating had definitely taken a toll on her self-control.

Once inside the steakhouse, the hostess led them to their seat. A waiter rushed right over. "Ms. Caspian, how are you this evening?"

There were times when being one of the prominent families had its advantage—other times, not so much. "I'm fine, Branek."

"Can I get the two of you something to drink?"

Since this was Kyle's first day as a dragon, she wanted something special. "How about your best Campovino?"

"Yes, ma'am."

Kyle leaned back in his seat, looking rather smug. "Thank you," he said.

"For what?"

"For not making fun of me, since it took me twenty tries to do a loop."

She leaned forward on her elbows. "You did an amazing job."

He grinned. "I had a good teacher."

Branek returned with two glasses and a bottle of the bubbly in an ice bucket. He poured the drinks and then returned the bottle to the ice.

Nessa held up her drink. "May you continue to enjoy your new life."

"As long as you're in it, I always will."

"You say the sweetest things."

"It's not hard when I'm with you," Kyle shot back.

Nessa sipped her drink. Someone on the other side of the restaurant let out a large laugh, and they both looked that way. Nessa's heart stopped. Dennis Taylor, Kyle's right-hand man, was sitting with her ex, Landry Madison. Just as she was about to comment on the odd friendship, Kyle slipped out of the booth.

"Give me sec, will you?" I want to say hi to Tom and Dennis." Had Kyle called Landry Tom? He scooted out before she could tell him the truth.

She'd never met his assistant Tom. She'd only spoken with Dennis after her foreman had been killed. During that event, Kyle had been somewhere else.

She had a mind to confront Landry right now, but something stopped her.

Oh, holy goddess! When she'd dumped Landry, he'd vowed to get even, but that had been a year ago. Since then, she hadn't given the man much thought. The fact he never showed his face at the Caspian mine made total sense now. He didn't show up because she would have recognized him.

Kyle slipped back into the booth, and she tried to wrap her mind around this new development.

He reached out a hand. "You're pale, and I can feel an incredible shock rolling off you. What's wrong?"

"I never mentioned this before, but I used to date a guy named

Landry Madison."

"Hon, the last thing I need to hear about is your former love life."

His shot of jealousy might have given her some pleasure in the past, but she was too shocked for anything else to register right now. "This is important. I dated him for only two months when I discovered he had a really dark side. Not only that, we didn't have a lot in common personality wise, and we always argued over stupid stuff. I finally had enough and broke up with him. That's when he confessed that he only dated me for a chance to worm his way into the Caspian family. Like that would ever happen. Right before he walked out, he vowed we would get what we deserved one way or another."

"I'll ask you again: Why are you telling me this?"

"I'm getting to that. Landry worked in the mines all of his life until his father died in a mining explosion—though not in one of our mines, thank goodness. Landry said he really struggled after that. The man was quite delusional, believing he was owed a life of luxury. That was when I wrote him off as a nut job and moved on. My brothers didn't trust him not to retaliate and insisted they watch me for at least a month after the Landry left."

"Did he ever come after you?" Kyle asked.

"No, but I'd see him around town for a while, and then he just disappeared."

Kyle downed his glass and then stilled. "Are you thinking this Madison guy might be behind the attacks?"

"I'd bet the mine on it."

"Why didn't you mention this before?"

Guilt stabbed her. "He hadn't entered my mind until now. What do you know about Tom Delaney?"

"I thought we were talking about this Landry guy."

"Go with me here."

"I know Tom worked for both DeLeon and Snar before coming to work for me."

"And when was that?"

Kyle looked off to the side. "A year ago, I guess."

"Right after I broke up with him."

"Excuse me?"

Chapter Twenty-Two

NESSA INHALED, HOPING Kyle would believe her. "Tom Delaney is really Landry Madison. The bastard must have been planning his revenge for quite some time, waiting for the right moment to strike."

Kyle shook his head. "I don't believe it."

"Why? He's an affable buy so he can't be a liar and a possible killer?"

"Something like that. He's always been such a straight arrow. He would never harm me."

This was going to be more difficult than she realized. "When you walked over to the table, did you sense something about Tom, such as a small vibration coming off his body or a scent that was distinct—not unlike cinnamon?"

His jaw dropped. "I did. Don't tell me he's a dragon shifter?"

"He is."

Kyle scrubbed a hand down his jaw. "He's always acted as if he feared dragons."

That should prove to Kyle just what a sleaze ball Dennis' assistant was. "He knew I'd figure out our criminal was a shifter, so that's probably why he never mentioned the fact to you."

Kyle's shoulders slumped. "He also was rarely available to question the mine workers. I'm thinking he must have been afraid to run into you." Kyle's face paled.

"Exactly. I bet he only came the day of the explosion because he thought I was dead."

Kyle finished off his drink. "I'm stunned. Both Dennis and I trusted Tom. As much as I want to confront him, I doubt he'll cop to the deception."

Nessa leaned forward. "He saw me look over at the table. He knows I know he's posing as Dennis' assistant." Now would be the time to tell her mate about her other secret. "Have you ever heard of the Guardians?"

"Of course. Everyone has." His brows pinched together. "Don't tell me you know who they are."

She blew out a breath. "Yes. I'm one, as are the rest of my family and the Sinclairs."

His eyes widened. "Well, I'll be damned. It's why your whole family rushed out to help those in Plux."

She smiled. "A lot of people helped, but yes. That's what we do, as well as a host of other things." Nessa inhaled. "I know I'm not an official part of this investigation, but I have an idea that might help you."

"Hey, my head is spinning so fast, I'll listen to anything."

"Then let's pay and get out of here."

Kyle pulled out his wallet. "I know that look in your eye, and I can feel waves of excitement rolling off you. What are you planning?"

She smiled. "You'll see." She held up a hand. "Nothing that involves fighting though."

The plan involved the Four Sisters of Fate. If anyone could help them, it would be one of them.

Once Kyle paid, they drove to the SinCas building, parked, and headed on up to the rooftop.

"Are you going to tell me what's going on?" Kyle finally asked.

"I didn't mention it before, but when a Guardian cloaks himself, no one can detect him except other Guardians. We however, can detect other dragons."

"That's awesome, but it doesn't tell me what you're planning."

"I can't be sure, but I get the sense that when Landry is in his human form and cloaks himself, I can't detect him, which makes him very dangerous. I want to even the odds."

Kyle smiled. "Let's do it."

They shifted and took off.

"It gets easier each time," he telepathed with quite a lot of joy in his voice.

"I wouldn't know since it was over a hundred years ago when I first shifted."

"You make me feel like a young pup."

Nessa inwardly smiled. Within minutes, she spotted the shop. She lowered her head in an effort to point. *"We're here."*

Kyle landed a few seconds after she did. They quickly shifted into their human form. "The shop's closed," he said.

"The sisters live in back. They usually don't mind being disturbed at night if it's for a good cause."

Nessa rang the buzzer at the front door and waited. Even without letting them know they were there, Nessa had the sense the sisters were always aware of any visitors. A few seconds later, the light in the back lit up and then the store lights came on. Primrose, the youngest sister—though youngest was a relative term where they were concerned—answered. While these sisters weren't shifters, they seemed to have been around for a long time.

"Nessa, is that you? What a surprise. Come in." Primrose glanced over at Kyle. "And this must be your young man." She smiled.

Kyle stuck out his hand. "Kyle Harper."

"How can I help you?" Primrose asked as she ushered them in.

Nessa hadn't seen her in a while. Her red hair had been cut short, giving her pixie face an even more youthful look. Tonight, she had on a long-sleeved white button down shirt over worn jeans. As usual, her boots were caked in clay.

"Did Magnolia tell you what happened at the mine?" Nessa asked.

"Why yes. Did the stone she gave you help?"

"Completely, and please tell her thanks."

"I will."

Nessa inhaled, hoping Primrose would be willing to help. "There's a shifter, who in his human form is able to become invisible. The problem is that I can't detect him."

"That's not good."

"No, it's not. Is there anything you can give me to help know when he's near? He's trying to kill us and must be stopped."

"Oh, my. That is serious." She glanced at the ceiling. "I do have a spray that if pointed in his direction would show his presence, but that won't do you any good unless you know he's there."

"Exactly."

Primrose turned around and walked along a row of shelves lined with different colored bowls. After she reached the end, she turned around and smiled. "I've got it! I'll do a spell to give both of you enough magic to detect all means of cloaking, whether he's in shifter or human form."

Nessa believed she could detect all cloaked dragon shifters, but maybe she couldn't. "How long does this spell last?"

"Forever of course."

Nessa had never heard of anything being forever. The Four Sisters only seemed willing to do short term solutions. "That would be great." She wasn't sure what else to say.

"Give me a minute to gather a few herbs."

Nessa's dad claimed the sisters used the herbs and potions to make the Guardians think the sisters were mere witches. The truth didn't really matter. If they said something would work, it would.

Primrose picked up a pottery bowl, went into the back room, and returned after a few minutes. "This should do it."

She waved the bowl full of who knew what around in a circle and said an incantation in a language Nessa didn't recognize. Primrose then set down the bowl. "Both of you need to place your hand over the top."

Nessa had no idea what that would do, but she was game. With their fingers splayed over the top, a bright white glow traveled up her arm toward her face. The area around her eyes warmed, and Nessa wondered if Kyle was experiencing the same thing.

After thirty seconds, their gracious host exhaled. "That's it. If you encounter this invisible man, you'll be able to see his outline and sense his presence."

Nessa didn't dare look over at Kyle. He was radiating disbelieve, but thankfully, he said nothing. "Thank you again," Nessa said to Primrose. "You've saved our lives."

She smiled, looking prettier than she ever had before. "I'm glad I could help."

Not wanting to overstay their welcome, they left.

As soon as Primrose closed the shop door, Nessa shifted. Kyle would want to discuss what happened, and she couldn't chance Primrose overhearing. He changed into a dragon, and when she took off, he followed.

"*Did you believe her?*" he telepathed. "*It seemed all smoke and mirrors to me.*"

"*None of the sisters have ever led us astray. Did you feel the warmth around your eyes?*"

"*I did.*"

"*I'm thinking that's how the magic was transmitted.*"

"*If you say so.*" He pulled alongside her, but he seemed to be lost in thought.

As the landscape fell below them, her plan for catching Landry turned clearer. "*I want to discuss something with you. How about we head to the SinCas building where no one can hear us?*"

"*I'd loved to be filled in.*"

He seemed a bit peeved, but that was understandable. Once they landed, they shifted and headed down to an empty conference room on the top floor. "Coffee or tea?" she asked.

"Coffee is good. What's going on?" Kyle asked.

He'd always been in charge of this whole investigation. "I've come up with a plan to lure Landry into a trap." She poured two cups of coffee, placed the drinks on the table, and then sat across from him. "I believe Landry suspects we're on to him."

"If he saw you look over, I'll have to agree." Kyle sipped the coffee but set it down right away.

Before she had the chance to detail her plan, her cell rang. When she saw the name on the screen, her heart stopped.

Nessa held up the screen. Tom Delaney. "Shit."

Chapter Twenty-Three

KYLE STIFFENED. "SEE what he wants, and put it on speaker."

She inhaled and gripped her phone tightly. "Madison."

"Such harshness," her ex said. "Though I understand your hostility. After all, I did pull the wool over your mate's eyes."

His gloating pissed her off. "What do you want?"

Kyle reached across the table and squeezed her hand. It helped slow her heart.

"I want you to meet me at DeLeon's burned out cabin."

She rolled her eyes. "And why would I do that?"

"Because I've hidden your sister in the woods. If you don't come, I'll kill her." The blood drained from her face, and Kyle's grip tightened as if he feared she'd collapse. Nessa couldn't be certain this wasn't a hoax.

"Why would you do that?" She was pleased her voice didn't shake.

"Because I want to cause you as much pain as you've caused me."

The only pain he'd suffered was not getting his hands on her family's fortune. "I don't believe you have Greer. Let me speak with her."

Landry laughed. "Suit yourself."

A second later, Greer yelled out, "Don't come!"

Landry returned to the phone. "You have ten minutes to get here. Don't bring anyone or I'll enjoy her sweet little pussy first before I claw out her heart."

"You fuck." Intense anger caused Nessa's body to glow a dark purple.

"Ten minutes, my sweet. And if I sense another dragon, Greer will die." He then disconnected.

She nearly crushed the phone.

Kyle slipped the cell from her fingers. "I know you need to go, but after I wait a few minutes, I'll be right behind you."

As much as she didn't want Kyle anywhere near the man who had tried to kill both of them, she wasn't sure she would succeed against someone who could truly become invisible. Even though Primrose had supposedly provided them with the ability to identify his location, she didn't want to bank on it, especially if Greer's life was at stake.

Nessa could tell Kyle this was her fight, not his, but knowing him, he'd follow her anyway. "Thank you. Give me enough time to find Greer first. I can't have Landry hurt her."

He nodded. "I'll call Birk for backup."

She huffed out a breath. "Having an extra dragon is great, but Birk shouldn't leave Lily. Landry might expect me to call him so he can go after your sister."

"Then I'll ask Logan."

"Perfect, but if he can't make it, I can handle Landry alone if need be." *I hope.*

Nessa pushed back her chair and hugged Kyle, praying this wasn't the last time she'd hold him.

"Stall him for as long as you can, until I get there," he said.

With that she ran out the door and up the stairs to the rooftop deck. How had Landry gotten the drop on Greer? *I bet he told her that I was in trouble. Naturally, Greer would rush to my rescue.*

She grunted her frustration. Nessa couldn't wait to sink her claws into that black heart of his. Hopefully, Landry didn't have any other abilities she wasn't aware of.

Landry had taken Greer in order to get Nessa alone. *Well, I won't be alone for long, sucker.*

Nessa shifted and took off. Before she knew it, she'd reached the wooden area where DeLeon's former cabin was located. The stench alone made finding it easy despite the dark night. She would have canvassed the woods for her sister from above, but her time was about to run out. As much as she wanted to attack the man right away, Nessa needed to find out where he'd taken Greer, especially if he had hidden her somewhere. Once Nessa knew for certain her sister was safe, she'd kill Landry. By the time the fight began, Kyle and possibly Logan would arrive.

Nessa dropped to the ground near the burned out building and shifted. "Landry, you got me here. Show yourself."

Primrose said she'd be able to see his outline if he was in his invisible form, but all she could sense was the wind. Hiding from her wouldn't serve any purpose, unless he thought he could sneak up behind her. Nessa spun around to make sure he wasn't about to do just that.

"Landry, you vile piece of shit, tell me where my sister is!"

Again, nothing. She glanced toward the sky, thinking he might be circling above, laughing at her. Only he wasn't. As she walked around the burned out cabin, she looked for markings of a dragon. A shaft of moonlight speared something white on the ground, causing her to stop. When she looked closer, Nessa discovered a scale— Greer's scale. Damn, she had been there.

Had Landry decided Nessa's time was up, and he was doing what he threatened to do to her sister? Shit.

"Kyle, Landry's not here. He must have taken Greer into the woods. I'm heading in there now—on foot," she telepathed, not positive how far their telepathic connection reached. Their relationship was still young, so the long distance might pose a problem.

Nessa rushed down the trail, fast enough to make good time, but slow enough to spot any evidence that her sister had been there, like a broken branch or even a partial footprint. Nessa had traveled maybe a hundred feet when she saw a reddish blonde hair snagged on a leaf. Thank goodness for her excellent shifter sight. Her heart sped up. Greer was leaving a trail—or so she wanted to believe.

For the next few minutes she called her sister's name.

"Nessa, where are you?" It was Kyle. His pain only added to her anxiety.

"In the woods, looking for Greer. I haven't found Landry yet either."

"I'm on my way."

"Be careful." Nessa didn't have to warn him, but she couldn't help it. *"Is Logan with you?"*

"I couldn't get a hold of him."

Damn it. He should have tried someone else. Like Anderson. It was too late now to rectify that oversight. At least Kyle would get there soon. Nessa needed to push onward. What seemed like a lifetime passed when soft moans finally reached her. Were they coming from Greer? Fearing it was a trap, Nessa stopped and looked around but saw no one.

"Nessa?" That was Greer's voice—faint and shaky.

"I'm here. Where are you?" Nessa asked.

The bastard was probably watching her right now. Damn his invisibility shield. So much for her new ability to detect him.

"In a cave," came the weak response.

A few hundred feet in front of her stood a sheer cliff. The base was littered with fallen rocks, probably blocking a few entrances that Greer would call a cave. Nessa ran down the path in the direction of her sister's voice. "Greer? Talk to me. I need to find you." Before Landry returns—assuming he isn't here now, that is.

It would take too long to find her sister if she had to search behind every nook and cranny. And where the hell was Landry? If Nessa could hear Greer's plea for help, he must be able to as well. Nessa's feet crunched the leaves and blocked out any more of her sister's pleas.

Once Nessa reached the cliff face, she tried to peer behind each of the large boulders. "Greer, where are you?"

"In here." This time, her voice seemed closer.

Judging the direction of her sister's voice, Nessa rushed up to one of the boulders and peeked behind it. Oh, goddess. Greer was leaning against the back wall—or rather, Greer's head was peeking above a pile of rocks. Getting her out would be difficult since moving the rocks might cause a landslide.

"I'm coming for you. Hold on." *Just as soon as I move the six-foot tall boulder blocking the way.* There might be another entrance into the cave, but she didn't have the luxury of time on her side.

"Kyle, I found Greer. She's been hurt. Take the path to the right side of the cabin and follow it to the end."

"Okay. Hold tight."

A SECOND LATER, Kyle landed at the cabin. He had to assume that his deceitful assistant was either following Nessa or lying in wait for her. *"I don't see Madison either,"* Kyle telepathed. *"Is he with you?"*

"No, but he can't be far. Greer's trapped in a cave. I'm having a hard time moving the rocks to reach her."

Nessa's anxiety rolled off her, ratcheting up his adrenaline. *"Where are you again?"* he asked.

"To your east. Just follow the path to the right of the house."

"Got it."

Kyle shifted into his human form since he needed to go on foot. He hadn't taken more than ten steps when Tom—or rather, Landry Madison—stepped from behind a tree. "Well, well," his assistant said. "I knew Nessa wouldn't follow my instructions and come alone."

Kyle stood taller. "She did come alone, and she found Greer."

"Good. Moving all those rocks should keep her busy. Actually, it's you I wanted."

Kyle couldn't figure out the man's game. "Is that so? Why?"

"If I kill you, Nessa will have to live the rest of her life without a mate. That would be such a shame."

Kyle huffed out a laugh. "I hope you don't think you can waltz in, offer her sympathy, and take my place."

He shrugged. "I don't see why not."

Kyle debated telling Nessa that Madison had shown up at the cabin, but it would be better if she worked on freeing her sister first. He could handle this guy. After all, he'd spent much of his youth battling it out on the streets. Sure, those punks were human, but fighting was fighting. Hadn't Nessa told him that a new dragon shifter was stronger and had more stamina than some old dragon? He hoped it meant he'd be stronger in his human form too.

"If you wanted Nessa for yourself, why did you try to kill her?" Kyle asked.

Madison held up a hand. "I didn't think she'd be down there when the explosion went off. I was merely trying to destroy the mine."

Kyle had to control himself to not beat the crap out of him. It was possible his former assistant wanted to fight in his human form, especially if he believed Kyle couldn't see him when he became invisible.

"When you had the chance to kill me, why not finish the job?" Kyle asked.

Madison shook his head. "I thought I had killed you the first time when I smashed your skull in with the rock. I sure as hell didn't anticipate you'd have such a thick skull."

"While this chit chat is nice, I promised Nessa I would help save her sister."

Madison smiled. "Be my guest, but be careful. After Nessa reached the caves, I set some explosives along the path. Poor Nessa will have to clean up your carcass if you step on one of the devices."

Madison might be lying, but Kyle couldn't chance he wasn't. Not able to take this man's murdering ways any longer, he charged. Before he was halfway to his opponent, Madison disappeared—but not completely.

Now Kyle wished he'd asked if the way to kill a dragon shifter in his human form was to stab him at the top of the heart. Hoping it was, Kyle mentally pictured growing his claws like he'd seen Nessa do. His anger must have been the needed ingredient because his hands transformed into sharp talons while the rest of him remained human.

Seeing Landry Madison's outline, he moved closer. As he drew near, his opponent rushed behind him and Kyle spun around. "We can do this all day, but I believe it takes energy to remain invisible. It's your choice," Kyle said.

Madison ran toward him, and Kyle thrust out his hand right at Landry's chest. At the last second, his adversary scooted to the side. Then suddenly, he appeared. "How could you tell where I was?"

"It's called magic. I inherited it from Nessa."

"You won't win, you know."

"We'll see."

Nessa's cousin Thane hadn't had the chance to train him yet, but Nessa was always giving him pointers. Without warning, a strong ache attacked him. Shit. It was coming from Nessa. She must be struggling to free Greer.

"Stay where you are, Nessa, no matter what. Madison set charges on the path that were meant to kill me," he telepathed.

"Landry is there? Shit. I'm coming to help."

Fuck. *"No. You need to stay with Greer."*

Without warning, Madison shifted, and Kyle had no choice but to follow suit despite the tight quarters. They both remained on the ground, because the trees blocked an easy exit. Kyle was fine with that as he was an expert in hand-to-hand combat—or in this case, claw-to-claw.

He went on the offensive and managed to stab Madison in the neck. Had his former employee not moved as quickly as he had, Kyle might have reached his heart. If nothing else, Kyle was tenacious when he wanted something, which meant he'd keep trying until he succeeded.

Keeping his opponent close, Kyle managed to swipe a claw at the dragon's face while avoiding a similar fate. Wiggling and ducking in an evasive manner seemed to confuse and tire Madison. Most likely, no one had ever fought him in such an unorthodox manner before.

Keeping him off guard seemed to be the best way to win.

"Kyle, are you all right?" came Nessa's sweet plea.

"Yes. I need to pay attention to Madison though."

He loved talking to her, but right now it would take all of his concentration to avoid death.

"Okay, don't you die on me!"

"I'm doing my best, love."

Madison must have not liked how the fight was going because a moment later he shot upward, smashing his way between the tree branches. Kyle debated following him, but he believed that was what the man wanted. Kyle lifted off the ground a few feet and moved closer to the line of trees, preventing Madison from diving at him.

There had to be something Kyle could do that Madison wouldn't expect. He couldn't remember if his opponent could see him if he cloaked himself, but it was worth a try. Concentrating on becoming invisible, his body disappeared from view. Knowing it took more energy to stay in this form, he had to make the attack quick and decisive.

Kyle spotted a long stick that he believed he could grasp in his claw. When he picked it up, it too disappeared. It was time to see just what he was capable of. He figured he had one shot at this, and he wanted to make it a good one. Nessa and Greer needed him, and he refused to let them down.

Focusing all of his energy on flying, Kyle rose straight up. His wings bashed against the branches, but he managed to power through the limbs. With his claw outstretched, he aimed the sharp stick at Madison's chest. He expected his foe to move to the side as he drew near, but it seemed as if he couldn't detect him. Yes! Retracting the sharp stick in order to give it more power, Kyle moved closer, but not too close for their wings to touch and give away his position.

Madison looked around and then beat his wings hard. It was as if he sensed something, but he didn't know what.

Now, his dragon commanded.

With as much force as Kyle could muster, he drove the stick forward and hit the mark—or so he hoped. He then flew toward his foe to prevent Madison from dislodging the stick.

Kyle's energy waned, and he reappeared, but Madison didn't react. His eyes glazed over, and his wings fluttered spasmodically. His mouth opened and a spit of fire shot out, but it wasn't enough to make Kyle lean to the side.

A second later, Madison's body turned limp, and he fell toward the ground, chest up. Kyle let go of the wooden spear and watched the horrid man spiral toward the terra firma. Once he crashed, Madison transformed into his human form, his body a tangled mess. When he didn't move, Kyle guessed he was dead. He sucked in much needed air.

As much as he wanted to rush to Nessa, he had to be positive this wasn't some trick on Madison's part. Kyle landed next to his prey. Madison's chest didn't move, and his eyes had turned black. Guess this was no trick.

"Goodbye Tom, you piece of shit, or should I call you Landry Madison?"

As if reality finally sunk it, Kyle refocused his attention on Nessa. Even though she had hiked in, Kyle couldn't afford not to believe Madison when he said he'd set charges at ground level to kill him. While Kyle was somewhat of an expert on explosives, he didn't want to chance that he'd miss one.

Remaining in his dragon form, Kyle flew eastward, hoping to spot the rock face with the cliffs below. He'd just have to figure out some way to save the woman he loved.

Chapter Twenty-Four

DESPITE NESSA'S SLOW progress and mounting irritation, a sudden wave of exhilaration swamped her. It came from Kyle.

"Are you all right?" she telepathed. Nessa stood, taking a rest from the back-breaking task of moving the big boulder.

"Yes, Landry Madison is dead. We are finally safe."

While Nessa was overjoyed at the outcome, her current worry over Greer didn't provide her with a lot of joy. *"Thank the Fates, but I really need your help."*

"I'm almost there."

A loud squawking sounded overhead, and she looked up. It was hard to recognize Kyle since his green scales blended in with the trees, but she could sense it was him.

Scrub brush bordered the rock face, but the top was bare. Wings fluttered and nails scraped against the granite as Kyle slid down the rock face. Losing purchase, he plummeted to the ground fifty feet from her. His animal lay limp on the ground, and she raced over to him.

"Kyle!" she yelled. The fall wouldn't have killed him, but he might be seriously injured.

Before she reached him, he'd shifted into his human form then pushed up on his elbows and grinned. "Hey."

She had to chuckle. Her mate was silly. "Hey, yourself. That was a stupid—albeit brilliant—stunt to pull." If she'd known exactly where Greer was, she would have flown there too. Kyle stood and brushed himself off. "You up for a little grunt work?" she asked.

"Absolutely." His hands and face were scratched, but those slight injuries would disappear shortly. The pride radiating off him from a moment ago disappeared and was replaced with high concern. He quickly hugged her. "How's Greer?"

"She's hanging in there, but her leg is pinned under the rocks. The space is too small for her to shift. Come on."

They both ran over to where Nessa had managed to move the boulder on the outside, but she'd yet to free Greer. They both squeezed into the cave.

"Dragon arms are stronger than human ones," Nessa said. "You will need to partially shift. We have to make sure we have a firm grasp on the rock before we move it, or it could crush her. Can you do that?"

"I hope so."

They changed their arms into dragon claws and wrapped them around the first rock. Greer grunted, spurring Nessa on to be careful. She'd always considered herself strong, but Kyle's abilities were far superior.

He tugged on one rock, but it didn't budge. "Let's both push," he said.

When they combined their power, the rock tumbled out of the way. Once they figured out the best way to free Greer, it went faster.

"The last one will be the hardest," she said, since it was sitting on top of her sister.

"Wait a minute," Kyle said. "Didn't you tell me that when you escaped from the cave-in that you heated the rocks to break them apart?"

"I did."

"How about if I try that?"

Holy crap. Nessa wanted to kiss him. She'd been so upset that she hadn't been thinking straight. "That's brilliant."

Kyle tossed her a brief smile. "In case my aim isn't perfect, why don't you wrap yourself around Greer to protect her?"

"Another great idea." Focusing on her inner dragon, she partially shifted to bring her scales to the surface. She then knelt next to Greer and used her body to block any projectiles. "Okay, we're ready. Concentrate on pinpoint precision. Your fire will be extremely hot. With it, you should be able to cut the rock."

"Got it."

Fire shot out of Kyle's hands. Rock fragments shot everywhere, but the few that hit her, bounced off her body. "You're doing great, Kyle."

The large rock took a lot of work to cut through. If she'd been doing it, she would have tired a while ago.

"A little bit more," he said, his voice deep and raspy.

A moment later, the rock cracked and rolled off Greer.

Her sister was finally free. Nessa returned fully to her human form and cupped her sister's face. "Greer?"

Her eyes fluttered, and then her head dropped to the side. Without a word, Kyle stepped close and scooped her up into his arms. "Let's get her some air."

Once they exited the cave, he set Greer down. "Now that your ex is dead, Lily is safe, so I'll call Birk and ask him to find a few men to clear the path back to the cabin."

"What do you mean?" she asked.

"I thought I told you that your evil ex claimed he'd set charges along the path, hoping to blow me up when I came after you?"

"That fuck. We'll have to fly out of here."

He looked upward. "There are a lot of trees in the way. Let's see what Birk says first."

Putting his cell on speaker, Kyle called her brother who asked a ton of questions. In the end, Birk promised to come with a couple of experts to disarm the area. The bad news was that it would probably take a couple of hours to search the entire path.

"Thanks, Birk," Kyle said. "Given Greer's weak condition, we'll find another way out."

"We'll still need to clear the path. We don't want some unsuspecting person killed," Birk said.

"I agree. And thank you."

Because that might take hours, after some discussion, she and Kyle decided the best method of extraction was to scale the rock in their human form until they were above the tree line and then fly from there.

Kyle and Nessa each wrapped an arm around Greer's waist. They partially shifted their free hand and legs into claws to give them a better grip. Despite that added advantage, it was slow going up the seventy-foot cliff. Once clear of the trees, Kyle shifted first, cradling Greer in his claws. Nessa followed. While it wasn't far, it seemed to take forever to reach the SinCas mining compound.

It was time to call Declan and have him heal her sister.

IT HAD BEEN two weeks since Landry Madison's death. Between Declan's extensive healing talents and Greer's own magic, she had healed nicely. The whole experience still shook Nessa though. To think she'd almost lost her sister. A knock sounded on her condo door. Yay! It was Greer.

Nessa rushed to answer the door. "Hey, good to see you out and about."

"I'm feeling back to normal." She placed a hand on Nessa's arm. "It's you I'm worried about."

"Me? Why?"

"When you stopped by the store yesterday, I could tell something was bothering you. Is it Kyle?"

Why would she think that? "No. He's wonderful, though he works too hard."

Greer chuckled. "Most men work too hard. I take it he hasn't found a new assistant yet?"

Nessa shook her head. "It bothers me that he blames himself for making the decision to hire Tom in the first place." Nessa rolled her eyes. "We both have that in common, I guess. I fell for Landry's charm too."

"I'm getting us a drink." Greer stepped into Nessa's kitchen. Cabinets opened and then shut. A minute later, she returned with two glasses of wine. "Here. Drink this. So how are you and Lily getting along?" She slipped onto one of the counter stools.

Nessa was finally able to give her a real smile. Greer was back to her usual helpful self. "Great. I think she's softening toward dragons."

"I'm happy to hear that. I've asked Birk about her, but as soon as I bring up her name, he shuts down."

Nessa sat next to her and sipped on her wine. "Like we said before, I'm more and more convinced that Fate has paired those two. Maybe he's being cautious and wants to give Lily time to heal."

Greer nodded and then waved her glass at Nessa. "The mine is back in full swing now, so why aren't you happier?"

"I am happy."

"Nessa."

"Fine. It's just that I miss the closeness Kyle and I shared when we were searching for Landry. It seems of late, we've both been preoccupied with our jobs."

"That happens, but you have to work at finding time for yourselves." Her sister took a long draw on her wine. "You know, he'd make a fine Guardian."

Nessa's heart jacked up a notch. "I've been debating asking Dad and Uncle Jamison about it, but I fear they'd say no because he's an outsider."

"They brought Kaleena's new mate, Finn, into the fold. And he was a real outsider."

"Being from Earth would qualify him as that. Here's the thing; I'm not sure Kyle wants to do what we do."

Greer leaned on the counter. "Have you asked him?"

She'd been afraid of what he might say. "No."

Almost as if he'd been standing outside the door listening to their conversation, the door unlocked and Kyle walked in. She hadn't expected him this early since he'd been working long hours.

Her traitorous body turned hot, and her purple scales glowed.

Greer set down her glass and cleared her throat. "Well sweet sister, your scales say it all. I'll let you two enjoy each other."

Nessa jumped up and hugged her. "Thank you."

"Be happy." With that, her sister headed toward the door.

Kyle hugged Greer and exchanged a few words before tossing his keys on the kitchen counter. "What was that about?" he asked once Greer left.

"Nothing."

"Really? You two seemed so serious."

Nessa smiled. "I'm good."

"If that's really the case, I'm going to take a shower. We had a small incident at Wilson Snar's mine, and I am covered in dust."

"Was anyone hurt?"

"Nothing serious," he said. "It was human error."

Greer had made her question her own motivations for why she'd been out of sorts. She wanted Kyle to be part of her family in more than just mating with her. "Mind if I join you?"

His eyes that had been dark blue in his human form, morphed into what she liked to call light sea blue. It was a combination of his old eye color mixed with that of teal—the color all male dragons possessed when stimulated.

"I was hoping I could convince you to get naked." He cupped her cheek.

"You never have to convince me." Right in the living room, Nessa stripped, and Kyle did the same.

He drew her near. "I've missed you these last two weeks. What with dealing with Tom's death and looking for his replacement, we haven't had a lot of time to ourselves."

"I was thinking the same thing." Nessa kissed him and every cell in her body exploded. She leaned back. "It's partially my fault. I've been preoccupied with the mine reopening. It has taken up a lot of my time. Thankfully, that is behind me."

"That's wonderful. How about we take the weekend off and go

someplace special? Just the two of us?"

Her pussy dampened. "I'd love that." Nessa dragged a nail down his chest. "I have another idea too."

Kyle's eyes widened. "What is it?"

"While I haven't asked my father or my uncle, I bet they'd be thrilled to have you become a Guardian."

His mouth opened. "They'd take me?"

She laughed. "I'm positive. They'd be thrilled if you said yes."

He hugged her tight and swung her around. "I'd love that!"

She couldn't believe it. Kyle would be a Guardian. Happiness swamped her. "Did someone say something about taking a shower and rubbing his hands all over my body?" She so loved this man.

"I wasn't specific, but I like the way you think." Kyle grabbed her hand and quickly led her into the bathroom. "If I start kissing you before I shower, I think you'll be sorry."

She grinned. "As much as I want you right now, I'm willing to forgo a bit of foreplay for the sake of cleanliness."

"Smart woman."

Nessa nodded at his big cock. "How come you're always in a state of arousal?"

He grabbed his cock and pumped his hand a few times. "I'm only like this when I'm around you."

They stepped into the shower, and he pressed the button to turn on the pre-set water temperature. Watching the liquid sluice over his sleek body had her dragon clawing for release.

Kyle was everything she wanted in a man. He was kind, protective, smart, and above all, honorable. Nessa grabbed the bar of soap and dragged it over his chest.

He immediately palmed her nipples, hardening them into peaks. "I've missed you so much."

"I've missed you too." Nessa stabbed a finger at his thigh. "Did I ever tell you how much I love your green scales? They're so…" She couldn't think of a description.

"Forest like?"

She smiled. "Like a forest—my favorite place to explore."

He rinsed his head and then plastered his chest against hers. The water bounced off his face and splashed her, but she didn't care. Having their bodies together like this was beyond joyous.

Kyle leaned down and kissed her. The moment their tongues touched, heat swamped her, and she slipped her hand between them and grabbed his cock.

He broke the kiss. "You're asking for it."

Nessa dropped her head back and laughed. "I can't get enough of you when you go all macho dragon on me."

"You haven't seen anything yet."

He pressed her back against the far wall and dropped to his knees. With a great deal of confidence, he spread her legs wide, and her pussy screamed for his tongue. The first lick had her standing on her toes and palming the back wall. Ever since they'd mated, her need for him had grown to epic proportions, which was probably why she was a little out of sorts. Needing someone that much was not in her nature.

But it was now.

Kyle reached up and cupped a breast. Her scales glowed, and heat rushed through her. Kyle changed tactics and slipped three fingers into her pussy. He then curled his fingers to touch her sweet spot. When he pressed inward, Nessa couldn't take it any longer and let out a yell.

Kyle smiled, stood, and moved in closer. She raised a hand. "Give me a sec to catch my breath. I have to taste you too."

"I don't think that would be wise."

Before he could talk her out of it, she scooted to the side and leaned over. With her right hand, she grabbed his cock, and with her left hand, she cupped his balls. His groans turned to grunts, and his scales pulsed that glorious forest green she so loved. Needing to taste him now, she drew him deep into her mouth, licking and swirling her tongue.

He clutched a handful of her hair as a shot of cum tinged her mouth. Wanting to experience all of him, she let go. Kyle reached behind her and shut off the water. A moment later, they were outside of the shower drying off as quickly as possible. Their gazes met, and he pressed her against the bathroom door. Not breaking eye contact, Kyle ripped the towel from her body. "I need to be inside you."

"Yes," was all she managed to say.

Kyle kissed her hard. He then spun her around and pressed on her back to bend her over. As soon as she palmed the door for support, he aimed his cock at her entrance and drove into her. Her inner pussy walls clamped down on him, needing to keep him inside her forever.

He reached around her and pressed lightly on her nipples, tugging and teasing. Nothing had felt so good. Desiring more pressure, she thrust her hips back.

"Nessa!" Kyle grunted.

Knowing they might be able to fight side by side and enjoy each other forever made this experience ever so special. His mouth came down on her neck. While biting her wouldn't give either of them any more power, Kyle seemed to need to mate with her again in his own way.

She lowered her head and reached behind her, but all she could grab was the side of his ass. When his sharpened teeth sank into her neck, her climax came on so hard that her knees buckled. Kyle lowered an arm and kept her upright as his hot cum filled her.

"You are my world, Nessa Caspian."

"And you are my realm."

"STAND STILL," NESSA told Kyle. She ran her fingers through his hair to straighten the strands that were a bit cockeyed.

"It's just dinner with your parents, right?"

"I think maybe the whole family will be there."

Kyle cupped her shoulders. "What aren't you telling me?" He'd been able to sense her excitement but not the cause.

"It's a surprise. Now let's go."

He knew questioning her wouldn't do any good when she wanted to keep a secret. Her parents lived outside of town, which meant it was easier to fly than drive. The evening was balmy, and the view of the city below was magical.

Once they passed the mine, they traveled another few minutes before landing on her parents' front lawn. Not having to be constantly on alert that someone might attack was such a nice change. They quickly returned to their human form.

"There's an awful lot of noise in there," Kyle said. "I thought you said this was an intimate affair."

She smiled. "It is, but I have a large family."

As soon as they stepped inside, Kyle was surprised all right. More than just the Caspians were present. The Sinclairs were there too.

The loud conversations died down, and everyone faced him.

Laird Caspian came over to them and patted Kyle on the back. "Come in, son. We have something to discuss with you."

Nessa had hinted that her family might officially offer him a position as a Guardian. Being able to help Nessa on her quest to right the wrongs of society appealed to him. He just hoped he could live up to the Guardian name.

Jamison Sinclair came over and stood next to Laird Caspian. "We'd like to formally thank you for all you've done for our family."

He was about to say that he was just doing his job, but that wasn't entirely true. "I love Nessa and will do anything to make sure she and her family remain safe."

Both men smiled. Nessa threaded an arm through his and looked up at her father and uncle. "Just ask him so we can get on with the celebration."

Laird Caspian chuckled. "Nessa always was impatient, but she's right. We would be honored if you would agree to be part of the Guardian family."

Just as he was about to answer, Kaleena and someone Kyle suspected was her mate, busted in. "Sorry," Kaleena said. "We had a little trouble with the portal location. Finn and I just returned from Earth. What did we miss?"

"We're waiting to hear whether Kyle is willing to become a Guardian."

Kaleena and Finn both grinned.

"Yes!" Kyle exclaimed.

He didn't even have the chance to shake either of the elders' hands because Nessa was in his arms, kissing him. Life with her would be one hell of an adventure.

THE END

Don't forget to sign up for my newsletter to receive three free books, as well as up-to-date information on my stories. If you prefer to only receive notices regarding my releases, follow me on BookBub.

smarturl.it/o4cz93?IQid=MLite

www.bookbub.com/authors/vella-day

I hope you enjoyed Nessa and Kyle's story. Next up is Birk and Lily's story, called KISSED BY FLAMES.

BIRK CASPIAN COULDN'T take it any longer—or rather his dragon couldn't handle not having the delicious Lily Harper in his life. Sure she was a human, but if he didn't convince his future mate to go out with him—and soon—not only would his inner animal explode, his work would suffer. And that could jeopardize the lives of a lot of people.

Birk folded his wings and extended his claws as he landed on the lush green grass of the park down the street from Lily's apartment. Once he shifted, he straightened his button-down shirt and made sure his hair was out of his face before making his way to her place.

With each step, his nerves increased, which was wrong on so many levels. Being the head of security for SinCas Gems and Metals, he was as tough as they came. So how could some blonde haired beauty with so many emotional walls bring him to his knees with a shake of her head?

Mate, mate, his dragon reminded him.

Like I could ever forget?

His problem was that Lily had refused to go out with him ever since his protection detail of her had ended, and it was causing him undo mental stress. It wasn't like Birk was some weak man. Far from it. He was one of the most respected of the Guardians, battling some of Tarradon's biggest foes. Yet here he was—desperate and dejected.

Lily will give in this time. I can feel it in my bones, his dragon said with what sounded like fake encouragement. *And remember to smile for goddess' sake. You look like an ogre most of the time with all your flexing muscles and perpetual frown.*

Fuck off. I got this.

Or so he hoped. He didn't need to explain to his dragon that his constant frown was because of Lily's negative attitude toward dragon shifters in general. His sour disposition also stemmed from the fact she didn't want to go out with him—now or ever.

He entered her building and strode up to her new wooden door he'd had replaced after her attack. Birk straighten his shoulders and knocked. The addition of the keyhole was his suggestion since the last thing she needed was her ex-boyfriend, Nelor Dobbins, another dragon shifter who'd burned her, to return.

Birk hadn't paid for the door repair to earn her favor, but he hoped it helped her understand that not all dragons were bad. From her reaction to him over the last few weeks though, she might never change her mind.

A china cup hit its saucer and tinkled lightly. Then the voices on the television lowered, but no footsteps neared.

He knocked again. "It's Birk, Lily. I need to talk to you."

As if she could float without making any noise, the knob twisted and her face appeared around the edge of the door. Devoid of makeup, Lily was the most beautiful woman he'd ever seen. Her creamy white skin and long blonde hair were in stark contrast to her gorgeous green eyes. And those naturally red lips were made for kissing. Her sweet lavender scent wafted toward him, making his dragon claw his insides.

Birk yearned to run his hand down her arm, but he didn't want to upset her.

"Is something wrong, Birk?" she asked, not stepping to the side to let him in.

Yes, a hell of a lot was wrong, but he'd keep that to himself. "I just stopped by to see how you were doing. Mind if we talk?"

She glanced behind her. He hoped it was to see if her place looked presentable and not to stall for time. He didn't sense she had company. "Sure," she said breaking eye contact.

When he stepped past her, he swore she was even smaller than the last time he'd come knocking. He was almost a foot and a half taller, but that only made him want to protect her even more.

He faced her. "Nelor hasn't show up again, has he?"

She jerked at that dragon shifter's name. "No. He won't come around. He knows the cops are still looking for him."

Birk's job as head of security at the mines meant he believed in following the rules. Hopefully, Lily appreciated that fact. But unless her brother told her about Birk being a member of the Guardians, she would have no idea just how much he cared about people. "No other strange men lurking about?"

When she furrowed her brows, he wanted to take back his question. He sucked at small talk, possibly because most of the women of Tarradon asked him out, not the other way around. Clearly being face-to-face with his mate evaporated his social skills.

"No. Once my brother's assistant was caught and killed, no one has threatened me. I'm invisible once more, just the way I like it." She tossed him a quick smile, but it didn't seem to hold much joy— only nervousness.

As much as Birk wanted to reach out and caress her face to soothe her sorrow, he didn't dare. "You're hardly invisible, Lily. You are not only beautiful, but you have an important job. People know who you are."

She broke eye contact once more. "Thank you."

Birk cleared his throat. "I came by in part because I wanted to see if you'd have dinner with me. Just so you know, I'm going to keep asking until you say yes." He winked, trying to act cool.

A wink? Are you kidding me? his arrogant dragon asked. *I'll be surprised if she doesn't shove you out the door right now.*

Lily let out a breath. When she touched his arm, heat swamped him, and he no doubt his ruby red scales were doing a dance under his skin.

Sheesh, Lily didn't need to see his brown eyes turn turquoise with lust or his scales flash under his skin to show how much she affected him. She was skittish enough as it was.

"I appreciate the offer, but like I've told you before, I'm not ready to date anyone."

Those words seared his heart. "Is it because I'm a dragon shifter?" Birk asked.

"No."

Her glance to the floor implied that was a lie. "It doesn't bother you that your brother is mated to a dragon?" And that Kyle was now one too?

Her lips twisted. "Not anymore. Nessa is a great person."

And I'm not?

His dragon growled. *Don't act defensive.*

Fuck off, you fire breathing animal.

"My sister is wonderful, but I'm only asking you to dinner. I promise not to shift or shoot fire at anyone." That was assuming he didn't have to protect some innocent person from harm.

"Birk, please. I know I owe you my life for protecting me all those weeks against Tom Delaney—or rather Landry Madison and his minions, but I prefer being by myself."

"I understand." Birk had no idea how to counter that response. He'd seen how joyous his sister was after mating, and he firmly believed that Lily could be just as happy if she gave him a chance. But just because she said no this time didn't mean he would give up. "I'll stop by again to make sure you're okay."

Lily tilted her chin upward. "I think it would be best if you didn't."

That was harsh. "If that's the way you want it, I won't then. Goodbye and take care, Lily." Those words sliced off a bit of his heart.

It took all of his self-control to walk out of the door and not punch the wall. She'd rejected him. Again. Had it been something he'd said? Birk had taken excellent care of her when those men were after his family and hers, yet he never once put the moves on her—and Fate sure as hell knew how much he wanted to.

Her brother, Kyle, told him Lily had also been emotionally scarred by Nelor, but that didn't make it any easier to accept her ultimatum. She was his mate and he needed her.

Birk wasn't one to give up. He was still convinced that with time and a little help from her brother and his sister Nessa, Lily would come around. The question was whether he could last that long.

As soon as Birk reached the front entrance to her building his cell went off. It was his cousin Declan who never seemed to relax when it came to managing the two mines.

"Hey, what's up?" Birk asked in his most cheerful voice. If he'd answered in a tone that reflected his mood, even his fearless cousin might become afraid.

"Where are you?" he asked.

"I just came from seeing Lily. Why?" Declan was well aware of Birk's need to connect with her.

"Are you free now?"

"Yes."

"Good. I could use your help at the gem mine. There's been an altercation between some of the men."

"What do you need me to do?" The employees who worked the late shift were probably just blowing off steam. Most likely Declan was calling to check up on him.

"I'd like you to coordinate extra security and send them right over."

That seemed lame. "I'll get right on it."

Instead of running back to the park where he could shift and head to the mine, Birk walked, stopping occasionally to plan his next move. He needed to win her over—but that event, however, was unlikely to happen soon.

Birk didn't think it was his looks that turned her off. Many women had told him he was exceedingly handsome, though he bet they were referring to his body more than to his face. Most likely his large build scared tiny Lily. Shit. It wasn't like he could change that. While he'd never met Nelor, it was his understanding that he was a big guy too. Lily had been attracted to that, until he went ballistic on her. Birk would never treat a woman or anyone with that kind of cruelty—unless he was in battle with an enemy and had to fight to survive. In fact, Birk had deliberately been passive around his mate, fearing she'd reject any man—or shifter—who was too aggressive.

He just needed to keep being himself, even though as of yet, it hadn't gotten him very far. Eventually, Birk hoped she would take a chance and see the type of person he was: a caring, giving, loving and highly protective man. Lily had been hurt. He understood that, but she had let herself judge everyone by that one experience and he didn't know how to get even a pinhole of light through the walls she built up around herself.

If you think you've been yourself, you're wrong. You've been nothing but a sullen, over protective ass. You haven't even tried to learn anything about her.

He didn't need this conversation with his dragon. *I know she works for an insurance company and grew up poor.*

If you know so much about her, tell me her favorite color or her favorite food. What is her best childhood memory? Who is her best friend?

A horn beeped and Birk jumped back to avoid being hit by a car. While a collision with a vehicle would hurt, it couldn't kill him. *"I would know more about her if she didn't push me away all the time. When she does answer my questions, it's with as few words as possible. Since she keeps saying that she wants me to leave her alone, it's kind of hard to learn about her."*

"I get it, but you have to try harder."

Perhaps. For sure, Birk needed help in the relationship department, though he didn't know whose advice he should seek. His cousin, Tory, was a people person, but he'd never live through the embarrassment of asking for her help. His sister, Greer, was class personified, but he didn't know how she could help.

Right now, he needed to get to the mine. Once Birk arrived at the park, he shifted into his dragon form, and flew there. The more he thought about it, he wasn't even sure why Declan had called him. His cousin was more than capable of handling a little ruckus.

As if on autopilot, Birk found himself over the mine a few minutes later. Not once during the short flight had he checked his surroundings for unfriendly dragons. Crap, he was losing it, and he blamed Lily for making him lose concentration—damn, sexy woman. Why couldn't she just go out with him? He was positive he could show her a good time.

Birk did have an ace in the hole. Lily's brother was mated to Birk's sister. If they had a get together, he'd be in the same room with her and could hopefully charm her, though that wouldn't show her what he was really like—a warrior, a protector, and a good man. Damn. Maybe he was destined to be alone.

When Birk landed and headed to the Sinclair Gem office, he didn't see any major catastrophe brewing outside the mine. When he stepped inside, Declan spun around.

"What took you so long?" His lips were pressed tight. Crap.

Birk shrugged. "I came right away."

"What did you do, fight crime for half an hour first?"

"No." Birk didn't need to justify himself to Declan. Okay, maybe he did. Declan Sinclair was boss over both the Sinclair and Caspian mines, but he was also his cousin.

"Did you contact your men to help out? Because if you did, no one showed up." Declan moved closer. Usually his cousin was easy going, but something seemed to have set him off today.

"Sorry, I forgot to make the call. I got a little distracted."

Declan stared at him as if he'd lost him mind—and that wouldn't be far from the truth. "You forgot? You never just forget. You are the most dependable person I know." He held up a hand. "But don't worry about the skirmish. My men took care of it." Declan gave him that death stare again and then chuckled. "Actually, I called you here to find out what's really going on with you. In the last few weeks, you've been distant and quite honestly unreliable."

Birk had never shirked any responsibility in his life. It was what made him so serious. "Nothing happened." Other than Lily.

"Bullshit."

"Fine. If you must know, when I was protecting Lily Harper I realized she's my mate." There. He'd spilled it.

Declan smiled. "Well, congratulations. You should be happy,

but clearly you aren't. Why?"

It was humiliating to mention his failure. "I can't get her to go out with me."

"Seriously?" His tone almost sounded mocking.

"It's because Lily is afraid of dragons."

"Hmm. What does her dragon shifting brother have to say about that?" Declan raised his eyebrows.

"Lily needs time to deal with what her ex-boyfriend did to her, but my dragon is giving me ulcers. I can't sleep. I can't eat. Hell, I can't even remember to call for help one minute after you tell me there is an incident at the mine. That's not like me."

Declan wrapped an arm around his shoulder. "I know. And that's what worries me. I'm sure you'll figure it out, but I hope you do it sooner rather than later. Why don't you take the weekend off? Think of Monday as a new start. If anything happens, we'll call you."

He'd suffered through too many weekends and none of them helped. "Thanks." *I think.*

Not wanting to talk about his humiliating experience to anyone else, Birk left the building and took flight. Just as he was about to reach his house on the outskirts of the city, he spotted The Wings Bar below. Even though he had an extremely high metabolism rate for alcohol, a few drinks would help loosen and relax him. If that didn't work, Birk would consider escaping to Earth for a fresh start.

HIDDEN REALMS OF SILVER LAKE (Paranormal)

Awakened By Flames (book 1)

Seduced By Flames (book 2)

Kissed By Flames (book 3)

WERES & WITCHES OF SILVER LAKE

A Magical Shift (book 1) – FREE

Catching Her Bear (book 2)

A Surge of Magic (book 3)

The Bear's Forbidden Wolf (book 4)

Her Reluctant Bear (book 5)

Freeing His Tiger (book 6)

Protecting His Wolf (book 7)

Waking His Bear (book 8)

Melting Her Wolf's Heart (book 9)

Her Wolf's Guarded Heart (book 10)

PACK WARS (Paranormal)

Training Their Mate (book 1)

Claiming Their Mate (book 2)

Rescuing Their Virgin Mate (book 3)

Loving Their Vixen Mate (book 4)

Fighting For Their Mate (book 5)

Enticing Their Mate (book 6)

Complete Box Set (books 1–6)

MONTANA PROMISES (Full length contemporary)

Promises of Mercy (book 1)

Foundations For Three (book 2)

Montana Fire (book 3)

Hart To Hart (book 4)

Burning Seduction (book 5)

Montana Promises Complete Box Set (books 1–5)

ROCK HARD, MONTANA (contemporary novellas)

Montana Desire (book 1)

Awakening Passions (book 2)

HIDDEN HILLS SHIFTERS (Paranormal)

An Unexpected Diversion (book 1) – FREE

Bare Instincts (book 2)

Shifting Destinies (book 3)

Box Set (books 1–3)

Embracing Fate (book 4)

Promises Unbroken (book 5)

A NASH MYSTERY (Contemporary)

Sidearms and Silk (book 1)

Black Ops and Lingerie (book 2)

SOUTHERN SHIFTERS KINDLE WORLDS

Bear 'N Dirty

Author Bio

Want 3 FREE books? Sign up for my newsletter.

COPY AND PASTE INTO YOUR BROWSER:
smarturl.it/o4cz93?IQid=MLite

Check out my latest interview on You Tube:
youtube.com/watch?v=sQo5pyyVMDI

Not only do I love to read, write, and dream, I'm an extrovert. I enjoy being around people and am always trying to understand what makes them tick. Not only must my books have a happily ever after, I need characters I can relate to. My men are wonderful, dynamic, smart, strong, and the best lovers in the world (of course).

I believe I am the luckiest woman. I do what I love and I have a wonderful, supportive husband, who happens to be hot!

Fun facts about me

(1) I'm a math nerd who loves spreadsheets. Give me numbers and I'll find a pattern.

(2) I love photography, so I'll be posting pictures—especially of my Costa Rican adventure.

(3) I also like to exercise. Yes, I know I'm odd. Not only do I lift weights, I love to hike and walk on the beach (yes, it sounds like an ad for a date).

I love hearing from readers either on FB or via email (hint, hint).

Social Media Sites

Website:
www.velladay.com

FB:
facebook.com/vella.day.90

Twitter:
@velladay4

Gmail:
velladayauthor@gmail.com

Google:
plus.google.com/u/0/116041077486216602121/posts

Instagram:
@dayvella